LORD EDGINGTON INVESTIGATES...

BOOK 12

THE
CHRISTMAS
BELL
MYSTERY

A 1920s MYSTERY

BENEDICT BROWN

COPYRIGHT

For my father, Kevin,
I hope you would have liked this book an awful lot.

FIDELITY

READER'S NOTE AND COMPETITION

This book may be the twelfth in the series, but I've written it so that new readers can enjoy it without knowing anything that's happened before. It doesn't give away spoilers from previous adventures, and I can promise that it is a fun, funny and festive murder mystery that is just right for Christmastime.

If you haven't read any of the other stories, all you need to know is that the former police officer turned roving sleuth, Lord Edgington, and his apprentice grandson, Christopher, are about to investigate a baffling case in December 1927. At the back of the book is a character list, a short glossary of unusual terms, and a chapter on my research.

I hope you absolutely love it.

Competition

As with all of my Christmas books (that's four novels and a novella at this point) there are a lot of hidden references to other Christmas films, books, and songs. There are ten in this book plus the example I'm going to give you. These include direct quotes or allusions to famous scenes, though some have had to be tweaked to fit the period and setting. For example, at one point Chrissy goes "dashing through the snow" which is obviously a quote from 'Jingle Bells' – however, this one was purely accidental, and I didn't even notice it until I edited the book.

Of the ten references, two are from my favourite Christmas book 'The Box of Delights' so I wouldn't expect a lot of people to notice them, but the rest are really famous. If you manage to find five or more, it might be worth e-mailing me at **bb@benedictbrown.net** with the list of references. The person with the most correct answers by the end of 2023 will win either a signed book sent anywhere in the world, or your name included in a future story – admittedly, some names are more suitable than others, and I can't really imagine Lord Edgington crossing paths with a Candy or Zach. (No offence meant to anyone named Candy or Zach!) If there's another prize you can think of, I'm open to ideas.

I'm eager to see whether any of you are as obsessive as I am when it comes to Christmassy content, so best of luck to everyone who tries!

CHAPTER ONE

The steam from the 10:17 to Banbury billowed around the station and, for a moment, I found myself lost within it. My head was still full of the week I'd shared with my friends in Oxford. Perhaps it was down to that festive time of year, and my excitement at returning home to see my family, but I felt a nostalgic warmth for events that had passed mere hours and days before.

The image of my former school friends standing in the junior common room in full Father Christmas regalia mingled with the memories of our late nights discussing every topic under the moon. My time visiting them had been a gift in itself, and our farewell at the station moments earlier already seemed like a treasured possession that I would hold onto for the rest of my life.

As the steam on the platform cleared, I caught sight of the young lady for the first time. Well, it was her long winter coat that stood out to me. It cut through the mist like a ship's searchlight. The shade was impossibly vibrant, almost like the arsenic green that Victorians wore before they realised how dangerous it was. Once the train had moved off, the space between us cleared entirely, and I could see her face. She was pale and elegant, her ash-brown hair piled on top of her head in a mess of curls and folds, but that wasn't what held my attention. The reason I couldn't look away from the beautiful mirage on that frozen platform was that I'd never seen a woman who looked so entirely alone.

Her face was free of all expression, as if she couldn't muster the courage to frown or cry. At her feet, a black leather suitcase stood patiently, like a loyal hound, and I was tempted to walk closer to see whether I could read her name on the label. That's what my grandfather, the renowned Lord Edgington, would have done. Detectives like him spot mysteries wherever they go and collect evidence on the off-chance that there is a crime to solve. For my part, I thought I might look a touch sinister loitering around her, and so I stayed where I was to wait for the train.

A diminutive station attendant stepped out of his wooden hut and, in a voice that was far larger than him, declared, "The 10:23 to Didcot will be calling at stops in the Cherwell Valley, including Radley,

Culham, Appleford Crossing and Didcot. Change at Didcot for the Great Western Mainline to London and Exeter. Snow on the line may cause delays."

He'd timed the announcement perfectly. The moment he finished speaking, I heard the chug, chug, chugging of my train from along the tracks, and a piercing whistle rent the air. The other people on the platform were clearly just as excited about the prospect of heading home as I was. There were families loaded with parcels for the holiday, tired businessmen stamping their feet to keep warm and— How was it possible? The girl in the green coat had disappeared from sight.

There was no time to think of her, though; the great hulking Mogul-class train was coming to a stop. The wheels screeched as the locomotive pulled its glossy wooden carriages into the station, and everyone moved a step forward to board all the faster. The doors opened whilst the train was still in motion and out leaped a few brave young gentlemen who thought nothing of breaking their necks. I've never been one for such daredevilry and allowed them a wide berth as they raced along the platform towards the exit.

Once all those who were getting off had done so, I looked for the right carriage and climbed aboard. My grandfather, or rather one of his servants, had bought me a first-class ticket, and I ended up with a compartment all to myself. As soon as I sat down in my seat, hoping to catch twenty winks or so before changing trains, I discovered that my mind had other ideas. I could think of nothing but the girl I'd seen. Perhaps it was the brightness of that vivid coat amongst all the greys, blacks and navy blues of our fellow passengers, but the image of her would not dissipate as the clouds of steam had.

Even as we pulled out of Oxford Station, and I got to enjoy the view of the perfectly snowy hills beyond the banks of the River Cherwell, she was still there in my mind. It was hard to know exactly why. Perhaps it was the idea that I might never solve the mystery she represented – never discover how anyone could be quite so forlorn mere days before Christmas. Or maybe I was still just as easily charmed as I'd ever been, and I was mesmerised by her beauty. A recent newspaper article on one of our murder investigations had said that "Christopher Prentiss is a hopeless (in more ways than one) romantic who, even after countless cases, still believes in the good within every person he meets." I can't say I disagreed with this description, though I did have to wonder who the journalist's source was.

Despite my supposed optimism, I sat on the train feeling as though the young lady's melancholia had leached across the platform to me until, at some point, I must have fallen asleep. We were already pulling into Culham when the door to my compartment slid open and I shot to my feet like a soldier preparing for inspection.

It was her! The girl in the green coat was standing a few feet away from me. I'm happy to say that she no longer looked so sad. I'm less happy to say that she was clearly bewildered as to why an uncouth oik of a nineteen-year-old was gawping at her. She froze in the entrance, as though she would change her mind and go elsewhere. Thankfully, I realised how peculiarly I was acting and sat back down.

I didn't dare look at her as she put her suitcase beneath the cushioned bench and took her place as far away from me as she could get within the six-by-nine-foot space. I didn't even sneak a glance at her as the conductor came in to check our tickets. No, it wasn't until I heard the sound of a faint bell that I couldn't resist it any longer. I'd been staring unseeingly at Charles Dickens's 'The Cricket on the Hearth' but risked a brief peek as I turned a page.

Now that she was that much closer, I found her wistful looks quite captivating. I suspected she was a few years older than I was, but there was a naïveté to her that struck me immediately. I tried not to get distracted by the ghostly blue of her eyes or the way the light rebounded off her hair as we rushed past all that snow. A chain with a tiny silver charm on it caught my attention as it dangled from her hand. That was the tinkling sound I had heard, but there was no time to study it closely. She glanced past me out of the window, and I had to go back to not reading my book.

I suppose I could have attempted to finish the story, but I was rather too distracted for that. Just as I was wondering whether I should close my eyes and feign sleep, she turned away again and began to sob. It was ever so quiet, just like the jingling of her bracelet, but try as she might to hide it, I knew she was crying.

I finally looked straight at her. She'd shifted her body to one side and faced the headrest in order to suppress the noise. The thought returned to me that she was just about the loneliest individual on Earth.

Some tiny chamber in my heart – that I wouldn't be able to identify with a medical encyclopaedia and a team of doctors – began to sting like it had been injected with rubbing alcohol. I so desperately wanted to help her but couldn't make my mind up what to do.

She put her hand over her mouth as her sobs grew louder, and I tried to think of what to say before remembering that I was terrible at that sort of thing and landing upon a better idea. I didn't like to leave her, but there was no choice. I dashed from our compartment and along to the buffet car. I was only gone for a minute or so, but I still worried that, by the time I came back, she'd have disappeared again.

"I'm very sorry, miss." I tried my best not to sound nervous or rude or both. "I hope you'll forgive me for putting my foot in other people's business... or rather for..." My words were in the wrong order and probably wouldn't have made much sense even if they hadn't been. Realising that the only solution was to take a deep breath and start again, that's exactly what I did. "I couldn't help noticing that something is troubling you, and so I bought you a cup of tea and a mince pie."

I held out my offerings, and she paused as though trying to decide how to react. Her eyes were enormous just then. They were pale, intense and clear, but with a hint of red at the corners where her sorrow had peeked through.

When her response finally came, it was soft and tentative. "You bought me tea and cake?"

"I'm not certain that mince pies count as cakes," I began before wishing I could just stop talking altogether. "Or rather... yes, tea and cake."

She held her hands out to take them and said no more. I couldn't stand the silence that followed. The only noise was the jickity-can, jickity-can of the train's wheels on the tracks, but they sounded like they were saying, *Try harder, boy. Try harder, boy.*

"My mother always tells me that there's nothing like a cup of tea for calming the nerves. Although, personally, I'm rather partial to sweets. Not just the boiled kind but, pies, puddings, pastries and—"

"Thank you," she said to save me from myself. "And thank your mother, too."

She warmed her hands on the china cup, and I thought that our exchange might provoke a smile, but then she noticed the bracelet that she'd laid on the armrest next to her and began to cry once more.

"I'm sorry." She might have wiped her eyes, but some fool had stuck a cup of tea and a mince pie in her hands. "I really am. I didn't mean to place such a burden on you. I'm simply not myself today."

I did something then that was quite out of character. Instead of jabbering out a load of absolute twaddle or becoming shy and returning to my book, I moved to sit next to her.

"There's no need to apologise. Really there isn't. As far as I'm concerned, you can cry your eyes out if it makes you feel better."

I thought this was nicely put and, now that I'd given her my permission, she started sobbing more loudly than before. As no other remedy presented itself, I wondered what my wise and compassionate mother would say in this situation.

"Whatever the matter is, things won't look nearly so bleak if you share your troubles." I gave her my most earnest smile and hoped for the best.

"It's my grandfather," she began and, for a moment, I wondered if she too was related to a genius who thought he knew more than everyone else and, more often than not, actually did. "Someone is going to kill him."

CHAPTER TWO

On hearing this news, I rather wished that I'd bought myself a cup of tea, or perhaps something stronger. We British are famed for not talking to fellow travellers on trains. Most people would think you forward for issuing a brief *Good morning* or a *How do you do?* It certainly can't be too common for someone to reveal a murder plot to a complete stranger within seconds of their meeting.

I was truly lost for words and could do nothing more than stare back at her, my mouth open and a sound escaping from it that reminded me of the perplexed grunting my father made when he was trying to complete a brainteaser in the paper.

"You probably think I'm half mad," she said. "The truth is that I've doubted it myself, but my family isn't like most people's."

Even as she took a sip of scalding tea, she stared at the bracelet again, and I got the impression that it was of great sentimental value to her.

"I can honestly say that my family isn't like any other I've met, either," I assured her. "But one thing we do have in common is that I love my grandfather and would be lost without him. So I believe I can sympathise with—"

My words did not have the effect for which I'd been hoping. Passing me the cup of tea – though sadly not the mince pie – she tipped her head back despondently.

"That's just it. That's why I'm so upset. My relatives are largely rotters and, if I had any money of my own, I'd leave home and never go back. St Audries is a lonely place; it's battered by the sea winds and quite inhospitable in winter. You see, I'm not crying because I'm worried about my grandfather. I'm crying because I'm so ashamed of myself."

"I refuse to believe that there's any reason for you to feel guilty."

Her response was firm yet somehow polite. "Then perhaps you weren't listening."

My parents would have told her that this was one of my most common failings. Instead of proving them right, I kept my mouth shut and waited for her to say more.

"I'm crying because I can't decide whether I wish someone would save Grandfather, or I'd like to lend a hand to whoever has it in for him." Her sobs had become so loud that it was difficult to decipher each word she said. "I only wish that green ostriches roamed more freely across the southern plains." I'm fairly certain that this was not what she said, but it sounded awfully like that.

"Of course you do," I replied and then did the first, and perhaps last, useful thing that I would accomplish that morning. I remembered that I had a clean handkerchief in my bag and went fishing for it.

When I gave it to her, I managed to catch a glimpse of the label on her suitcase. It said H. Bridport, Somerville College, Oxford, which didn't help a great deal.

"I am ashamed," she reminded me. "Ashamed to have such wicked thoughts but, if you'd met my grandfather – if you had any sense of what kind of person he is – you'd understand why I feel as I do."

"If he really is a monster, it sounds to me as though you're quite reasonable in your feelings."

She didn't reply but picked off a piece of the sweet pastry on the top of the small, sugary treat I'd given her. I was quite shocked that I hadn't bought two. How much longer would that have taken? What had this girl done to me that I was already ignoring my appetite?

"I don't know why I'm telling you this." With her morsel consumed, she took a moment to gather her thoughts. "I'm not normally so forthcoming with people I don't know, but there's something very honest about you."

Her gaze caught hold of me again, and my heart seemed to tremble. Though I had faced any number of savage murderers, and even solved one case myself by this point, I was powerless before her exquisite blue eyes.

"Perhaps I can help you." I tried to sound sincere, but my voice went squeaky.

"There's nothing anyone can do." She glanced away, and it was almost a relief. I didn't feel quite right when she looked at me so intently.

"You must at least tell me why you think your grandfather is in danger. I couldn't live with myself if we went our separate ways without knowing that much."

She turned back and somehow found the courage to trust me. "Grandfather is a very rich man. In fact, he's a lord."

"I think I can imagine what it's like to be related to such a person." I managed not to smile.

"Oh, I don't think you can. He controls everyone in my family as if he were our sovereign ruler."

"You're right. I haven't a clue what that would be like."

She took back her tea and sipped it quietly. "Ever since my parents died, I've been under the old miser's power. I'm certain there are jollier orphanages in Britain than his cheerless estate."

"That still doesn't explain why someone wants to kill him." I felt dim for not grasping more of what she was trying to communicate, and I tried to state things more clearly. "You're saying that he's a rich old man with a grand estate, and you're afraid someone wants to murder him?"

"That's it in a nutshell."

We'd made it to Appleford Crossing by now. We'd be arriving at the end of the line at any minute, so I raced to get the information I needed. "You can't think he's going to be killed just because he's a rich old Ozymandias."

"I don't. I think he's going to be killed because someone keeps trying to kill him."

I had to pause then, as I had not been expecting this. My grandfather had often told me that the number of people in this life who have been convinced that someone was trying to murder them is far greater than the number of people who have actually been murdered.

"Back in the summer, when my family were all there together, first, someone tampered with his wheelchair," she said to convince me. "He might well have rolled off the cliff if his butler hadn't stayed nearby. Then an old marble bust fell from the terrace and landed inches away from where he was sitting. Finally, just before I left for university, someone put foxglove seeds in the mug beside his bed. Luckily, a servant noticed, and he came to no harm, but it simply can't have been an accident."

It was my turn to fall silent. It was an interesting series of events, to say the least. The first two incidents could well be dismissed as unfortunate mishaps, but everyone knows that foxgloves are poisonous. Whether a few seeds in a drink would have been enough to kill is another matter, of course, but I couldn't dismiss her fears out of hand.

"Very well. It does sound suspicious. But who do you think is to blame?"

She looked down at the empty cup. "My cousins stand to gain the most. Luke, Flossie, Nathan and Silas." Her face became more strained, as if each name on the list was nastier than the last. "In fact, any one of them might have done it."

"I have come to see over the seven or so minutes I have known you that, while you may not adore your grandfather, you clearly don't wish him to suffer."

"Then you clearly know more than I do." She could no longer resist and took a big bite of mince pie. I didn't blame her.

"The situation is simple. You must go to the police as soon as you get home. They'll know what's best to do. I promise they will."

She waited until she'd finished her mouthful before answering. "I've already spoken to the local constable. He said that it was a series of accidents and nothing more. And…" I thought she would cry again, but she fought the emotion. "I'm not sad for my grandfather. I'm sad at the thought of the minutes, hours and days ahead of me. I have to spend two weeks with my sorry excuse for a family, and it's supposed to be Christmas."

Ouch! That chamber in my heart started stinging again. A murder plot against a troublesome old man might have elicited a certain amount of sympathy, but the idea of this charming young woman having to undergo such an ordeal at Christmastime made me think that I should forget about my train home and follow her wherever she needed to go.

"That's just horrible. I can't tell you how sad it makes me."

It seemed incredibly unlikely that we'd be able to crack the case before we arrived at our destination, and I felt the pull of separation already forcing us apart.

Brushing the crumbs from her hands, she smoothed her soft coat over her lap, then stood up to get her bag. "Thank you, kind stranger. I may not be looking forward to my holiday, but these eight minutes have been perfectly pleasant compared to what's ahead."

The train was slowing down, and I saw the sign for Didcot. There was nothing I could say to make things better, nothing I could do to extend those last few seconds in her company, and so I just sat there holding her cup. She pushed down the sliding window and put her arm out to open the door, and I just sat there. She offered a sad smile, and I just sat there.

It was only as she stepped down from the carriage that I found my words again. "I don't even know your name," I called, and she paused to look at me one last time.

"It's Holly," she replied, and I should probably have imagined something quite so serendipitous. "Happy Christmas, stranger. The mince pie was delicious."

And then she was gone. Like every fairy in every Christmas pantomime I'd seen, she disappeared in a puff of thick white smoke… well, steam, but they're basically the same thing.

I should have been thinking about the connecting train I needed to catch – or running after her to enquire whether she was in need of a husband with limited detective skills, a penchant for birdwatching and a love of Charles Dickens. At the very least, I could have told her about my grandfather's friends at Scotland Yard, but I was still rooted to my seat. I looked at the spot where she'd been sitting and there was her ticket. I went to pick it up and noticed a glint of silver on the arm of the chair.

"Holly, wait!" I shouted as I rushed to the door before remembering that I had a bag of my own, and then remembering that I was holding a china cup from the buffet car. I grabbed my suitcase, ran from the compartment to leave the empty teacup with another young lady – who was not nearly so mysterious or tragic as Holly Bridport – and then I jumped down from the train.

I looked along the platform to see if I could spot her remarkable green coat, but there was no sign of it. The station was busy, and a train had just pulled in on the other side of the tracks. There were two possibilities. Either she had rushed to catch the 11:04 to Bristol that had just been announced or, like me, she was heading into London on the 11:15. Actually, the third option that I didn't want to consider was that she lived nearby and had left in a car, but I was already hurtling along the platform, my red scarf billowing out behind me.

I took the stairs to the footbridge three at a time and had to dart and squeeze through people just as the stationmaster blew his whistle. I made it over the tracks and raced down the steps once more, but I was too slow. The train was pulling away. The chimney was chug-chug-chugging, and the wheels were picking up speed.

I stood at the bottom of the stairs looking into each passing carriage, but there was no sign of her. I stood on my tiptoes to see better, but she just wasn't there. As the last carriage went past me in a blur, I rather wished that I'd kept hold of the teacup so that I could have thrown it in frustration.

No longer caring whether I caught my train or not, I wandered back to the other platform. Trains come by on a regular schedule throughout the day; young women like Holly Bridport don't turn up too often. I felt just as heartsick as when I'd lost sight of her the first time. I sat down on a bench and kept expecting to see her emerge from the waiting room or talking to the guard, but I would not be so lucky.

Not even the sight of a brand-new King-class train thundering through the station on its way to London could cheer me. Nothing could make up for the unsettling feeling that my encounter had left behind. I looked down at the silver chain that I was clutching and tried my level best to imagine how I might return it to her.

CHAPTER THREE

"Christopher," my grandfather whispered between songs, "why aren't you singing?"

We were standing in front of a row of houses in the village that bordered our estate. A sweet-voiced choir of our employees from Cranley Hall were preparing to sing 'God Rest Ye Merry Gentlemen' as a small crowd of enraptured children had formed in the glow of their open front doors.

"I *am* singing," I lied in the surly voice that I had taken as my own ever since I'd returned from Oxford. When he didn't try to convince me otherwise, I felt a little guilty and joined in with the next song.

> **"God rest you merry, gentlemen,**
> **Let nothing you dismay,**
> **For Jesus Christ our Saviour**
> **Was born upon this day,**
> **To save us all from Satan's power**
> **When we were gone astray:**
> **O tidings of comfort and joy,**
> **comfort and joy,**
> **O tidings of comfort and joy."**

"That was beautiful," an old man declared as he came out of one of the snow-laden cottages when the song was complete. "But you're not getting any money from me. Now hop it!"

"I beg your pardon?" My grandfather stepped away from the group to respond. "We're not here for your money. We're here to spread goodwill at the holiest and most charitable time of year."

The man before him was a good decade younger than the spritely lord, but the two couldn't have looked more different. The unappreciative churl had not a hair on his head and appeared to have been sculpted by a child from a large block of clay. The process had left him with a very rounded stomach and unusually skinny arms.

"I'm not interested in your kind of charity. The hardworking people of St Mary-under-Twine don't have money to hand over to a toff like you."

My grandfather was evidently disconcerted by this encounter and looked at his factotum, Todd, for assistance.

"I believe the gentleman is referring to the tradition of carollers asking for money for their songs, M'lord."

This brought a grumble of agreement from a few of our footmen and a gardener or two.

"That is the custom, Your Worship," our oversized maid, Dory, replied.

"And *you* are not having *any* of *mine*," the bald chap with the disproportioned body replied. "Now hop it!"

"But I'm not here for your money, Mr…?"

He waited expectantly, but the man really wasn't in a co-operative mood. "You won't be having my name neither, Lord High And Mighty. Now… hop… it!"

The children – who had presumably stayed to hear another Christmas carol rather than an argument – looked apprehensive in the dim light. Todd gave his employer a pointed look and Lord Edgington realised that, in the spirit of the season and Christian forgiveness, there was only one way to resolve the unpleasantness.

"You're absolutely right, my good man." He reached into the inside pocket of his long grey morning coat and emptied his wallet of all the coins he had. "Christmas is a time for giving." He walked to the end of the row of houses and presented the first child there with a shiny silver piece. "A time to think of others before oneself." The next boy only got a copper, but he seemed just as happy. "What right has some snooty aristocrat got to go swanning around the village demanding peace on Earth and good will to all men? My sort have made their living off the backs of the working man for centuries."

His challenger had come to the end of his garden path to see what the barmy lord was up to. "Well, I wouldn't go that far, but I suppose you have a point."

My grandfather had finished in the first house and walked to the second. "Too many people in this world fail to practise what they preach. It's all very good talking of charity once a year, but words are cheap." With the children suitably rewarded, he moved on to his staff. All coins were soon distributed, and so Lord Edgington presented our cook and pageboy with a one-pound note each.

The belligerent man's previously grumpy face had been transformed by this act of kindness, and he clearly couldn't wait to discover what he would receive.

"Personally, I think that your attitude is the right one," my grandfather told him. "And so I have something far more precious to offer you than coins or even bank notes."

"That is very kind of you, M'Lord." The tiny chap was bristling with excitement, much like his neighbour's children would be in three days' time as they ran to their living rooms on Christmas morning to see what treasures Father Christmas had brought. "Really, very kind indeed."

"For you, my good man, I would like to offer my very best wishes for the season and a happy New Year." Grandfather tipped his top hat and walked off along the street singing.

> **"Here we come a-wassailing**
> **Among the leaves so green;**
> **Here we come a-wand'ring**
> **So fair to be seen."**

The look of shock on that grumbletonian's face was enough to dispel any negativity that may have previously clouded around me. I joined in with the song as the choir followed their master.

> **"Love and joy come to you,**
> **And to you your wassail too;**
> **And God bless you and send you a happy New Year**
> **And God send you a happy New Year."**

We stopped in front of the illuminated Christmas tree in the middle of the village and some Yuletide revellers who had been busy drinking to one another's health in the pub next door came out to enjoy the scene. The landlady brought us all hot cider, and it warmed us inside and out. Without the impish killjoy who had threatened to derail our evening's festivities, we were free to bask in the warmth of togetherness.

Well, that's how I felt until we returned to Cranley Hall, at least. Once our lovely staff had dispersed, and I was left to dwell on my thoughts, I felt just as blue as I had for days. It was not simply that I wished to return a treasured possession to the melancholy figure I'd met on the train; I was worried about the danger in which she might now find herself. If someone was trying to kill her grandfather, who was to say that she wouldn't be next? I had no way of knowing whether she was even alive.

"All right, Christopher. That is enough," my mother told me at dinner. The rest of our family still hadn't arrived for Christmas, and I would normally have been overjoyed to spend some time with her, but… well, you know why I wasn't. "You look like a dog who's lost a paw. Now tell me what's wrong."

Our golden retriever Delilah clearly considered such talk undiplomatic as she whimpered and disappeared beneath the tablecloth. Her reaction summed up how I felt about the world rather wonderfully. Why isn't it socially acceptable for humans to hide under tables from time to time?

"I've been trying to get the story out of him ever since he returned from Oxford," Grandfather told his daughter, before a possible explanation dawned on him. "Is this about your education, Chrissy? Are you upset that I suggested you should train to be my assistant rather than go to university?"

I groaned, which at least told him that he was some way off the truth. I should probably have just told him the story, but I felt certain he would tell me I was being a love-struck dimwit and that I should forget the whole sorry episode.

He blew out his cheeks in dismay. "I have honestly got more sense out of my dog this week than I have from that boy."

Delilah produced a well-timed growl from her hiding place. If I were she, I would have given his ankle a vengeful nip.

My mother has always been the most diplomatic person in the family (and the whole of England, for that matter). She left her place at the long table that was laid out with elaborate decorations and bronze charging plates, even though there were only three of us for dinner that night.

"Christopher, my love, we have no wish to interfere, but we're worried about you. Things won't look nearly so bleak if you share your troubles." Gosh, where had I heard that before?

I looked from my mother to her father to the upright footman by the door. I knew they meant well, but that wasn't going to help me. While I didn't want to make them sad, I couldn't bring myself to reveal the whole story, so, I mumbled, "… train journey… blue eyes… quite heartbreaking…"

"I'm sorry, Christopher," my grandfather replied with a curious frown, "while I like to think that I have perfectly adequate hearing for a man of my age, I am not fluent in the language of glum adolescents. Could you please try to enunciate?"

"Oh, very well." I sighed – also like an adolescent – and gave in to the pressure. "I said that, on the train journey from Oxford, I met a girl with the most incredible blue eyes. She told me that someone is trying to murder her grandfather, and I find the whole thing quite heartbreaking."

"That certainly wasn't what I was expecting." My grandfather looked at his daughter in wonder, and Mother looked back much the same.

While it is the temptation of every young man to believe that his elders could never possibly understand him, I knew better. My grandfather didn't merely possess a fine mind; he had a sense of compassion that was almost as rare. So why was I so dismayed?

Thankfully, my mother knew to treat me with the softest of kid gloves. She coaxed the story out of me that I was so reluctant to divulge. "You poor thing. You're worried about the young lady you met."

"That's just it." Full of nervous energy, I shot from my seat. "Wait, no! Actually, you're miles off. I'm not just worried. I'm petrified for her, and I don't know what to do about it."

"I totally understand your position." Grandfather stood up to look more commanding as he delivered his inevitable retort. "If only we knew someone – a detective, for example – who might have some knowledge of how to locate people without a great deal of information."

I wasn't quite as stupid as he thought. "I have considered that, but all I know about her is her name."

"Which is?"

"Holly Bridport."

Delilah had reappeared by this point. There's nothing she likes more than following her beloved master about the place, and she must have sensed that he would indulge in a bout of pacing.

"And you met her on a train from Oxford a few days before Christmas, is that correct?"

"It is," I replied, and his pacing commenced.

"Which might suggest that she herself is enrolled on a course there?"

"It does indeed." The image of her luggage label flashed in my mind. "I saw on her bag that she goes to Somerville College."

"Ah ha!" He clapped his hands together jubilantly. "So we've already discovered more about her than you previously claimed to know."

I remained unimpressed. "Yes, but I've already explored that possibility, and it didn't get me any closer to finding her."

I should mention that my mother is almost as good a detective as her illustrious father, and she soon elaborated upon the scant details I had provided. "You mean to say that you called the college, and they wouldn't help you?"

"Precisely. Or rather… not quite precisely. The porter to whom I spoke told me that anyone who could answer my question had already left for the holiday. He also told me that they wouldn't have given me information about a student unless I was a policeman or a member of her family."

Grandfather stopped in the middle of the room and declared, "You must know more than you're telling us, Christopher. How long did you spend on that train talking to her?"

"I believe it was nine minutes by the time she alighted at Didcot."

He nodded, as though pleased with the precision of my answer. "Jolly good, but that surely proves my point. It is very difficult to talk to anyone for that length of time and not glean some pertinent fact about them, especially as you've already told us she was in a distressed state."

It was nice to prove him wrong for once. "You clearly underestimate me…" I realised that this wasn't right and corrected myself. "Or perhaps you overestimate me. It's hard to know."

"Nine minutes…" Walking to the window to look at the patchy snow outside, he would not be dissuaded. "In that time, I imagine that you did what you could to comfort the distressed young lady with the beautiful blue eyes." He spun back to me, and his own grey glare was rather penetrating. It pricked and prickled me. "Was there a buffet car on the train?"

I already had a sense of the magic trick he was about to perform. "Yes, but—"

"I put it to you that, as a sensitive, well-mannered boy with a love of food and drink, you saw this damsel in distress and desperately thought up a way to make her feel better. Running to the buffet car, you purchased refreshments and returned to your carriage to deliver them as a heartfelt offering."

My mother beamed brightly. She even murmured something like, "Good boy, Christopher," under her breath.

"Tea and a mince pie," I confessed.

"I beg your pardon."

"That's what I bought her: a cup of tea and a mince pie."

Without saying a word, Grandfather conveyed the fact that he had understood my meaning but did not approve of the loose grammatical formation of my original comment. He was particularly skilled when it came to silent communication. I believe it was all in the eyebrows.

"There we go. You bought her a cup of tea and a mince pie. You displayed your kind, charming nature, and I have no doubt that you learnt any number of significant details about her."

"Charming?" I had to laugh at the idea.

"Of course you are, Christopher," my mother promised, and though this was not the most impartial view, my grandfather supported it.

"There is such a thing as too much modesty, my boy. Doubting yourself will get you nowhere in life." He came a few steps closer to make his point. "You may not see it, but people often warm to you quickly in our investigations. Now, what more did she tell you?"

Even though I had gone over my conversation with Holly any number of times, I tried hard to think of something I'd overlooked. "She said she has a number of scheming cousins who would be only too happy to get the old man's money. Her parents are dead, and she is under her grandfather's care. She said that he is a cruel, controlling person…" I picked over her words again, but nothing new came to mind. "The only thing that I thought might help us find her is this…"

I reached into my pocket where I'd been keeping her silver chain and train ticket ever since I'd left Didcot.

"An unstamped ticket?" Grandfather sounded perplexed.

"Not the ticket, the jewellery!" I let it hang from my hand, and he came to inspect it.

"It's a charm bracelet," my mother told us. "I'd say it was far from uncommon."

"I'm afraid you're right, Violet." He held out his hand then, and I dropped the chain into it." It is real silver, but it could be purchased at nearly any jeweller's. The only unusual about it is the charm. There are holly leaves and small berries etched onto the bell. I would assume it was given as a Christmas present."

I presented my own analysis then. "I've thought about it a lot, and I believe that it must have come from her parents. From the way she looked at it when we were talking, it was clearly important to her. That's another reason why I wish to find her again."

Mother put her hand on my arm. "You must think harder, Christopher. There's bound to be some essential detail that will lead us to her."

For once, I was disheartened by her excess of faith in me. "That's easy to say, but I've been racking my brains for days and nothing useful has come to me. That poor girl is in trouble. The miserable old lord who controls her will be murdered, and her horrid cousins will claim their prize."

Grandfather was shaking his head in disapproval before I'd finished speaking. "Are you saying that her grandfather is a lord?"

"Yes. What of it?"

He sighed and left the room.

CHAPTER FOUR

Delilah was the first to follow him. She cantered after her master, and my mother and I were close behind. The dear creature is always disappointed if she's left out of things, and I could tell how proud she was to be included in whatever new adventure we were about to enjoy.

Unfortunately, we only went a few rooms down the corridor to the library. I don't know how our dog felt on the matter, but I was disappointed that we wouldn't be blasting off the estate in one of my grandfather's many sporty cars to hunt down Holly Bridport. My heart only sank deeper when Grandfather seized the ladder that he used for accessing the drier, dustier and far less interesting books above head height. In fact, he extracted just about the two most boring tomes in his vast collection.

"'Burke's Peerage'," he murmured, before moving off in search of another on the opposite side of the room, "and 'Who's Who'. We should find the answer in one of these."

Mother and I took a book each and sat in the armchairs beside his desk.

"Bridport? Wasn't that her name?" she asked as she nimbly skipped to the appropriate page.

"That's right," I replied without looking up. My edition of 'Burke's Peerage' dated back to 1915, and I couldn't say whether it would have the information we needed, as mother beat me to it.

"Here we are, The Viscount Bridport – Arthur Wellington Alexander Nelson Hood, C.B. of Cricket St. Thomas, Somerset."

"He's not the man we need." Grandfather appeared to know more than any printed material could tell us.

"And why not?" my mother responded in the same indignant tone that I would have used.

"Because the second Viscount Bridport died three years ago. I remember reading his obituary in the paper. I believe that his heir lives in Guernsey, or Italy, or somewhere like that."

I know that geographical knowledge is not my strong suit, but even I failed to see how the British isle of Guernsey was in any way like Italy. They're far apart... aren't they?

"So a relative, perhaps?" My mother's eyes narrowed just as her father's did whenever he was thinking over some juicy conundrum.

"Or perhaps Holly Bridport's mother was the daughter of the rich old man we need to find and, without knowing his surname, we've reached another dead end." Forgive my pessimism, but even with Lord Edgington on the case, I didn't hold out much hope.

Delilah whined in sympathy, but Grandfather would not be defeated.

"Let's think about this rationally." He marched over to his desk and pushed a pile of papers clean to the floor. For a man with a staff of at least fifteen, he had a strange resistance to anyone tidying his library, and it was in a particularly messy state that week. On the now clear desk, a large map of Britain was visible. "The deceased viscount may still be related to Miss Bridport, and he was from Somerset. Where did she go when she got off the train?"

"When I realised that she'd left the bracelet on her seat, I tried to catch her, but she had already crossed the platform to catch the train to Bristol."

"A city that borders Somerset." As if he'd planned this whole sequence of events, grandfather pulled away the map of Britain to reveal a very similar one, this time with red, green, mauve and brown lines running all over it. I didn't need to read the title at the top to make sense of what I was seeing, but I did all the same.

"Map of British Railways." For some reason, I kept reading. "Bartholomew's – Cartographers to the King."

Mother put down her book and came to see why her father was making so much fuss. When she was my age, she had followed the then police superintendent on a number of his cases in London. However, she evidently hadn't learnt that the one thing that made him happier than investigating a murder was the chance to plan a route to the scene of the crime.

He ran his finger between Didcot and Bristol, and I looked at the key at the top to confirm that mauve lines signified those of the Great Western Railway.

"From Bristol, she could have changed for a train to Taunton and from there…"

"To Exeter?" my mother suggested in an uncertain voice.

"No, Exeter is in Devon; that's no use." He had his finger pinned to the town of Taunton as his eyes cast around for the next obvious spot. "From Taunton, she could have gone…"

"Anywhere." I was just the life of the party that night!

"Now, now, there's no need to be hasty."

If anyone could work out this thorny puzzle, it was my grandfather, but he wasn't studying a list of evidence; he was looking at a map of an entire nation. There was nothing to tell us where Holly had gone after she left Didcot.

"There's no need to be hasty," he repeated, and his eyes moved from point to point.

I could only imagine that he was reading the name of every village, but there were hundreds of them. I'd probably visited Somerset at some point in my life, but even if I hadn't, I was certain that it was a pretty place covered with fields, hills and countless settlements. The chances of our finding the right one were infinitesimal. Grandfather was so excited to have a miniature mystery to solve that the air seemed to seep out of him as he accepted defeat with a sigh.

"You mustn't think the worst." Mother put a hand on my shoulder, and I must admit it made me feel a little better. "Just because the young lady was worried about her grandfather, there's no reason to think that any harm will come to him."

Thankfully, our disappointment would soon be eclipsed by the arrival of approximately ninety-five per cent of our loved ones. We heard the sound of tramping feet in the hall and rushed out to see what was happening.

"We weren't expecting you until tomorrow. Mother's voice rose in cheerful surprise as she ran down the corridor to embrace my father, kiss my brother on the cheeks and civilly shake her mother-in-law's hand.

Father was not the most effusive person, but he was smiling from one ear to the other. "I couldn't wait any longer, so I left my office early, picked up Mother and drove straight here," He explained, as my grandmother looked disapprovingly at me.

I wondered what the terrifying creature was about to say. Though she had softened a touch over the last year, she was known for her icy looks, withering asides and comments on my weight.

"Hello, Christopher. You look…" She turned her head to inspect me before landing on the right words. "…*very well*, and it's lovely to see you. Come and shake your grandmother's hand."

To tell the truth, I was a little shocked, but did as I'd been told.

These were just the first emissaries, and we would soon be joined by a selection of old friends, first, second and possibly third cousins, and a few people I didn't actually recognise.

The only thing that I regretted about that fine evening was that they'd all arrived too late for dinner, but we retired to the grand salon for drinks, and Cook sent a Tunis cake, a trifle and plenty of shortbread biscuits up to us. The cake was topped with a thick layer of dark chocolate and various green and red marzipan fruits. The lemony sponge underneath was just delicious and, if someone had told me that there would be no presents that year, I'd have said, *Fair enough! I'm happy with my lot.*

My cousin Francis had become a dab hand at the piano since I last saw him – or perhaps he always had been and no one had told me. He entertained us all evening with Christmas carols, and the supposedly stony and uncompromising Lord Edgington led us in a beautiful version of 'Away in a Manger'. The night of the twenty-second turned into the morning of the twenty-third, and the festivities kept rolling. With Cranley Hall dressed in every colour of Christmas, and our friends and relatives all there for the celebration, there was nothing that could dampen my mood. Well, nothing except the memory of poor Holly Bridport.

Even as we exchanged presents – and Grandfather gave me a really very nice pair of leather slippers, to match the near identical pair my parents had already given me – the image of the girl in the green coat kept coming back to me. I would catch flashes of her in the face of my elegant cousin, Cora, and something about my friend Scarlet's voice reminded me of her. It was almost as though she were haunting me.

We were supposed to be going to see my father's extended family in Tatchester on Christmas Eve but, not only did I not like my father's extended family – who made my grandmother look like a deeply warm and emotional person – I couldn't bear the thought of never seeing Holly again. And so, instead of staying to play Musical Chairs or Reverend Crawley's Game, I returned to the library to think.

Mother was right. There had to be a way to work out where the young lady lived. A lingering feeling in my brain, like the ghost of a thought that once was, told me that I'd forgotten a significant fact. Holly had spoken of an estate, so her grandfather presumably owned a substantial piece of land. It would also make sense for her to live in Somerset, as her father's family were from there and the train she'd caught was heading in that direction. I returned to the original map we'd consulted and went over every square inch of the county.

"Christopher, I have something to tell you," Grandfather eventually popped his head into the room to reveal.

It was the wrong moment, and I shooed him away with one hand as I seized a large briefcase of travel maps from one of the shelves. I could barely lift the thing onto the desk but, once I had opened the leather flap, I began to flick through the thirty-seven charts therein. They were one of Grandfather's prize possessions, and there was one for every region of the country including... Well, as it happens there wasn't a specific one for Somerset, which made things more difficult. Instead, I took out the maps for Bristol, North Devon, and Dorset.

"It really is a marvel to see you hunting for clues," Grandfather stated in an impressed manner. Although I appreciated the compliment, I was still too busy to pay him any attention. "You're like a seagull following a trawler."

Perhaps it was this poetic interjection which helped stir the first memory I required.

"The sea! Holly mentioned the sea wind. The estate must be by the coast somewhere."

He didn't reply, but stood looking cheerful as I laid the maps on top of one another as best I could to piece together the coast of South West England. It felt positive to be doing something to find her again, but I scanned the most promising area, and nothing screamed, *Here's the girl you're looking for!* In fact, there were so many towns and villages about the place that my head began to swim.

"If you've exhausted your search," my grandfather began when he saw that I was struggling, "I have another present that you might enjoy."

"Shhh!" I replied like an impatient librarian and continued my search. "I believe that Holly must have told me the name of the place where she lived. It's on the tip of my brain, but I can't quite find it."

I scoured the coast from Land's End in the south-westernmost tip of England right the way up to Sharpness Dock on the River Severn. I spotted all sorts of ridiculous place names – Simonsbath, Westward Ho! and Velvet Bottom would surely have made me titter when I was less mature. Oh, fine. I smiled just a little at that last one. Sadly, nothing looked familiar beyond dull, geographical features that my old teacher, Mr Anders, had pointed out to us on the map at the front of his classroom. He used to bore me to death trying to make us memorise every last element of…

Sorry, I can't finish that sentence as I'm falling asleep just thinking about it.

My point is that… well, I'm not quite sure any longer. The memory of Mr Anders's phenomenally monotonous voice has overshadowed everything else. What I can say is that I failed to find Holly's family estate, and so Grandfather came to lend his support.

"If you let me tell you what I came to say, I think it will make you feel better."

I wouldn't give up. I couldn't give up. I tried one last time, layering the maps in a slightly different order so the point that had previously been obscured by the edge of one of them was now visible.

"The present I wish to give you…" my dear companion told me, but I had to interrupt him.

"St Audries Park!" I yelled with great joy. A tiny fragment in the top left corner of the Dorset map had been hidden by the border of another one but was now visible. It didn't even look as though it was a part of the coast unless you examined it very carefully, but there was the name I needed. "Holly lives on her grandfather's estate in—"

"St Audries Park! That's what I was going to tell you. I rang an old friend last night. He's a retired assistant chief constable for the Oxfordshire Constabulary, but still knows a lot of the local officers there. A detective went to Somerville College this afternoon and got the address of Holly Bridport."

I was a little taken aback, not least because he'd failed to run into the room shouting *St Audries Park, St Audries Park! Let's get in the car right now, and we can be there by midnight.*

"So you cheated," was my initial response. "I've been applying every rule you've taught me to find the location, and you called a friend to find the answer."

Rather than react to my sharp tone, he smiled. "That's correct. I made the most of our resources."

"Well, Grandfather..." I needed a moment to make sense of all this. "I think that's just brilliant."

CHAPTER FIVE

While Lord Edgington loved nothing more than choosing a route across Britain when investigating a new case, I rather enjoyed the more general planning involved. The when, why and how immediately came to my mind but, as there was a Christmas party still taking place in the grand salon, my grandfather suggested we put off discussing any more details until it was over.

It had been my grandmother's preference before she died to invite the Cranley Hall staff upstairs to spend time with the family on Christmas Eve. My grandfather had failed to continue this tradition during the dark years of his mourning, but I was happy to see that it was alive once more. Our maids, footmen, pageboy, grooms and several gardeners had joined the family for drinks and a sample of Cook's sensational Christmas pudding. Every last one of them was dressed in their finest clothes, and Grandfather sat in a comfy chair in the corner, surveying his subjects like a king on a throne. Being the benevolent overlord that he was, he handed out small presents and (hopefully far more valuable) envelopes to each member of staff.

The hors d'oeuvres that our normally eccentric cook had prepared for the evening were delicious, with barely a pickled whelk or Couilles De Mouton in sight. The decorations were spectacular, perhaps because I'd been too busy with our recent investigations to have anything to do with them. The tree in the corner of the room grazed the ceiling and was threaded with strings of silver bells and beads that shone in the light of the chandeliers. In fact, everything was just perfect and filled me with the joy of the season, but I still wished that everyone would go to bed so that I could plan our escape.

My cousins, who had come together that day from the furthest corners of Surrey, were in such a fine mood that the games went on until the early hours of the morning. It was a lot of fun but also enough to put me off Christmas for life. Eventually, I could take it no more and sidled over to my grandfather to pretend that I was really very interested in a gloomy old painting of one of our ancestors.

"Pssst…" I said, but he was clapping along with a game of Nuts in May and didn't hear me. "Grandfather, I think we'll have to get up very early tomorrow morning. If not, my granny will never let me leave."

His only response was to sing along with the players. "Here we come gathering nuts in May on a cold and frosty morning!"

"Grandfather," I tried again, but a grateful maid came to talk to him, and I would fail to communicate my message until the party was over.

"Don't worry, Christopher," he whispered once everyone had said goodnight and we were walking along the corridor to mount the stairs. "I have everything in hand. Be packed and ready by six o'clock in the morning, and we will sally forth on yet another Christmas adventure without the rest of our family knowing the slightest thing." He laughed fiendishly and looked over his shoulders at our chattering relatives. "They can't possibly imagine what is afoot."

He took the stairs to his luxurious suite, and I continued on to the sparse and desolate icebox of my own lodgings in the wing reserved for unloved guests. I really should have made more of a fuss about the room he'd chosen for me back when I first moved there three years earlier. Minor concerns such as chilblains and pneumonia did not disturb me that night, though, as my head was full of the voyage we were about to make to the far coast of England. I predicted it would take us five hours to arrive, which meant we would be there by lunch time at the latest. Of course, that didn't explain how we would infiltrate the house where Holly and her odious grandfather lived, but I trusted that my grandfather would formulate a suitable plan.

"You're suggesting we simply knock on the door?" I replied with disbelief the next morning after he'd explained his grand scheme.

"That's right."

"But that's ridiculous." We were standing at the front of Cranley Hall in near darkness. There was frost on the ground and my bones felt as though they'd been left out in the cold overnight.

"In what way is it ridiculous?" He allowed himself a tut. "When our car skidded off the road last year and we got stuck in the snow, we simply called at the nearest manor house. If you remember correctly, they gave us permission to enter the house and investigate any murders that happened to occur whilst we were there. I don't see that this is any different."

"Yes, but…" I was certain there was an argument against his half-baked idea, but I couldn't quite muster one.

"Trust me, my boy. Everything will go exactly to plan. We'll turn up at St Audries Park, pretend that we're lost in the snow, and the old miser who owns the place will have to let us shelter from the elements until help is at hand."

I was reluctant to believe him, and yet his predictions so rarely failed that I did not contradict him. "Very well, Grandfather. I just hope that we get there soon."

A hungry look crossed his face, and I knew that he would take my words as an invitation to drive like a lunatic across the country. Fittingly enough, it was at this moment that dear Todd pulled up in Grandfather's Bentley 3 Litre. On the one hand, I was relieved that we would not be travelling in one of his tiny sports cars with only a leather roof to protect us against the wind and cold. On the other, I was instantly reminded of what a beast of a machine it was.

"It comes with guaranteed one-hundred-mile-an-hour performance, you know?" Though he had owned it for over a year, he had not grown tired of reminding me of its top speed.

I didn't answer but presumably turned a little green. Staring out at us from the passenger seat, our dog Delilah looked quite nervous about the journey herself.

"Pssst," a voice in the darkness psssted. "I'm coming with you!"

We strained to see who was there as my dear mother emerged from the shadows dressed in a long black frock.

"How did you even know that we were going somewhere?" I had to ask.

"It was obvious, Chrissy. You were shifty-eyed all last night, and I know how much this young lady's safety has been playing on your mind. I assume we're going to save her?"

Grandfather did not approve of stowaways, but he was evidently reluctant to refuse his own daughter. "Violet, my dear, you have other plans today. You're supposed to be driving to Condicote."

"To spend another miserable weekend with Walter's boring cousins? I'd rather kill a few days in a nice draughty prison somewhere. And besides, Father, you were supposed to be coming with us."

"Ah, yes..." he began. "You see, the thing is—"

"I'm coming with you," another voice declared, and the sound of boots on the gravel path announced my father's arrival. "I can't stand my cousins. They're all quite mad. One of them addresses his children by naval ranks, though the closest he's ever got to a ship is the boating lake in Hyde Park."

"I would love you to join our burgeoning investigation." Grandfather spoke in a firm tone, as if he was about to talk some sense into them. "However, this is a sensitive matter, and we will need—"

"Good, you haven't left yet," my Granny interrupted, and I could see my grandfather's patience ebbing away. "I'm coming with you."

"Mother?" my father was surprised to see her.

"I must escape from our dreadful relatives. They surely can't object if there's a murder that needs investigating." She turned to one of her favourite foes. "There *is* a murder that needs solving, isn't there, Edgington?"

"We hope there will be soon," I answered, and that was when Grandfather finally lost his temper.

"Now that's enough. Loelia, your relatives are coming to your house today. What will they do if they get there and discover that there's no one home to entertain them?"

She snorted before replying. "Oh, don't worry about that. They'll soon find someone else to bother. The whole lot of them are parasites."

"Mother," my father chastised, "you're talking about our family."

"That's right." She turned her haughty stare upon him. "The very same family we all sneaked out of our rooms before dawn on Christmas Eve to avoid."

Grandfather would not be deterred and raised his gloved hands in the air. "Now listen, all of you. Christopher and I will be travelling alone to St Audries. It is the only hope we have of stopping a potential crime."

My mother knew him too well and had a rebuttal to this seemingly foolproof argument. "Is that actually true, father?" She batted her eyelids to look even more innocent than normal. "Are you really travelling alone, or will you have a selection of your servants following behind in a convoy of cars?"

Considering how cold it was out there, he looked oddly warm all of a sudden. "Ah, now… I might have mentioned our plans to a few members of staff. There is really nothing I can do if they choose to bring along several hampers of fine food and drink, but that does not mean I gave them instructions to do anything of the sort."

It was at this point that two more cars drove around the house. Both were large Rolls Royces, stocked full of baskets, boxes and the aforementioned hampers. I was glad to know that we would not be relying upon the hospitality of the people whose house we were invading.

"Todd," Granny barked as our chauffeur stopped the Phantom behind my grandfather's Bentley. "Violet, Walter, and I are coming with you. Bring around your master's Daimler. I'm happy to drive it."

Lord Edgington had never looked so stunned. It was as though someone had pickled him, or prepared him for a state funeral, or both.

It would fall to his son-in-law to reason with the formidable old woman. "Mother, you haven't driven in at least twenty years."

Loelia Prentiss was not the sort of person who changed her mind. "So it's high time I got behind the wheel. We'll see you there, Edgington."

I could tell that my grandfather's temper was bubbling like a volcano, and so I steered him towards his car before he could shout or spew lava everywhere.

"Everything will be fine," I promised as I sat him in the driver's seat.

"This investigation is already a disaster. Why don't we just invite your brother and cousins along and be done with it?"

I took this literally for some reason. "Because Albert is spending Christmas with friends this year, and I'm sure my cousins have other commitments."

The expression on his face just then said, *Christopher. I was being sarcastic,* so I looked for something else to cheer him.

"The good news is that Granny doesn't know where we're going, and you're a very fast driver."

"You're right. I am." The thought of breaking the land speed record heartened him somewhat. "Of course, the staff know where we're going, and your grandmother can follow them, but at least we'll have some time to investigate before they arrive."

With no more encouragement needed, he pressed the button to start the car and the Bentley's motor produced a slight shudder, as if affronted by the cold. Delilah barked her approval and jumped onto my lap when I took my place in the passenger seat.

"Christopher?" Grandfather asked as he navigated the burgundy automobile around patches of ice on the path off the estate. "Would you like to say it, or should I?"

It took me a moment to know what he meant, but I yelled out one of his favoured phrases before he withdrew the offer. "Drive like blazes, and don't spare the horses!" The Bentley's engine roared, and I had second thoughts. "Actually, if you could drive at a moderate speed and be careful on the roads, that would be preferable."

CHAPTER SIX

"Christopher, why are you laughing?" Grandfather asked after we'd been driving for an hour and I had, more or less, worked out which roads we would take.

"Oh, no reason. No reason at all." I tried to snigger a little more quietly.

It's really quite incredible that we managed to chart a route from Surrey to the western coast of England without hitting any famous places. There were no major cities but, to make up for that, there were plenty of towns with ridiculous names to enjoy. I found Mudford Sock, which was located a mere five miles away from Queen Camel. After that, I spotted Tinker's Bubble, Cannard's Grave and Four Forks. I believe my favourite had to be the imaginatively titled Street, which was really not so very far from Coat. And, of course, there were plenty of far ruder names that a polite young gentleman like me could never possibly repeat.

"Christopher?" he asked again when I could hold in my cachinnation no longer. "Are you laughing at the word 'Bottom' on that map?"

I promise I was trying to be grown up about it, but there were just so many of them around. "No, of course not." I managed to remain serious for a few seconds before I noticed the best Bottom of all, and my laughter broke free. "I'm sorry. I really am." It was actually quite painful. "I don't mean to be immature but—"

"Tell me the name, Christopher." His voice became stern, and Delilah whimpered.

I replied in a hushed voice. "It's… well, it's… Galloping Bottom."

His bright white moustache seemed to twitch disapprovingly before he put me out of my misery.

"I suppose that is mildly amusing." His laughter wasn't nearly as enthusiastic as my own, but it came as a real relief. "Though, if I'm not mistaken, there's an even better example on the Dorset coast. If you look between Durdle Door and Bat's Head, you'll find a Scratchy Bottom."

I had to put my whole hand in my mouth so as not to squeal. "Stop it," I begged. "Please stop it. It's inane and childish, but I can't help finding it funny."

By the time another hour had gone by, I'd managed to stop laughing. To precipitate this, I read aloud the entry for the man in Burke's Peerage whom I took to be Holly's grandfather.

"The Viscount Rivers, (Peregrine William Rivers) of St Audries Park, West Quantoxhead. Born 1848 – a baronet, J.P. and high sheriff for West Somerset. Educated at Eton and Christ Church, Oxford..."

I believe it was around then that I started nodding off. The next thing I remember was, "Husband to Lady Catherine Polly Rivers (deceased), 3rd daughter of 2nd Earl Fortescue, by whom he has issue, Magdalena Bridport (deceased)..."

I'm not sure whether I was making much sense, but Grandfather didn't complain. All I recall is the odd phrase as the exceedingly tedious tome went into detail on the man's extended family. "Nathan Rivers, (great-nephew) born... Florence Rivers (great-niece)... his brother, Theodore Acland (third cousin twice removed) both of Bicknoller... married Elizabeth Stevans..."

After that, I certainly didn't laugh or, indeed, open my eyes again until we stopped to fill the car with petrol and buy some much needed refreshments. The sugary sweet gingerbread star and angel biscuits we bought were just what I needed and gave me the energy to fall immediately asleep again when we got back on the road.

To be quite honest, I slept for much of the rest of the journey. It was a dull, overcast day, and Grandfather kept pointing out famous churches or, even worse, significant hills, so it's hardly surprising that I struggled to stay alert. And when I woke again, we were passing through a wholly different world from the one in which I'd fallen asleep. It was white, pristine, and beautiful.

"You see, boy," my chauffeur mumbled, "everything is going exactly to plan."

I certainly kept my eyes open, though not just to enjoy the snow. My grandfather was a skilled driver, but I had to keep pointing out the dangers I spotted to ensure that he didn't kill us on the slippery road.

"Watch out for that car," I told him on any number of occasions. "There's a fence coming up on the left," I felt the urge to explain from time to time. And, just the once, I mentioned, "I believe there's a bull in that field."

"Thank you, Christopher. That's enough." He did not appear to appreciate my observations. "Were you afraid that the immense creature would jump into our path?"

"You never can be too careful when it comes to bulls."

He looked at me dubiously but managed to bite his tongue. When we left the Wiltshire Downs behind us and reached lower land, something occurred that really didn't fit the old genius's plan.

"Oh. That wasn't supposed to happen." He looked ever so perplexed as he stared across the flake-free landscape. There weren't even any patches of snow from previous weeks. As far as the eye could see, the scenery around us was the dull green, brown and grey of a mild winter.

"It may be hard to claim that we need shelter from the snow if there's no snow within fifty miles." I managed to hide my amusement, though he did not seem worried either way.

"Fear not, Christopher. Much like the tide, the weather will turn in due course."

Although I was rubbing my hands together at the idea that I had finally trumped my all-knowing mentor, his prediction would (predictably) come true. As we got to within a few miles of the coast, high hills rose up on the horizon. And where should St Audries Park be but nestled right amongst them?

Grandfather smiled to himself the whole way there. By the time we pulled off the road on the other side of the Quantock Hills, my neck was hurting from shaking my head so much. I noticed one more unusual name on the map not far from where we hoped to spend Christmas, but I decided not to mention 'Dead Woman's Ditch'. My negativity hadn't helped anyone so far. If I'd pointed out such a bad omen, Grandfather would only have grumbled.

We passed an attractive church topped with sloping roofs of frosty white. St Etheldreda's was raised above the road, as though looking out across the horizon to see whether the weather would change any time soon. I thought it rather lovely, especially sheathed in snow like that, and my mind immediately turned to the young woman we'd driven across the country to help.

We continued the drive along a narrow lane, and the wheels of the Bentley began to skid. It would have been rather funny if we really had ended up veering off the road. When they arrived later, our servants could have driven into the back of Grandfather's car, and my father could have gone into theirs. It would make our acting far more believable when the time came to explain our presence to Lord Rivers.

We drove past a gatehouse and up to a pair of tall metal gates. Although they were imposing, with their twisted black, wrought iron metalwork, they were also wide open, and we glided on through. There were lines of large privet bushes shaped like spinning tops on either side of us, which drew the eye towards the jewel of the estate.

The ancient manor house was built in a Tudor Gothic style with an ashlar façade contrasting with red sandstone features. The most noticeable thing about it was the giant tower that had been stuck to the front, as though a child had decided that his home was not castle-y enough and needed more battlements. It made the asymmetrical building entirely uneven, but I thought there was something rather fantastical about it. I almost wondered whether Holly would let down her hair from the top of that tower so that we could climb up and save her.

There was a frozen lake to our right as we drove around the property, and if I'd had any doubts about just how cold it was outside the toasty vehicle, they were soon answered when Grandfather stopped the car some distance from the house. He opened his door, and a wind sucked out the warm air we'd enjoyed over the course of the journey. It felt as though someone had thrown a handful of icicles at my face, and so I pulled on my grandfather's arm to get him to stay there just a little longer.

"We've already made our first mistake," I told him. "If they see this car, they'll know we haven't had an accident."

He could evidently see the sense in this, and I was glad of another thirty seconds of comparative warmth as he closed the door and parked out of sight behind a hedge. As I'd been in the car for so long, my legs felt as though they'd been glued into position. Delilah was clearly desperate for a run, though, and sprinted to the house across the untouched expanse of fluffy snow. So that was her exercise done for the day.

"Grandfather," I asked as we followed her footsteps, "do you know what we're going to say when we get inside?"

"Of course I do. It is the foremost rule in a detective's notebook that, much like chess players, we must always plan several moves ahead. I know what I will say when that door swings open and, from that point, I have several other potential paths through our time here."

If nothing else, this was a good distraction from the blizzard we were traversing and those cold sea winds that Holly had mentioned. I was a little jealous of Delilah who, though I could not make her out at first, was sitting patiently under the carved stone porch looking perfectly cheerful when we arrived.

Now that I was closer, I could see that there was ivy growing up one wall of the snow-dappled tower. The whole central column of that building was oddly balanced with an octagonal turret attached to the side of the square block that rose above the main house. I had to wonder whether the castellated feature had been added after the building was complete or the original architect was just a little eccentric.

Stepping beneath that sheltered porch felt like breathing again after an underwater dive. I stamped my feet to get the snow off, and Grandfather shook his coat.

"Here we are then." He was relishing the chance to indulge in some amateur dramatics, but I was more nervous. I still didn't think it likely that the miserly old lord inside would welcome us with open arms, especially as there were three more carloads of people to come.

Grandfather raised his hand to press the bell, but the door was already swinging open, and one of the most crumpled and creased old gentlemen I'd ever seen stood before us in some distress.

"Lord Edgington, I don't care what you're doing here, but I'm very glad you've come. These people are trying to kill me!"

CHAPTER SEVEN

The man before us was not a lot older than my own beloved ancient, but looked as though he'd been compacted by whatever troubles were weighing him down. In fact, we towered over him, as he eagerly ushered us into the house.

Grandfather looked more than a little surprised by this welcome. It would seem that this was not one of the possible outcomes for which he'd planned. "Our car skidded off the road and—" he began, but our host interrupted him with an impatient wave.

"Yes, yes, there's no need to explain all that." The little lord adjusted his monocle to look at me. "I'm sure you have an excellent reason to be here, and I say welcome, welcome, one and all. My name is Peregrine Rivers, and you've arrived just in time."

Though he was effusive in his greeting, there was a note of bitterness to his words which told me we were not entering a happy home... Well, that and the fact he'd claimed the other members of the household were trying to murder him.

"That's very kind of you." Grandfather took the opportunity to prepare the man for what was to come. "I should probably mention that a few members of my family may take the same wrong turn as we have and potentially skid off the road on the same icy patch. Oh, and my servants may well be with them."

The short-set lord walked with a shiny silver cane, which he brought down on the flagstones with a satisfying *clink*. "Never mind that, man. My life is in danger."

"Yes, of course it is. And that's why..." Grandfather's acting was not up to his usual high standards, and he stumbled over his words. "Or rather, you must tell me all about it."

As Rivers shuffled further along the hallway with excruciatingly slow, small steps, I finally had the chance to take in the scene before us. There was a long entranceway leading up to a bifurcated staircase that plunged down from the floor above and forked off on two sides. Standing on the bottom step was a man in his early thirties who, even from a distance, I could tell was a soldier. No, he wasn't wearing a uniform. It was the way he held himself, and his evident muscularity.

Dressed in a black woollen blazer and carefully pressed navy-blue trousers, he observed us coldly.

Sitting on the step just next to him was a rather different prospect. Although I took the pair to be brothers, this second fellow was far more suave than the soldier. He wore a maroon velvet suit with black piping and had a perfectly trimmed goatee that lent him a devilish aspect. He had the same dark eyes in narrow slits as his companion and, even before he spoke, I felt that there was something duplicitous about him.

"What a nice surprise," he practically purred as I approached. "We weren't expecting guests this Christmas. My name is Nathan Rivers, and this is my brother Silas." You see! They were brothers! I wasn't such a bad detective after all.

He held out his hand, and I realised what was so odd about his behaviour. It wasn't merely that the owner of the house believed that at least one of these people was trying to kill him; it was evident that there had been an enormous row just before we'd entered the building.

I could see it on the faces of everyone there. A butler stood beside the first door off that warmly lit corridor, looking quite uncomfortable – not merely because of the tightness of his waistcoat. Just inside the sitting room beyond him, there was a woman of perhaps fifty. She held one hand to her mouth, to hide her presumably troubled expression, and then I finally found the person I really wanted to see. Holly was hidden by the shadowy overhang of the cantilevered stairs, and if she'd looked frightened the first time I'd met her, she was petrified now.

"Yes, it's lovely to meet you," I told Nathan as I accepted his hand. "My name is Christopher Prentiss. I'm sure you recognise my grandfather." I paused for effect then. I was hoping to strike some fear into the man, but his tiny black eyes – like raisin pips hidden within two seashells – showed no alarm.

"Of course, Lord Edgington is a living legend, though I feel I should tell you right now that my great-uncle Peregrine has a fanciful imagination. He's been screaming and shouting for months over the idea that someone wishes him dead, but I've yet to see the proof. Isn't that right, Silas?"

He turned to his brother, who did not appear to possess the power of speech but nodded his agreement.

I believe I mimicked Nathan's smug tone. "Whatever the case

may be, my grandfather will discover the truth."

The smooth character put one arm around my shoulder as we followed the two lords along another corridor to what I took to be the older part of the house. Suddenly, the walls and fixings went from the typical grandeur of a Victorian manor to the plain stone of a medieval building.

"Don't sell yourself short, Christopher," Nathan continued, and I realised that he knew more about me than vice versa. "I've read the articles on your exploits in London this past autumn. There was a rather nice write-up in The Chronicle. It sounds as though you outdid yourself, solving that business in the West End. Two murders, and you got to the bottom of them in just a couple of days! That's good going in my book."

He really did not appear to be concerned by our presence, but then silver-tongued charmers like Nathan Rivers are born with lies in their mouths and know how to hide their true feelings. I'd only just met the man, and I already disliked him.

We'd come out in what, I was fairly confident, would turn out to be called the Great Hall. I'd been to any number of houses with such rooms, but this one was rather special. It had high stone arches that looked as though they'd been pilfered from a church, an ornate minstrel's gallery at one end and an immense, blackened chimney piece which dominated one wall. Above it, there were countless family coats of arms. I noticed the Bridport one, with a sea serpent and a crow, that I had seen in the book in Grandfather's library. The Rivers shield was given prominent billing, of course, and showed a centaur shooting an arrow at a neighbouring sparrow. Its motto was written in large letters underneath. It read "Fidelity," and I thought, *That remains to be seen.*

Lord Rivers was still shuffling across to a large chair in front of the fire. It was not just that he was slow; he had a pronounced limp in his right leg and had to rely on his cane to support his weight. Delilah walked along at her master's side, but was clearly struggling to move so slowly and, once the two men had sat down, she made up for this torturously stiff journey by doing a quick lap of the room before settling before the fire.

"I'm sure you think it's strange that I should welcome you to my house in such a manner," our host began, "but I speak the truth. As of this morning, it is impossible to ignore the fact that someone in this house is trying to murder me."

"I have no reason to doubt you," Grandfather replied, thus cleverly avoiding having to say whether he actually believed the man whilst appearing to suggest that very thing.

"Now, listen." Lord Rivers had a directness about him that made every sentence he pronounced sound like an accusation. "I am a rich man. I would estimate that everyone in this house – including the servants – would benefit from my death. I'm a blunt, cantankerous old meddler, and I've pulled the strings of my young heirs for my own pleasure for decades. I love to watch the little worms wriggle on the end of my line as they try to outdo one another to see who I will favour in my will. My uncle did it to my brothers and me, and I'm upholding the tradition."

Grandfather listened to this rapid, rasping account of the Rivers family's sordid history, but he said nothing.

Holly's grandfather looked about the impressive space. "Obviously, I'm only interested in leaving all this to a male heir, so my one direct heir is out of the picture. I've got several great-nephews who fit the description, but with all that's happened this year, I'm beginning to doubt whether I should pin my fortune on them at all. In fact, I greatly believe that one of them must be to blame."

Lord Edgington presented his first question. "What exactly do you believe they have done? You said that I would find it hard to accept that someone wants you dead, and yet you haven't explained what makes you believe that to be the case."

He wagged his finger at us then… or perhaps he was trying to point and his shaky body did the rest. "You're right, Edgington. I must explain everything from the beginning. It started back in the summer. I had several close shaves with a falling sculpture, a surprisingly well-lubricated axle on the wheelchair I use for walks along the cliffs, and that was followed by a near poisoning. Each could have been an accident, but this morning was different."

He paused and looked about the room. I hadn't realised it until now, but the brothers grim-and-slimy had not crossed the threshold. They must have retreated into the house, as the only other person there was the butler we'd already seen. He had silently appeared beneath those churchly arches while we were talking.

Rivers shifted in his seat before explaining. "When I woke up this morning, the door of the water closet in my bedroom was ajar. I pushed it to, and a large stone block tumbled to the ground. No one goes in there but me. If I'd been a bit livelier, it would have cracked my head open."

With his hands on his own amethyst-topped cane, Grandfather selected a delicate response. "That does sound fairly conclusive. Whoever is responsible for the attacks has surely given up trying to make your death look like an accident, which suggests that the attempted murderer has become more desperate for some reason. Can you think of any circumstance that has changed recently to explain this development?"

Lord Rivers shined his monocle on his black fuzzy waistcoat as he considered the question. "I'm no genius. That's why I need you. The only things I've ever been good at are hunting and fishing. My first suspect in all of this would be Silas – that sullen slab of stone whom we passed on your way here. I know he doesn't like me, and he's done the least of the lot of them to win my good opinion. I assume it's because he's the oldest and thinks that St Audries Park should be his by right." He paused for a moment and his eyes widened. "He wasn't always so bad, but the war changed him. The Lord knows how many Germans he killed over there. I've heard tell that he was a real savage; one more notch on his knife won't worry him in the least."

Grandfather was clearly overjoyed to be thrown into a new investigation and, even if no one had been murdered (yet), his brain was racing with possibilities. This was his real Christmas present – and I think it was better than the black silk tie I bought him, which he assured me would be perfect for funerals.

"What of the other potential heirs?" he asked. "If Silas is the obvious culprit, then, in my recent experience at least, he probably had nothing to do with the attempts on your life."

Lord Rivers's face was twisted into a particularly bitter expression which rarely left him. His lips parted as though he were about to answer, but it would take another fifteen seconds before he formed a response. "The easiest thing to do is bring everyone together. I'll call them for you."

He put both arms in the air and clapped, but he had so little strength in his hands that this action resulted in little more than a quiet pat. "Ripon!"

The butler must have heard every word we'd spoken, as he knew what was required of him and sped off to do his master's bidding. We waited for him to return, and Lord Rivers lit a cigar but did not offer one to his guests. In fact, we hadn't even been given a glass of water, and I believe I know why. It would be easy to put the man's bad manners down to the shock he had received that morning, but I think it owed more to the fact that, as his granddaughter had told me, he wasn't a particularly nice person. He viewed Lord Edgington not as his social superior, but as a man who had come to do a job for him. To Peregrine Rivers, a detective, regardless of his rank and breeding, was on a par with the plumber who came to fix a leaking pipe or the postman who brought his letters. Lord Rivers was not the kind of man who shared his cigars with labourers like us.

I felt a flutter of excitement when I saw that Holly was the first to arrive. She came into the room speaking, as though she didn't want us to say anything before she could.

"Grandfather, who are these men?"

"You'll find out soon enough."

He turned those cold eyes upon her as though he barely recognised his own kin. It was hard to describe their colour, neither blue nor grey nor brown, but a hazy mix of the three which left him looking quite alien. They were overshadowed by two impressively wild and hairy eyebrows that moved with every laboured breath he took. To be quite frank, I'd rarely met a man who looked so well prepared for a trip up the celestial stairs to St Peter's gates.

He was the perfect murder victim, as he was inordinately wealthy and surely couldn't fight back.

"Stand over by the window and wait for the others." He barked out the command to her before turning back to us. "That's my granddaughter, Holly. Sadly, her mother – my only child – was a woman, or we wouldn't be in the mess we're in now. It's all my wife's fault, and she's not even here for me to blame."

As I said, he was the perfect murder victim and, if someone didn't get it over with quickly, I felt I might have to do it myself.

The next person to arrive was a young man of a similar age to the brothers we'd met, but with a far more pleasing demeanour. He had a sprig of mistletoe pinned to his lapel in honour of the season and his cheery, moustachioed face would have made a nice decoration for the top of the tree. Despite this favourable impression, I became rather disheartened as this triggered the realisation that we were yet to see a Christmas tree in the house. I crossed my fingers that there would be one in the dining room or a pretty salon somewhere.

"Morning all." The newcomer bounded through the room, apparently unaware of whatever had happened before our arrival. "Have I missed anything important this morning? I really must set an alarm in future. Even if I'm on holiday, I can't bear to let the day get away from me." He caught sight of Grandfather then and had to pause. "Lord Edgington?" I believe the words *what are you doing here?* were probably on his lips, but he resisted, and his great-uncle issued another order.

"Luke, dear boy. You can probably imagine why I allowed these gentlemen into our house on Christmas Eve. There's been another attempt on my life."

"That's terrible, Uncle Perry." He had real concern in his voice and walked over to check that his elderly relative was all right. "I hope you aren't hurt?"

"Hurt?" The old lord— Wait, this could get confusing as there were two old lords there. I'll try that again…

"Hurt?" The grumpy lord let out a brief note of laughter from his dry throat. "It'll take more than a lump of stone to kill me, but I appreciate your concern." He kept his eyes on his great-nephew as he spoke to us once more. "Luke is a good lad, unlike some of his cousins."

Holly was standing out of view of her relatives, and I noticed a slight flicker of her eyelashes as her grandfather spoke. I couldn't tell why, but she clearly didn't think so highly of Luke as the old lord… sorry… as the grumpy lord did.

Conversation continued, and I had a chance to look at her properly. It felt as though we were back on the train to Didcot together. The gown she wore was a similarly vibrant green to the coat she'd had on that day, but there were small red trimmings attached to it. A collar around the bateau neckline was in red banding, and the cuffs of her long sleeves were similarly finished. Their colour matched perfectly with a sash that hung loosely at her waist and, though I couldn't see her shoes for the length of her flowing skirt, I can only conclude that they were of a similar hue.

The brothers came next, followed by the middle-aged lady who had been in the front sitting room as we arrived. She wore a silvery dress but extravagant pearls and was accompanied by a far younger man with short, blond hair and grey eyes. He was dressed more professionally than the other members of the party – in a cream suit that was more in keeping with a summer garden party than a Christmas gathering. I had to assume that he was an employee rather than one of the family, and I noticed a nervous look about him as he took his place beside Holly.

"My dear," Lord Rivers called across to the lady, "it was good of you to come." He paid no such courtesy to his other young relatives, and, once a few members of staff had arrived to join the line of suspects, it seemed that we were ready to begin.

I must say that I felt for them all at that moment. They made me think of the condemned men from the Great War who were lined up before a firing squad at the Tower of London. I believe I even felt a twinge of sympathy for Nathan, and it was only a few minutes earlier that I'd decided I detested him.

Uncle Perry, as he was apparently known, rose unsteadily from his seat, and there was a curious moment as my seventy-seven-year-old Grandfather rushed forward to stop Rivers from toppling over. For a second, I imagined the pair of them keeling over on top of one another, but Lord Edgington was a sturdy beast, and he steadied the feather-light patriarch with ease.

Lord Rivers rolled his shoulders as if to regain his pride and then shuffled over to the waiting line. The people there no longer looked like condemned prisoners. With him in front of them, they resembled naughty school children standing before the headmaster.

The fierce character pointed at my far softer grandfather. "In case any of you don't recognise him, that man is Lord Edgington, the Bloodhound of Scotland Yard. And the boy standing next to him is… Actually, lad, I didn't catch your name."

I was about to answer when Silas finally spoke. "It's his grandson, you old fool." He had a deep, almost croaking voice that perfectly fitted his dark features and immense frame. "If you'd opened a newspaper in the last two years, you might have known that."

Our host grinned as he savoured the news he was about to deliver. "Lord Edgington and his grandson will be staying with us for Christmas. They're here at my request, and they won't leave until they find out who is behind all of these nasty tricks."

I can only imagine that he'd intended to walk along that line to glare into their eyes one by one. For this tactic to have worked, he would have needed to move a great deal faster. He'd only made it past the butler, maid and cook by this point, and they seemed less moved by the speech than the man's own kin.

"You can't do that, Uncle Perry," Nathan replied. "It's Christmas. We don't want strangers in the house. This is the one time of year we pretend to get along."

"Until Boxing Day at least," Silas groaned, "by which time we're normally at each other's throats, and Flossie and I are clamouring for a good old-fashioned duel in the English garden."

"I'll be your second if you like," his brother joked.

Lord Rivers interrupted them. "And where is young Flossie? I wanted everyone here, not just the ugliest of the lot of you."

The butler, Ripon, stepped forward to answer this question. "Miss Florence was not in her room when I went to look for her, M'Lord."

Rivers peered back along the line in the direction from which he'd come. I don't believe he had the strength to retrace his steps, and so he shouted from where he stood. "That doesn't do me any good, does it!" He seethed on the spot for a few moments before turning to my grandfather once more. "These are your suspects. I'll leave you to get to know them on your own."

"Why? Where are you off to?" Nathan clearly had no fear of his ill-tempered great-uncle.

"I'm due for my siesta. Not that it's got anything to do with you." Though he had started his long walk across the room, he really wasn't built to make a dramatic exit.

"Wait a moment, I thought that siestas were in the afternoon, not the morning?" Why was this the only thing I said in our whole time there? Why was this the point I wished to clarify?

"And I'll have one this afternoon, too." His cane went click, click, click towards the far door, and he shouted something back over his shoulder. "Look after our guests, Holly."

He finally made it out of earshot, but the others remained in position against the sandstone wall with its high mullioned windows. The family still looked nervous, and I thought I could see the first hints of the real Nathan Rivers. He was the sort of person who wanted everyone to think he was big and brave when, at his core, he was nothing but a scared little boy. As I had been that very thing not so very long ago, I was rather good at spotting them.

Grandfather cleared his throat a little artificially and addressed the troops or what have you. "This is all rather strange." Far fleeter of foot than the potential victim, he walked down the line with his hands behind his back and his long grey coat hanging over them.

Goodness me. No one had even offered to take our coats. What was the world coming to?

"You see, I hadn't expected to come here today to investigate a murder. We merely skidded in the snow on our way to spend Christmas with family, and yet here we are." This was far better acting than he'd previously managed, but he paused for a moment to decide what he wanted to say. "I will need to talk to you all before long—"

"You're wasting your time." We'd already heard much the same from Nathan, but it was his brother this time who looked to get rid of us. "Peregrine Rivers is a toplofty crackpot, and anyone who believes a word from his mouth is a fool."

Grandfather was only a few feet away from the burly brute and studied him without saying anything.

"I'm afraid I have to agree with my cousin," Luke spoke up, and my picture of him as a reasonable, easygoing sort was called into question. "Well, not the way he said it, but the general message. Our great-uncle has been paranoid for some time. There used to be a small village nearby with eight or so houses, but he forced out all the villagers and bought up their land because he thought they were plotting to take over the estate."

"And that was back when we were children," Nathan added. "Just think how bad he is now."

Lord Edgington appeared interested in the account but would not be thrown off a case so quickly. "I appreciate you telling me this, but I couldn't forgive myself if something happened to Lord Rivers. I'm sure you understand why I can't leave St Audries until I'm confident that he is not in any danger. And besides, my car slid off the road and we can't go anywhere until the snow thaws."

There was a rash of conversation that travelled along the line and mainly consisted of discussion of the terrible weather, the unlikelihood of Rivers being murdered, and some talk of what Christmas dinner might offer that year.

"Holly, was that your name?" I asked the young lady I had driven one hundred and fifty miles to see. "Perhaps you could show us to our accommodation as your grandfather suggested."

CHAPTER EIGHT

We were taken upstairs by the girl who we'd had to pretend not to know. Even as we left the others behind and she showed us to a suite of rooms in the tower, she acted as though we'd never met before. It was only when the door was closed behind us that she felt she could speak freely.

"I can't believe you're here." She held her hand to her chest, and I was worried for a moment that she might topple over in shock.

Now that I saw her again, I realised that there was something rather old-fashioned about her. It was not just the long dresses that she wore, or the way her hair was pinned on the top of her head like a Victorian matron's, there was a fragility to her that was more suited to the stereotypical image of women from the last century who were not allowed a voice of their own. I must admit that it made me want to do whatever it took to take care of her, which presumably wasn't very enlightened of me.

"After what you told me on the train, we had to come," I explained. "At the very least, I had to return this."

I reached into my inside pocket to extract the silver chain with the Christmas bell. It swung freely between my two fingers and caught the light coming in from the snowy world outside.

"You found my bracelet!" Her eyes were suddenly so expressive, so full of light and life and I knew that, even if we achieved nothing else, our trip there was worthwhile. "I thought I'd lost it for good."

"You left it on your seat in our compartment. I ran after you, but you were too fast. Or perhaps I was too slow. I really can't say."

She turned towards the window as though she wished to examine her treasure on her own. "My mother gave it to me when I was a child. She called it my Holly bracelet. I've been heartbroken thinking that I would never see it again. I went to the station every day in case someone had handed it to a guard."

I suddenly felt silly for not doing this very thing. "I'm so sorry, I should have thought. I really—"

"No, no. You didn't realise."

I believe we both became aware of my grandfather at this moment.

He was sitting on a green leather chair at a small bureau, keenly watching our exchange.

"Don't mind me. It's nice to see you so happy." I felt he could have said more, but he left it at this.

As Holly was now too self-conscious to continue, I decided that I would have to steer our conversation to a more significant topic.

"We may not have much time to talk, so we should be quick. I imagine you've realised by now that my grandfather is a detective. I would have told you on the train, but I couldn't get my words out."

"Of course. I know who you are, Lord Edgington." She looked past me at the man who really mattered. "Before you arrived, my grandfather had the most terrible argument with Silas and Nathan. Even Luke was involved, and I haven't seen his sister Flossie since. Everyone in the house butted heads. I believe I may have been the only person not to lose my temper."

Grandfather looked at her with a curious twinkle in his eyes, and I wondered what he was thinking. "You seem frightened of your own relatives, my child. Why is that?"

Fear was evidently a part of Holly Bridport's very being and, as she answered, she had to wrap her arms around herself to stop from shaking. "It's him. It's Grandfather. He can be so unkind. I know he's never loved me. He tells me all the time. I'm his closest relative, but he hates me because I don't bear his name."

Something about her bearing since I'd first seen her there told me that she wasn't one of the family so much as an unpaid skivvy. As she finished speaking, we heard her name being called below.

"I have to go." She turned before I could say anything, but Grandfather was unwilling to end the discussion so soon.

"No, child. Give us two more minutes."

She held her hand against the door but did not open it, and so he continued.

"What was the subject of the argument upon which we intruded?"

She swallowed and looked away from him once more. "My grandfather was his usual angry self. He was doing all he could to rile Silas. I'm no admirer of my cousin. He has a thin skin and a violent temper, which is a terrible combination, but my grandfather brings out the worst in him. So then his brother lost his temper. Nathan…"

I would say that she hesitated again at this moment, but that pale creature rarely did anything else.

"You can tell us, Holly," I tried to reassure her. "That's why we're here. We came all this way to help you."

"I know, Chrissy. I really do, but that doesn't make it any easier to say. I'd never expressed my thoughts to anyone outside of this house before I met you this week." Despite this, with her eyes now tracing the swirling pattern of the thick red carpet beneath our feet, she found a way to continue. "Nathan... well, he told Lord Rivers that he wanted to kill him."

"You heard him use those words?" Grandfather asked and received a nervous nod of the head from Holly.

"That's right. We all did, and Nathan was about to charge straight at my grandfather when he opened the front door and, as if you'd timed your arrival for that very moment, you were both on the doorstep."

"Holly?" a woman's voice called again, and I heard footsteps coming up the snail-shell staircase we'd just ascended.

"Before you go," my grandfather continued. "You must tell us who the two people are who are not in your family. Not the servants, but the young gentleman in the cream suit and the lady dressed in grey. I take it that they provide some assistance to your grandfather?"

He could be a little demanding sometimes, but the expression on his face told her he was only looking out for her interests.

"Mr Acland is a sort of clerk. He helps Grandfather with his paperwork and the running of the estate."

"And the woman with the pearl necklace?" Grandfather pushed her to speak, as she clearly didn't want to reveal anything else.

"That's Victoria Stevans." She froze for the length of one deep breath. "She was my grandmother's companion and she..." I swear that she shuddered then, as though she couldn't bear to speak of the woman. "Well, she stayed on here after her former employer died. My grandfather is very kind to her."

I extracted five potential conclusions from this restrained account...

One: Holly did not like Victoria Stevans.

Two: Lord Rivers *did* like Victoria Stevans.

Three: Victoria Stevans was a moneygrubber who had probably stolen her pearl necklace from the lord's dead wife.

Four: Victoria Stevans almost certainly murdered Holly's grandmother.

Five: Victoria Stevans most likely killed Holly's parents and was no doubt the one plotting against Lord Rivers.

I must admit that these baseless presentiments were unlikely to be true.

A knock on the door echoed about the room and Holly jumped so dramatically that she almost hit her head on the ceiling – again, that's not actually true.

The door swung open and there was Victoria Stevans. "You promised you'd help me get things ready, Holly. It's Christmas Eve and there's a lot to do."

Holly did not look at the woman directly, but replied in a polite, controlled voice. "Yes, Mrs Stevans. I'll come right away."

The middle-aged… Sorry, I don't really know how to describe her. She was Holly's grandmother's companion who, for some reason, had stuck around St Audries Park long after her employer had died. Whatever she was, she glanced from my grandfather to me and then nodded without betraying a single emotion. "Gentlemen, the preparations for lunch are under way. I'm sure that Lord Rivers will welcome your presence at the table with us."

She gave another nod and swept from the room with her long skirt sweeping the floor behind her with a satisfying swoosh. Holly pursed her lips together apprehensively and followed her out.

"Well, my boy," Grandfather purred once we were alone, "what do you make of our time here so far?"

It was hard to know what to say. "It has certainly been dramatic. And Holly's relatives are just as monstrous as she suggested when we first met."

His serious expression transformed at this moment and his moustaches looked quite chipper as they pointed up excitedly. "Yes, it's wonderful, isn't it! This is just the sort of mystery I enjoy solving. Family rivalries, two mysterious characters embedded in the household, a cruel old lord and his diabolical descendants: it's like the plot from some wonderfully gothic novel. My first question has to be, did you set this up as a Christmas present, Christopher? Are they really just actors?"

He was so enthused by the possibility that he began to shift from one foot to the other as he took in his grand bedroom, which had a smaller chamber leading off it for me. The suite was in the square tower that I had seen from outside. There was a large, curtained bed in one corner, upholstered all in red to match the carpet and wallpaper. It was a good-sized room but terribly sparse. Despite the expensive fixtures and fittings, there was too much space, and it was not as cosy as I would have liked.

"No, of course I didn't stage anything for your enjoyment."

"Oh, come, come." He stopped to look back over his shoulder. "You can tell me; I'll still go along with the game if that's what it is. And you must admit that the story of a beautiful young lady breaking down in tears on a train is a little far-fetched. How did you even find a compartment to yourselves on a busy day so shortly before Christmas?"

"Just chance, I suppose." He clearly wouldn't be convinced, so I took a sterner tone with him. "Now will you please believe me that a man's life is in danger, and we must take this case as seriously as any other we've investigated?"

"Yes, of course." He sounded a touch chastened. This was rare for him, and it didn't last long. "And what a sumptuous case it is. It's as tasty as one of Cook's famous hors d'oeuvres."

As he anticipated the delights – both culinary and criminal – that lay ahead, I tried to concentrate on the danger before us.

"We have two clear suspects to consider. Silas and his brother Nathan struck me as nefarious types from the moment I met them."

He had stopped before the wide, bisected window in the bay that looked over the front lawn. "From what I heard, Nathan thinks very highly of you. You have begun to make a name for yourself as a detective." His brow creased, and he reconsidered my words. "But what possible evidence do you have that they are untrustworthy? Are you basing everything you know on a superficial judgement? Has the man's devilish facial hair convinced you of his guilt?"

I wasn't sure how to react for a moment. I would have liked to deny his observation out of hand, but he was quite right. "I wouldn't say that exactly, but Holly has told us of her cousins' machinations in trying to inherit this place. And it sounds as though Lord Rivers has played his potential heirs against one another for years."

He clicked his fingers three times before responding. I have no idea why.

"Now you're talking, my boy. Now you're using your brain. Whatever else we might think of our suspects, the key to understanding this interesting collection of people must come down to Lord Rivers's will, if one indeed exists. He makes it sound as though the question of who will inherit the estate is in the balance."

"I thought much the same. Of course, he heavily implied that Luke is his favoured candidate. Perhaps it will turn out that Nathan and Silas are innocent, and the seemingly cheerful great-nephew is the real instigator."

He walked back across the room to shake my hand. It came as something of a surprise.

"Christopher, I applaud you." He could be a very literal man and pulled his hand back to do just this. "Not so very long ago, you would have come into this house and assumed that all the young ladies were angels, all the gruff fellows were swine, and any bright character with a cheerful word to say couldn't possibly be to blame for the crimes. You have grown up a lot this year, and I sincerely congratulate you on your progress."

"What you mean is that I've become the cynic you always wanted me to be!" I had a brief laugh at his uncomfortable reaction, but soon reassured him. "Don't worry, Grandfather, I am not yet a stone-hearted doubter through and through. I still believe that every girl is as innocent as the day she was born." I winked at him, and I believe we would have continued our dissection of the facts, but everything was about to change.

We heard screams from somewhere in the house. They were only faint at first, but they touched off a rash of further noises. Feet pounded along corridors, doors swung open and slammed shut, and my grandfather launched himself from the room. Unlike our host, he could move at a fair clip when the moment required, and I had to run to keep up.

We shot down the old stone staircase in the octagonal tower that was adjacent to our room. It was easy to know where to go, as we could follow those noises like a trail of stones through a forest. We cut through the house and selected a door under the grand staircase that would lead us towards the back of the property. We followed a narrow corridor that took us past grand parlours, and I noticed an extremely attractive dining room, but there was no time to wonder what we would be eating that weekend. Well, not much at least.

We turned off into a games room that bordered a large salon in the far back corner of the house. Almost everyone was already gathered there ahead of us. There was a line of people, just like in the Great Hall a short while earlier, but this time they weren't waiting to be inspected. They were trying to make sense of the sight before them. Lying on his back on the hearth, with his hands by his sides in an oddly meek position for such a belligerent person, was not Lord Rivers as I had expected, but his great-nephew Silas. There was a bloody hole in his temple, and I had to assume he would have one on the other side where a bullet had passed through. I could see no sign of a gun, which I took to suggest that the killer wasn't finished with his plan.

Grandfather pushed through the crowd to see for himself. He moved slowly as he approached the poor man, then knelt down to close his eyelids.

"No, it can't be," Nathan shouted, like a stubborn fool trying to strike a bargain with death. "Not Silas."

"I'm sorry, young man," Grandfather proclaimed in a strangely distant voice. "Your brother is dead."

CHAPTER NINE

Though Silas's fate was surely evident before we arrived, my grandfather's confirmation of the fact still shook the place. I was surprised to see the family's butler fall back into a chair and hold his head in his hands. It was hard to know whether this was the reaction of a man who loved his young master, or simply that most people – unlike my grandfather and me – are unused to coming across such sights of a morning.

The person who looked most distressed, however, was a girl of about my age with curly, chestnut brown hair whom we had not previously seen. She was dressed in a festive white and red checked dress and, when Grandfather stood up from his examination, she fell to her knees a few feet from the body. Luke went over to put one hand on her shoulder, but he could find no words to comfort her. I concluded that this was his sister Flossie, who had not been around to welcome us before.

Holly appeared from deeper in the house at this moment. There was a door in the corner of the bright salon which looked as though it led to a staircase, and, from there, presumably the bedrooms on the upper floors. She was evidently the last to know, as even her grandfather had hobbled in as we arrived. And she did not react as many of the others had. If anything, she looked resigned to this sad reality. Holly didn't cry or scream out. She quietly joined the others and leant against a chest for support, as if standing would have exhausted too much energy.

"And so it has come to pass," Grandfather mumbled to himself. The jaunty air he had previously exuded had dissipated. He looked down at the body for a few moments before addressing the flock. "Ladies and gentlemen, I can only imagine how distressing this must be for you. Your loved one has met a terrible end that I would not wish on my worst enemy." I knew for a fact that this was true, as at least one of his worst enemies was rotting in gaol. "There is nothing we can do to bring poor Silas back to life, but with your assistance, I will do all that I can to find his killer."

I realised then that as much as this speech was designed to comfort them, it also served to warn the culprit that he would not get away with whatever plan he had in mind. Feeling just as confident of this fact as my redoubtable mentor, I went to stand next to him and scanned every face in that room.

It was Nathan who provided the first response. "And when you find whoever did this, I will wrap my hands around his throat and choke the life out of him." He spoke through gritted teeth, and I had no doubt that he meant every word he said – which in turn made me wonder whether he meant a single word he said.

From the first, I had noticed something just a smidge too theatrical about Nathan. Judging by his perfectly coiffed black hair and beard, which appeared to have been shaped with a pair of nail scissors and ruler, appearances were everything to the man. Even as he mourned his brother's passing, there was a note of artifice in his voice that made it hard to believe him.

"You'll do nothing of the sort," Lord Rivers snapped, and he walked right up to his young relative to look him in the eyes from fifteen inches away. As he was only a short man, this was as close as he could get. "You'll let Lord Edgington do his job, and the courts will decide what becomes of the blighter who came after me and Silas."

What he lacked in stature, the old man certainly made up for in grit and aggression. His proclamation had more of an effect than my grandfather's even, and everyone there fell quieter. People froze where they stood, and the sounds of the room rushed in around us. A flaming log was crackling softly in the fireplace, and I believe that, had a window been open, we might even have heard the snow landing gently on the ground.

"Thank you, Lord Rivers," Grandfather replied when the moment suited him. "I will need to know more about Silas and so, for the moment, I wish only to speak to his brother." He turned to the still crestfallen butler, then thought better of it and looked for the maid. "You may call the police to inform them of the death."

"There's no chance it's just a tragic accident, is there?" Luke suggested hopefully. "I know that Silas liked messing about with weapons. In fact, it was his favourite thing to do. Isn't it possible that he slipped and the gun went off?"

"I'm afraid not." Grandfather was already shaking his head before he spoke, and there were clearly any number of problems with this theory. "For one thing, there is no sign of the weapon that killed him. Furthermore, while you will all have noticed the bullet hole through his temples, there is a further wound to his heart, which I believe rules out suicide."

I glanced down to see the evidence for myself and now spotted the blood stain beneath the dead man's jacket. I should have probably already questioned such a glaring incongruity, but I began to wonder why no one had heard the shot.

"Who was the first to find the body?" I asked rather abruptly, and Holly jumped again, as she had in grandfather's bedchamber.

The staff had begun to wander from the room, but Luke's sister, who had seemed so distressed by Silas's death, lingered to answer. "It was me. I was coming out of the orangery and heard a noise like someone falling to the ground." She looked up at the simple glass chandelier on the ceiling and corrected herself. "Actually, I heard shouting and two quite similar sounds some seconds apart, but I didn't think anything of them at the time. I had to lock the orangery, and it took me a couple of minutes to cross the lawn and come in here."

"Thank you, my dear," Grandfather offered her a truly sympathetic smile. "I will talk to you in due course. You should go somewhere to rest for the time being. You've had a trying time."

Victoria Stevans came to guide the startled young lady away. Perhaps realising she was expected to offer a similar level of kindness, Holly skipped to catch up with them. In a moment or two, we were alone with Nathan and his fallen brother. The still-breathing of the two took a seat as far from the body as possible. His hands shaking, he took a case from his pocket and attempted to light a cigarette with a match. He was too nervous, and so I went to help him. If my mother had been there, she would have told me how important it is to show courtesy to our fellow men, even if we don't think highly of the fellow in question. What with it being Christmas, I decided to heed her message for once.

As Nathan puffed on the cigarette, Grandfather called me back to look at the victim.

"The wound to the heart is strange," he told me. "I thought perhaps he'd been shot twice, but the cut in his shirt is too fine for that."

He knelt down to pull aside Silas's jacket. There was plenty of blood, but the hole in the shirt was barely noticeable and definitely not the work of even a small-bore bullet. Grandfather donned his gloves to open one button and lift the white cotton from the skin so as to better inspect the wound.

"My guess would be a knife of some kind, which is stranger again. Why would the killer use a knife if he was holding a gun? Or, alternatively, why shoot Silas if he'd already stabbed him?"

This was the typical sort of conversation we had whenever the great Lord Edgington inspected a body, but I must say that it felt odd with the victim's kin present.

Nevertheless, I replied in a whisper. "Perhaps he didn't want to make too much noise. Perhaps he stabbed him in the heart…" I hadn't got much further in my supposition than this, but a second half of the equation presented itself. "…and he wanted to make sure he'd done the job so shot the man anyway."

"I suppose that is a possibility." He clearly considered this an unlikely proposition.

"You know why this happened, don't you?" Nathan called over to us. He put one foot up on his knee and stared into space. "He was the eldest. If Uncle Perry had been killed without making a will, Silas would have been the one to inherit St Audries."

"I don't see how that's relevant, as Lord Rivers is still alive." It generally falls to me to point out the obvious, and I did a sterling job this time.

"Oh, for goodness's sake!" Nathan had lost the layer of slippery charm he'd had when we arrived, but there was still a great deal of arrogance in the way he spoke. "It's really not hard to understand. The killer had a good go at murdering Uncle Perry, but the old dog wormed his way out of it each time." (This was one too many animal metaphors for my liking, but I didn't interrupt.) "So he had a break and went for the next in line. He can see to the old lord later."

With Grandfather's examination complete, we walked over to Nathan, but he still wouldn't look at us.

"There is a certain logic to what you're saying, but perhaps you'd prefer to hold this discussion elsewhere?" Grandfather tilted his head in the direction of the door, but Nathan just shrugged.

To be fair, his brother wouldn't come back to life no matter how far from the body we went. Instead, we took our places in a pair of armchairs in front of his sofa. The room was a little unloved compared to the others we'd seen. It had the feeling of being surplus to requirements, located as it was in the most distant corner of the house. The decoration was decidedly dull and Victorian, and though the space was clean, neat and warm, there was not much else to recommend it.

"Very well. I accept your point."

Lord Edgington mimicked our suspect's posture. I wondered whether this was an intentional tactic to intimidate the man, and so I decided to do the same. I soon changed my mind as we looked silly sitting in identical poses, and

"If one of your relatives were hoping to inherit Lord Rivers's estate," Grandfather continued, "by killing off the relevant parties in the wrong order, he might hope to obscure the motive."

Nathan was no longer so distressed as he had been, and his cold laugh travelled across to us. "You're just as clever as they say, aren't you Edgington?"

"Perhaps you've never spoken to a marquis before, but people don't tend to refer to me by my surname." My grandfather was not normally the sort to care about titles, but the man's attitude had clearly got his back up. "However, I have no doubt that you're clever, too. Perhaps you killed your brother first to make it appear as though you weren't to blame. As he was older than you – and, from the look of things, Lord Rivers is unlikely to leave you his estate of his own free will – it would be a smart trick to start with Silas."

Nathan didn't respond. He pulled more putrid grey smoke into his lungs and held it in for as long as he could as though he wished to punish his insides with that burning sensation that was familiar to me from the single puff of my father's cigarette I had once taken.

When Nathan eventually replied, it was not to address the accusations put to him. "I'm impressed. I really am. I never imagined that you'd be as good as the papers say."

I could sympathise with his loss, but that didn't mean I liked the man, and so I turned the screw a little tighter. "You're an admirer of Lord Edgington's work, isn't that correct? Perhaps you got your first kill out of the way quickly to avoid funking out at the thought that he would catch you. There's definitely something haphazard about the way your brother was murdered. The killer took a risk in shooting him with so many people nearby."

He shook his head and produced another small cloud. "Don't be ridiculous, you goose. If I was worried about your grandfather catching me, I would have simply waited until you'd left the county. After all, the New Year is just as festive for a killing as Christmas Eve."

Something in what he'd said appeared to undermine the very idea of his innocence, but I didn't particularly like being compared to a farm animal, and so I left it to Grandfather to challenge him again.

He leaned forward to do just this. "The fact is, I have met few killers who believed I was their match, and plenty who underestimated me. Whoever murdered your brother has made that same mistake."

"Oh, so you don't think I indulged in a little holiday fratricide after all? How very sporting of you."

Grandfather nodded, as if to imply, *Of course I don't!* When I knew what he was really thinking was, *Don't get ahead of yourself, sonny boy!*

"As it happens, I believe that you will be of great help to this investigation. First, you must tell me about Silas. For the moment, I have a good idea of who hates whom in this family, but not a great deal more."

Grandfather was a wizard with words. It was not just that he had a vocabulary that would have put Alexander Pope's to shame; he knew when to employ it more sparingly. He was a real master at extracting the information we required from our suspects, and I watched as the effect washed over Nathan.

"I can see how that might help." He nodded to himself, as though this was his idea and he was content with it. "Well, my brother was… different. He came back from the war quite changed." He had the same hungry look in his dark eyes as when he'd introduced himself. "There's not a lot more to say about Silas as, since then, his life has remained just as it was. He hated living here but had nowhere else to go. He was, to all intents and purposes, a child."

"A child who loved weapons, according to your cousin."

Nathan wasn't intimidated by things like facts and brushed this aside. "Precisely. He killed a great number of men in his time in the army. He was a sharpshooter and a blasted good one at that. He

74

made a name for himself at the Battle of Belleau Wood and continued through the Hundred Days' Offensive. When he wasn't picking off enemy soldiers from a distance, he would cross no-man's-land to raid trenches with nothing but a knife."

"Do you believe that this disturbed him in some way?" Grandfather was clearly judging the man before us. Nathan's evident pride in his brother's violent past was difficult to stomach. "Do you think, just perhaps, that it robbed him of a sense of right and wrong once the war was over?"

Our suspect had been enjoying the chance to weave his tale and seemed upset by this interruption. "No, I'm saying that Silas was a hero. Think of all the men he saved by killing those Jerries." He replied in such a rush of verbiage that he had to take a breath. "And what has his moral compass got to do with anything? He's the one lying dead on the floor. We should be discussing the disturbed individual who did it to him."

Grandfather made no sign of having noticed this surge of anger but maintained his calm delivery. "So Silas never got married, never bought a house of his own. He returned from the war a stunted individual."

"That's more or less it."

"Did he have any enemies?"

"Not one… except everyone to whom we're related."

"Any friends?"

Nathan brought one hand down on the arm of the sofa. "He had me."

"You loved him, and he loved you?"

"That's not the word he would have used, but we were brothers." He examined his nails as he spoke. "We were loyal to one another. We promised that, whichever of us inherited the estate, we would share it equally."

There was a slight glow to my grandfather as he moved the conversation on to exactly where he wanted it to go. "Which brings us to the question of who you are, Nathan Rivers. I've only been here for a short time, but I believe I have ascertained certain facts about you."

Nathan leaned back to view the detective from a different angle. "Please, Lord Edgington. Impress me."

He didn't need to be asked again. "You are an orphan. Or at least, your father is dead, though I suspect your mother is, too." If Nathan was surprised by this, he didn't show it. I, on the other hand, had to cover my mouth, as I couldn't imagine how he'd divined such a fact. "You have set your hopes on you or your brother inheriting this estate, but despite your honey-mouthed ways, things haven't gone to plan."

"You don't know me at all."

Grandfather smiled in that uniquely innocent way of his. He could be as friendly as a kitten and dangerous as a scorpion at the very same time. "Oh, I think I do. I think that you believed that, as Peregrine had no sons of his own, the pair of you would one day be wealthy, and so you've done nothing with your life."

Nathan finally looked up at him. He was trying not to show any emotion but, if *I* could see how rattled he was, I can only imagine what my grandfather had discovered.

"I'm confident that you have borrowed against your prospects over the years and now, with your would-be benefactor entering his eighties and still refusing to depart this mortal coil, you find yourself in a precarious position."

I would have liked to stand up and applaud. Grandfather normally only used his skills of mind reading – or whatever he was doing – to unnerve me. I'd rarely seen such a display in front of a suspect before, and this alone was worth the price of admission – by which I mean a snowy drive across England.

Nathan huffed out a long, troubled breath, which only made me believe that my grandfather had described him to a tee. "What possible evidence have you got that any of what you're saying is true?"

"Well, for one thing, you haven't denied it."

He looked at me then. He really must have been struggling if he thought I would be able to help. "I… Why would…?"

"Nathan Rivers…" Pulling back his shoulders, my grandfather spoke more forcefully. "…you are a man of some charm who, I have no doubt, has lied, swindled and cheated to get by in life. With your hope of a comfortable existence ripped away, I could well imagine you plotting to murder Lord Rivers, and your brother too, if it were necessary."

Shooting to his feet, our suspect attempted to show us just how offended he was. "How can you say that? Silas was the only real family I had, and now he's gone. Have you no heart?"

"How can you stay in the room where your brother was murdered to have a conversation? You didn't even find a blanket to place over him. Have you no heart?"

I simply adored my grandfather at that moment. He was an absolute marvel with a mind like a complex machine. The grimace that he'd provoked on Nathan's usually smug face was perfection itself.

Our suspect marched across the room as if to storm out, but he had more to say. "Now, listen here. I'm not a killer. You can call me a philanderer, a dangler and a rake, but whatever other sins I may have committed, I have never once physically assaulted another man."

"And yet you threatened to kill your great-uncle before we arrived this morning." It was a touch brazen of me to run into the fight and land the last blow, but that took nothing away from my pleasure in doing so.

Something about Nathan's expression put me in mind of a burning building. He really should have left when he had the chance. "I didn't kill my brother or plan to murder Uncle Perry. You should be looking to my wonderful cousin Luke or the old man's fancy woman if you want answers. I can promise you this; I am not the one you need!"

CHAPTER TEN

"That was remarkable, Grandfather," I said once we were alone. "How did you know so much about that slippery fish?"

He attempted to hide his smile, but his moustache had other ideas and curled up a fraction. "I suppose I have learnt a thing or two during my years as a detective."

I wouldn't let him get away with such coyness and pressed him for more. "I can imagine how you knew his father was dead – that was the only thing that made sense if he and his brother were in line to inherit this estate – but what about his lying and double dealing?"

"Nathan Rivers is a man who projects total confidence, but something about the way he speaks points to an underlying core of insecurity. With such people, all you have to do to unravel them is find a loose thread and pull."

This was hardly a comprehensive explanation, and he soon continued. "I have met many men in my time who have lived their lives in expectation – be it of the future success of a business venture or the promise of an inheritance. Most of them overextended themselves in anticipation of this change in fortunes. It was no great stretch of my imagination to see that Nathan fitted this sorry profile, and he confirmed the rest himself."

I was a touch disappointed that he hadn't used any form of wizardry. "So you could have been wrong about everything?"

"I could have, but I wasn't."

"But you—" I decided to cut that argument short. "Do you think he really is the killer?"

"To tell the truth, I do not know. It is too early to draw such conclusions, but we have already discovered plenty of motives to explain the killer's plot. Lord Rivers is the obvious target, and I'm inclined to believe our initial hypothesis. The poor man lying before the fireplace would have had to die at some point anyway, and the fact that the viscount is still alive was no reason for the killer to delay the rest of his plan. We already know that he has given up on the hope of making the murders look like accidents. That means he is exposed and possibly quite desperate."

The more he told me, the more questions came to my mind. "And the shot? Why did no one hear it?"

Grandfather glanced about the room for the solution. "It would be possible to dampen the sound to an extent if, for example..." He stood up then and went searching behind the sofa. There were floor length curtains hanging on either side of the wide window and, hidden behind them, he soon found what he was looking for. "As I suspected..." He held up a red velvet cushion, and I had a flash of a memory from the time he'd sent me running about in search of cushions for some reason. "The killer wrapped this around the gun before firing. It wouldn't have muffled the sound entirely, but then it didn't have to. It did enough to disguise the sound. Remember what Flossie heard before she came in here."

I managed to catch his meaning. "She said that there were two distinct noises. The first was presumably the thud of Silas falling to the floor, perhaps after he was stabbed. And the second could have been the gunshot."

I felt this was a realistic version of what had happened. The killer would have needed a moment to take a cushion and, had Silas still been on his feet at the time, he would presumably have fought back, so it stood to reason that he'd been stabbed first. I'm not sure that this would help us catch the swine who'd killed him, but it was nice to feel sure of at least one detail.

"Come along, my boy." Grandfather used the end of his cane to peel back the dead man's jacket once more. "Have you any further hypotheses for why he was both stabbed and shot? Surely one would have done the trick."

"I haven't a clue. If it wasn't to finish the job, then..." With a bit more pondering something eventually came to me. "Perhaps it was anger that did it. Perhaps the murderer detested his victim. Nathan said that his brother had nothing in his life – no better half, job or interests beyond weapons – but maybe that wasn't true. Maybe there is more to discover about the victim than we currently know."

He turned away for another look around the room, but he soon came back to me. "It's a shame there's not a short novella we could read that summarises the different players involved. It would make our investigations easier if we sent an officer ahead of us to interview the suspects, extract what he could from them, and type up his notes in advance."

"Yes, that would be handy," I agreed, "but we'll be lucky if the police make it here in the snow, let alone do our jobs for us."

"You know, I think we should have Christmas off next year." His eyes were rather misty for a moment. "A festive celebration with family and not a body in sight would be a nice change." I thought this a strange wish, considering how eager he had been to come on this adventure.

He lingered there, saying nothing for a minute longer. I wondered if it was my job to decide what to do next, but then the bell for the front door rang, and we dashed from the room to discover who it was. It was hard to know whether I wanted to see a platoon of police officers on the doorstep or my family and friends.

"Ahh..." my mother said as we reached the entry hall. The butler had opened the door to her, and I could tell from the way she looked from him to my grandfather and then back to the butler that she couldn't decide whether to tell the truth and risk contradicting whatever fantastical story her father had invented, or lie and risk contradicting whatever fantastical story her father had invented. "I'm... Or rather, we..."

"Violet, my dear mother," I said quite unnaturally. "How nice it is to see you. We have already told Lord Rivers about our unfortunate accidents in the snow. I'm so glad that you're finally here."

"That's right," she murmured, still unsure of the ruse. "It was an unfortunate accident... and other things my son said."

"Is there any brandy at hand?" My father was rarely interested in our investigations and had his own priorities. "It's cold enough out here to freeze the fingernails off a fox."

They came in carrying a bag each, to which the butler soon saw. I had to hope there were enough guest rooms to go around, especially as Granny was just behind them. I would say that she looked frozen, but her cheeks always had that slightly pinched quality to them.

"Has anyone been murdered yet?" she whispered as she stamped the snow off her boots on the coarse mat before the door.

"Well, yes," I admitted.

"Jolly good. I can't stand mystery novels that take forever to get to the first killing. All that character development and scene-setting! Who needs it? Throw me into the deep end, that's what I say."

Grandfather looked a little vexed that she would compare one of our cases to – of all things – a mystery novel, but before he could say anything, she stuck her head back through the door to shout to our servants.

"This way, all."

A moment later, Todd appeared carrying a wooden chest. He was soon followed by our ancient footman, and even poor Henrietta the cook had been roped into carrying my grandmother's luggage. They rather reminded me of the Three Wise Men, recast for the modern day.

"Really, Granny, why did you have to bring so many bags?" I should have learnt by now never to question the indomitable woman, and she turned to peer down her nose at me with a tigerish glare.

"Never you mind, you impertinent boy!" And with that, she followed my father and mother into the first salon they found, where they set about pitching camp for the weekend.

"Thank goodness you brought more staff with you," Lord Rivers said and went to welcome my family to his beautiful home. I must say that he did not look particularly distressed that his great-nephew had been murdered, but then Silas did not seem like the person to inspire such emotion. And to be fair to his great-uncle, the victim's brother had threatened to murder him that morning.

I waited for Grandfather to tell us what we needed to do next, but he looked just as confused by the situation as I was.

"How very odd," he murmured. "You would think that he might take exception to so many people invading his house on Christmas Eve."

Before I could respond, I noticed something through the cracked-open door opposite the sitting room. Our insolent dog had sneaked in there and was looking very comfortable in front of the fire.

"Girl," I rasped, both as quietly and loudly as I could. "Delilah, I'm not sure you're allowed in there."

I walked a little closer, but she just looked back at me, tongue lolling, tail wagging, as if she couldn't see the problem. As far as I could tell through the narrow opening, the room was some kind of office. There were shelves all over the walls, but there wasn't a real book in sight. Instead, they were filled with files, folders, and publications connected to money or business or some such thing.

I pushed the door wider and tiptoed inside. "You can't stay here. Go into the sitting room with Mother and Father. I already feel guilty for colonising this house. You don't need a room to yourself."

I was about to take her by the scruff of her fluffy neck – or should that be the fluff of the neck? – when someone spoke.

"She's fine where she is. It's nice to have some company for once."

There was an old desk at the end of the room which looked sturdy enough to sail across the Channel. Behind it sat the young clerk we had already seen twice that morning. I should probably have responded but, by the time I'd found my voice, my grandfather had followed me into the room.

"Ah, you must be Mr Acland," he said quite confidently, though, personally, I had forgotten the young man's name by this point.

"That's right, but you can call me Philip." He had a ponderous manner and considered every word he produced. "And you're Lord Edgington. I've read so much about you, my lord." He was exceedingly well spoken for a man of his status, and I had to wonder what terrible crimes he'd committed to end up as Lord Rivers's assistant. Working for the old miser who had made Holly's life so unpleasant can't have been easy.

"It's a pleasure to meet you." Grandfather did not introduce a topic of conversation or pose a question. He stopped halfway into the airy room to see what Acland would do next.

The man hesitated for a few moments before continuing in a faltering voice. "If the truth be told, I wanted to speak to you… to both of you, of course." He walked over to the door to close it. "You see, I can't say I'm entirely surprised by what happened this morning."

"We know all about the supposed accidents that occurred over the summer," I intervened unnecessarily, then remembered that I really must stop putting words into our suspects' mouths.

"I'm not referring to the accidents, though I doubted from the beginning that was what they were. I mean the behaviour of certain people here. I am a lowly employee – barely more important than the cook or maid – but I have noticed some unusual things about the family."

Grandfather nodded and walked to the desk to take a seat in front of it. I'm more of a lurker than a sitter when it comes to our interviews, so I remained on my feet. Delilah moved to occupy the spare chair before her master signalled that would not be allowed.

He looked at the witness for a moment, then nodded and began. "As an outsider familiar with the way of things here, you may be the person who is best placed to assist us."

Acland was still hovering near the fireplace, and so Grandfather pointed to the other side of the desk for him to take his place once more. "When you are ready, you may share your thoughts on the case."

CHAPTER ELEVEN

"I don't wish to get anyone in trouble."

"Why, of course," Lord Edgington replied in an exaggerated tone, and we both knew what he was doing. "You need not fear such a thing. Whatever information you give us will be treated with care and discretion."

Philip Acland had unusually bright eyes. They seemed to have an extra source of illumination behind them, like coloured glass ornaments with candles inside.

With his mind apparently now set at ease, he explained a few of the connections we'd been missing. "It isn't just during the summer that there have been problems. Silas lived here all year round and never failed to cause arguments."

"What of the other cousins?" Grandfather asked. "Do they also live here on a permanent basis?"

"No, no." He shook his head. "Holly is at university in Oxford. Nathan has a house in London somewhere, and Luke and Flossie inherited their parents' substantial property not so far away."

"Did they inherit the money to go with it?" I had to ask, not only because their diminished finances might provide us with a decent motive for murder, but as I knew many old families were struggling to live within their means these days.

Acland turned his head to look at me, much as a robin on a hedge will peer curiously at an intruding human. "As it happens, they didn't. Lord Rivers has always been the wealthiest in the family, and the other branches have struggled for some time. In fact, if Luke isn't chosen to inherit, he will almost certainly have to sell Grenham Manor, where he and his sister grew up."

Hurray for motives. Aren't they just wonderful?

"How interesting." Grandfather spoke in a detached tone that I would not have been able to maintain. "However, it seems to me that Luke is the favourite to inherit. That is certainly what Lord Rivers has implied. There is no doubt that he approves of the boy."

Luke couldn't have been less than thirty, but I suppose he seemed like a whippersnapper to someone my grandfather's age. I could only marvel that he managed to tolerate my youthful ignorance as much as he did.

"It's not the best idea to trust what Peregrine Rivers says to people's faces. It's what he whispers behind their backs that holds the most weight." There was a touch of anger in the way Acland spoke then, and I thought it a risky comment to make about one's employer.

Grandfather evidently agreed with my judgement. "You don't think highly of him."

"I wouldn't say that. He has always been generous to me, but I hold no loyalty to him. I'm sure that the feeling is more than mutual. If he didn't like the food his cook produced, he would fire her. If he isn't happy with my work, he will do the same."

His questioner nodded a few times. "I understand that you help with the management of the estate. Is that correct?"

As though to prove his worth, Acland tidied a pile of papers on the desk before him. "Among other things, yes."

"Which must give you some insight into what goes on here."

I thought that the young clerk did well at this moment to pause and assess exactly what my grandfather was asking. Far too many suspects speak without thinking. If they also happen to be guilty of a crime, the chances are that their loose tongues will end up convicting them.

"Precisely, and that's why I thought I could be helpful to you. I have no direct interest in what goes on in this family, and so I'm more likely to tell the truth."

"Hmmm," my grandfather replied softly. "*More likely* is an interesting phrase, but I take your point. Perhaps you can start by telling me whether you have come across a will which would leave St Audries to a particular member of the Rivers family in the event that the viscount dies before he nominates his heir."

"If there is one, I've never seen it. Though that doesn't mean it doesn't exist. I have only been working here for a few years, after all."

"And before that?" I asked to give my grandfather a chance to rest his voice. The question made me wonder how old the man was. He had a rather ancient air about him but was probably around the same age as my brother. I would say he was twenty-five at most.

Acland acted as though he were surprised to find himself in the very situation he had engineered. "I'm from the area. I grew up nearby."

Grandfather returned to the issue which would surely shape our investigation more than any other. "Have there been any discussions about a future will? Has one been drafted for example?"

"The matter has been discussed." One moment, Acland seemed as though he wished to reveal the family's every secret, and the next he was tight lipped and ambivalent. "But my real point was that you cannot necessarily trust what Lord Rivers has told his potential heirs."

"You mean to say that he has promised different things to different people."

He smiled. "No, I mean that he has promised the same thing to different people. He takes great pleasure in setting those around him at odds with one another. He has even tried to do it to me on occasion, but I'm not interested in his games."

I wish sometimes that there was a tube one could purchase that could be connected to another person's ear in order to access their thoughts. I would love to have known what my grandfather was thinking throughout this conversation. There was currently no reason to believe that Philip Acland was responsible for Silas's death, but there was something unusual about him that evidently intrigued the renowned detective, and I would have liked to know what it was.

"I suppose you think I am quite disloyal talking of Peregrine in such a manner." Acland fidgeted with the end of his blue tie as he spoke. "But everything I have said is common knowledge here. He takes pride in his duplicitousness. I believe he would have made a capable spy if the chance to become one had ever arisen."

Grandfather allowed his hand to drop to the side of his chair and stroked Delilah's ears absentmindedly as he replied. "You're absolutely right. He has told us a lot of this himself. And that being the case, why do you think you can be of aid to our investigation?"

Acland took a deep breath as though he was about to get a burden off his chest. "The likely culprit could be one of the potential heirs – and the male ones at that. There is no way that Florence or Holly would benefit by killing off the men in the family, as there would surely be a distant cousin who could be found to take their place. That leaves Nathan and Luke as likely culprits, but there are other possibilities."

He came to an unexpected stop just as it was getting interesting, and so Grandfather helped him along with a nice simple, "Oh, yes?"

"Yes." The pendulum had swung in the other direction and our witness now held the trump cards. "Mrs Victoria Stevans is not merely an employee here. She was Lady Rivers's companion before she died."

"We already knew that." There I go, jumping in again when I should keep my mouth shut.

"Did you know that she is Peregrine's mistress?"

"It has been implied." At least I had a smart response for him.

He was not discouraged by my jaw's complete lack of slackness and moved on to a third piece of relevant information. "Well, I very much doubt you know how much she despises her employer."

"The employer whom you do not despise?" Grandfather reminded him.

"That's correct. My feelings toward Peregrine are neutral. Inwardly, I may not think highly of his behaviour, but I understand why he behaves as he does." I found this coldness of manner quite off-putting but had decided to let Grandfather speak instead of silly me.

"And what about Mrs Stevans? Do you understand why she behaves as she does?" The real interviewer had gradually become more hostile. He had moved on from the idea that Acland was an impartial helper to treating him as a manipulative third party and perhaps even a suspect himself.

"I understand how difficult it must be for a woman in her position, but I don't know exactly why she hates the man with whom she shares a bed."

There was something terribly distant about the way he spoke. It was as if he were an anthropologist describing the habits of some ancient civilisation. I couldn't tell whether this made it more or less likely that he was manipulating us.

Grandfather may have noticed the same thing but, unlike me, he knew how to deal with such complicated witnesses. "Well, Mr Acland—"

The young fellow smiled. "Please, call me Philip."

"As you wish." I thought he might call him Mr Acland again just to make a point, but he resisted the temptation. "You have brought our attention to a few different suspects. Nathan is the dead man's brother and evidently Lord Rivers's most outspoken critic. Although, from his attitude this morning, I believe that he may once have occupied a better-favoured position in his great-uncle's affections."

"You're exactly right." The rather colourless man suddenly sounded enthusiastic. "There was a time not so long ago when Nathan followed Peregrine around like a pet dog, and it seemed obvious who would inherit the estate."

I would have asked what had gone wrong, but Grandfather had been interrupted and wished to finish his thought.

"Nathan may have been the likely heir, but judging by his behaviour this morning, he is furious at the thought of his reduced prospects. And then there is Mrs Stevans who may have her own reasons for wanting her employer dead. But there are other people in this house you have dismissed. You said that Rivers's granddaughter and great-niece couldn't possibly be to blame for the attacks on him, or for Silas's death. That is only true if we assume that the motive behind all of this is the inheritance of the estate."

Acland's eyebrows jumped higher up his forehead. "Isn't it the likely explanation?"

"It is." Grandfather breathed in slowly to delay his next comment. "But were you the killer, would you risk carrying out your plan if everyone could guess the motive?" Just for a moment, he made it sound as though he thought Acland was to blame.

"That would depend on how desperate I was, but I suppose you have a point." The man pouted for a few seconds as he considered this. "What other reasons are there?"

"It takes passion," I replied under my breath, before finding more confidence. "People kill for money all the time, but that doesn't make it easy. In my experience, killers have to believe in themselves and their own right to succeed above all else. There's normally a mix of love, hate and fury when someone kills a person they know; the promise of riches is not generally enough to transform an innocent man into a killer."

Acland's hand closed tightly around a golden fountain pen that had been lying on the desk. "So you're saying that Holly might have killed her cousin and tried to murder her grandfather because her own parents should have been the ones to inherit St Audries Park?"

"It's a possibility," Grandfather replied.

"No, it isn't," the clerk was quick to respond. "Did you know that Holly's parents were killed on the Lusitania? Their boat was torpedoed by the Germans during the war and, though he might not have done a very good job of replacing them as her guardian, Peregrine actually saved her life. She was supposed to go to America, but he kept her behind so that he didn't have to go to some infernal garden party on his own. She was only eight when they died. I don't believe that she would ever kill her grandfather, no matter how much of a beast he is." He had become more insistent since starting on this topic. "And no. She wouldn't have killed her cousin, either. Even the most distant and objectionable relatives become important when you've had the sort of life that poor Holly has."

His words brought back memories of the spring of 1915. I don't recall much about the war except the odd significant image. I can picture a drawing in the papers of the armistice being signed on a train carriage in France, and I'll never forget the day the men from my village came back home to their families. I was terrified of a photograph of a long line of enemy soldiers walking along a ridge somewhere in Germany, and I remember the sinking of the Lusitania just off the Irish coast.

I was six years old, but the picture of the ship's bow sticking up into the air as its funnels continued pumping out smoke has never left me. I had bad dreams about it for weeks, so I could only imagine how Holly must have felt.

Silence had fallen between us. Perhaps we were all recollecting that same terrible sight.

Even Grandfather took his time to respond. "I see why you would want to protect her. It makes sense that you called us in here—"

"I didn't call you—"

He spoke right over Acland. "That you would call us in here to share your view of what has happened, but you haven't offered one single impartial fact. Maybe Nathan is the killer – that must be what everyone is thinking. Or perhaps Luke is desperate to preserve his childhood home and will pick off every last member of the family in order to achieve his goals, but we can't rule out anyone just because you feel he or she is innocent." He stood up then and clutched his cane in two hands. "I'm sure that you meant well, but we cannot resolve this case on the back of vague sentiments."

With this said, he nodded sternly and marched away. Delilah was at her master's side before I had the chance to stand.

"Goodbye for now, Mr Acland," I remembered to say as I reached the door. "It was a pleasure." As my mother often reminds me, it costs nothing to be polite.

CHAPTER TWELVE

"That was interesting, don't you think?" Grandfather asked, and I was surprised how much he sounded like me.

I considered being obtuse, rude or dismissive in reply, as he so often could be, but decided that wasn't my style. "Absolutely. Acland wanted to take us by the hand and guide us through the case as though he were the arbiter of who could be the killer."

He wandered along the hallway to look at the snow through the frosted-up windows beside the front door. "Precisely."

I really wasn't used to his agreeing with me. I kept expecting him to say something patronising like, *Is that really what you think, Christopher?* Or *No, of course not, Christopher.* Or, *Christopher, how did you manage to get piccalilli on your jacket when the only food we've eaten today was the biscuits when we stopped to buy petrol near Andover?*

"The question is," he said instead, "why would he seek to influence our opinions so?"

"I was wondering the very same thing. Do you think he really believes what he told us, or is he trying to protect someone in the house?"

He seemed ever so pleased with me until he noticed a stain on my lapel. "Christopher, how did you manage to get piccalilli on your jacket when the only food we've eaten today was the biscuits when we stopped to buy petrol near Andover?"

"How do you know it's piccalilli?" I countered, though I realised this was no great defence.

"Because I…" he replied rather grandly, "…am a detective, and I know you very well."

I couldn't deny that I had a penchant for piccalilli, but before I could say anything more, there came a psssting from the sitting room. The door opened a fraction, and someone peeked out of it.

"Pssst," came the sound once more. "Christopher, over here."

I recognised my grandmother's voice, and Delilah went over to push the door wider.

"You'd better come in here too, Edgington. I have something important to tell you." She beckoned us forward, and we were helpless to resist.

"What is it, Loelia?" Grandfather asked in an urgent tone. He clearly hoped that she had discovered something vital.

Still standing in the doorway with my parents in the room behind her, she looked along the corridor to check that we wouldn't be overheard. "It's the maid."

"Which maid?" Grandfather was taking her far too seriously, whereas I waited to hear what she would say.

"The maid from this house, of course. I don't know her name." She spoke as if we had suggested something entirely unreasonable. That the house was perched on the back of an elephant, for example, or that the inhabitants of the local village were all flying lizards.

"Well?" Grandfather prompted her. "What about the maid?"

Granny took her time to answer. "I don't trust her. I think she must be the one who killed... whoever was killed."

The great detective stopped still. He was presumably quite mystified by her claim. "Ah, so you're offering a tip. We will take it under consideration."

Granny seemed perfectly happy with this outcome and offered some evidence in support of her statement. "She was mincing around out here for the last ten minutes. I simply don't trust people who mince."

I cast my mind back to the moment of my family's arrival, and I recalled seeing the young maid there in the hallway. I hadn't thought anything of it at the time, as I'd assumed she was keeping the place tidy.

"Granny," I began, the expression on my face perfectly illustrating my befuddlement, "don't you think it's possible that she was working rather than merely mincing about? She did have a feather duster in her hand."

"Yes, Christopher. And that is why I don't approve of such things."

It was my grandfather who afforded her a reply. "You don't approve of feather dusters?"

"Quite right!" I thought she might explain this view, but she clicked her heels together like a soldier and retreated to an armchair beside yet another roaring fire.

Sitting on the other side of the hearth, my parents had settled in nicely. My mother was lost in a good book, and Father was enjoying a glass of brandy.

94

"Christopher?" he looked up at me expectantly. "I don't suppose you know whether lunch will be served soon? I'm starting to feel rather—"

Before he could say the word *peckish* – which would almost certainly have set my undernourished tummy rumbling – the St Audries Park butler arrived with an announcement.

"Ladies and gentlemen, lunch is served in the morning room." When we all looked hopefully in his direction, and no one moved, he continued. "The morning room is at the back of the house adjacent to the room where young Mr Rivers's body was found." Sixty per cent of the people there were none the wiser, so he finally said. "If you follow me, I will show you the way."

This sparked some cheerful noises from the assembled guests – though perhaps "guests" is too strong a word for whatever we were. Uninvited interlopers might be a better description, but we were certainly happy to discover that a meal was on the cards.

We followed the butler to a room on the far side of the Great Hall, and I was beginning to get a sense of the shape of the strange house. It must have been built in stages over the centuries, as it had not been constructed in a square around a central courtyard as I would have expected. If anything, it was like a squashed Z shape, and we would be having lunch in the diagonal that joined the two more substantial wings of the house.

As we walked into the morning room – which was essentially a dining room that they presumably only used during the day – all heads swivelled in our direction. The various members of the household looked thoroughly dejected, and our arrival did nothing to lighten the mood. Nathan directed a glare in my direction, whereas Holly was back to staring off at a point in the distance that only she could see.

My father has never been the best at judging the atmosphere in a room and decided it would be a good idea to go around introducing himself. "Walter Prentiss," he said, shaking first Luke's hand, then Flossie's, and so on around the table. "I'm Christopher's father. Lord Edgington's son-in-law." I hoped he would stop there, but he just kept going. "This is my mother, Loelia, and my wife, Violet." The less they reacted, the more apprehensive he became and the more he jabbered. "People say that men often end up marrying women who resemble their mothers, but I don't think that's true in my case."

I was hoping someone might interrupt just to put the poor man out of his misery, but we were oddly enchanted by the inappropriateness of the scene. It was a bit like when you drive past a dead deer at the side of the road, and you can't help but look into its sorry eyes.

"I work in the city," he tried one last time and, when this still produced no response, he finally reached one of the free seats and sat down. Daddy was a resilient sort, and I knew it wouldn't trouble him for long.

Grandfather stationed himself at one end of the room opposite a grand chair where Lord Rivers would surely sit when he arrived. Mother took the seat next to him, and I was interested to see that both Victoria Stevans and Philip Acland would be eating with the family, too. The only problem was that there was space at the long, oval table for eleven, and they already looked rather squashed in together. As a result, one of the staff had positioned another much smaller piece of furniture nearby with a single place set at it.

That's right; I would be eating at the children's table.

Lord Rivers arrived in his usual slow, shuffling manner. If anything, he looked more decrepit than he had that morning and now seemed to limp with both legs. I had to wonder how long it would be before his body gave up entirely and he would be restricted to his summer wheelchair. It was not just that he was old and infirm; there was something terribly fragile about him, as if his bones were made of shattered glass.

One thing that was undiminishable, however, was his fiery personality. Even before he sat down, he started shouting across the room in his usual blunt tone. "This doesn't have to be a wake, you know. Silas is dead, but who here can say that you actually even liked him?"

I thought Nathan would answer him, but he looked down at his cutlery as though trying to remember which fork to use first. Sadly, there was a whole side of the table whose reactions I could not spy from where I was sitting.

"You see," Lord Rivers continued, "you can't even say that you loved your own brother. Silas was a cold, strange person. He was still family, of course, and family is important. But I won't have any talk of the innocent angel we lost, as it wouldn't be true."

To my surprise, it was Holly who spoke back to him. "You're

right. My cousin was strange, and he could be violent and cruel too, but he had a softer side that I will never forget. And it simply isn't Christian to discuss his failings after what he endured in the final moments of his life."

I couldn't see her face, but her words conveyed the emotion that was simmering inside of her. What they didn't convey was any evidence of Silas's supposed tenderness and, though the room fell silent in expectation of a few examples, none were forthcoming. It made me wonder why she had made such a claim in the first place.

It fell to her cousin Luke to try to conjure up a few words in Silas's memory. "He was an intelligent man. You could talk to him on all sorts of topics when he was in the mood."

"Not that he ever was," Nathan murmured.

"And he had a good sense of humour," Luke continued, shoring himself up with these words. "I believe he knew exactly who he was, and he wasn't afraid of other people's opinions."

Lord Rivers raised one hand, and I thought he would complain again about the reappraisal of the dead man's personality. Instead, his response was calm and considered. "That is all true. Silas may not have been a sociable or gregarious character, but he was loyal to this family and this country." With the help of his cane, he struggled back up to his feet and leaned forward in his usual slow manner to seize the wine glass that Todd had recently filled. "I retract my previous words. Silas deserves to remain in our thoughts. He was not an angel, but he shouldn't have died as he did."

He raised his wine, and we all did the same… well, except for me. I'd only been served a glass of grape juice. On the one hand, this made me feel rather immature, and on the other it suited me perfectly, as I still hadn't developed a fondness for wine.

"To Silas," he said, and the refrain echoed around the table. This moment of unity was only undermined by the subsequent message he delivered in a cold, hard tone. "And if the killer imagines that I will be next, then he can think again."

With his piece said, he sat back down, and I found the whole scene very odd. Nathan, Holly, Luke and the old lord must all have had their reasons for the parts they had played in this brief piece of theatre, but I couldn't begin to tell you what they were.

I looked at one half of my grandfather's face to see his reaction, but he was as inscrutable as ever. My grandmother, meanwhile, was having a wonderful time, and only looked disappointed that no one had started an argument. She was the kind of person who is at her most contented when she has a reason to shout.

I noticed that some small concessions had been made to the season. There were unpulled Totem crackers laid between place settings, and a green centrepiece with four candles was burning brightly on the main table. I had a single sprig of mistletoe in front of me, but then space was severely limited. Our staff were collaborating with the servants from St Audries Park to deliver the feast, and I was eager to see what they had conjured up together. Todd and Halfpenny worked alongside the resident butler, and one or another of the maids occasionally appeared with laden trolleys from which they would serve.

We ate the first course in tense silence, and I would like to tell you about the glances that were exchanged around that table – as family member suspected family member, and everyone there watched for some sign of who the killer might be – but I was assigned to the children's table and could not make out a great deal. Still, the fricasseed turkey with a helping of goose liver pâté was worthy of my concentration. It was truly delicious, and I wondered which of the two cooks had created the tasty dish.

I was in no doubt as to the artist behind the second course, however. The eccentric tastes of Henrietta, our faithful domestic from Cranley Hall, had evidently led to the choice of *eggs a la tripe* served with a matelot of tench, and there were certainly some strange looks as the plates were delivered.

"I'm terribly sorry, Master Christopher," Todd told me when he brought quite a different option to my little enclave in the corner. "I think we have a case of too many cooks failing to communicate effectively. Mary, the cook from St Audries, heard that Lord Edgington's grandson would be eating and prepared a dish for the young lad she imagined in her head. I didn't like to tell her that you're a grown man, but if you'd prefer the fish and eggs, I'll fetch you a plate."

"No, no, Todd," I replied most generously. "I wouldn't want to disappoint the poor woman. Sausages, mashed potatoes and roast tomatoes suit me just fine." I believe this is what I tried to say but, as I was already shovelling the delicious food in front of me into my mouth before he could take it away.

I positively launched myself at the task of enjoying such hearty fare, while the two most diplomatic members of our party attempted to strike up conversation. Mother was a singularly unifying force there and managed to get Mrs Stevans and Philip Acland to share their memories of childhood Christmases. Flossie seemed to have a similar attitude and engaged her cousins in conversation on the other side of the table. I might have said that it was almost convivial for a time, though I knew that someone was bound to spoil things before long. I had rather expected it to be Nathan but, with his dessert consumed, Lord Rivers did the job.

Wait! You have my apologies. Here I am brushing past dessert as if it wasn't the most important word in that sentence. For all her quirks, dear Henrietta knew how to make sweets like no one else I'd met. Her vicarage pudding was an unparalleled triumph, and though not typically associated with Christmas, it had just the right mix of dried fruits, wintery spices and a sticky exterior to whet our appetite for the festive meals ahead of us. Oh, and the pint of custard with which it came was simply too delicious to describe.

"I've had enough of this forced jollity," Lord Rivers eventually declared. "As much as I enjoy thinking back on happy times, I find it less cheering when I know that someone here has been trying to kill me. I'm off for my afternoon nap, and there had better not be a snake in my bed or something else set to squash me flat. I may be old, but I've got plenty of living still in me."

He rose unsteadily and tottered from the room at such a reduced pace that it greatly limited the drama of his bellicose statement.

CHAPTER THIRTEEN

Grandfather seemed to have forgotten that we were involved in an investigation and spent the next half an hour enjoying a digestif and discussing current affairs with the gentlemen. Nathan had retreated to his room, and so there was a place for me at the table. I sat between Flossie and Holly who, now that I thought about it, had rather similar names.

After a few minutes' polite conversation, Flossie turned to ask something that I couldn't have imagined her saying in a millennium or longer. "Christopher, would you like to see my parrots?"

I didn't quite know how to respond. Was *parrots* a youthful slang word that I hadn't previously encountered? Were they a fad of some sort – like a new type of cigarette card that people were collecting? Perhaps it was a euphemism for something rude that I didn't understand.

I felt quite out of my depth, but rather than revealing my ignorance, I said, "Oh, yes. I very much would!"

With a smile, she hopped up from her seat, and I followed after her. We walked past the room where Silas's body still lay, before arriving at a door at the side of the house that gave onto a large rectangle of white. I can't be much more precise than that, I'm afraid. I could maybe postulate that there was a formal garden underneath the snow, but the only sign of any such thing was a basin in the middle with a three-bowl fountain sticking out of it. More importantly, on the far side, there was an elegant outbuilding with a glass roof and windows covering one wall. I had to assume this was the orangery where my companion had been when Silas was killed.

"It's coming down rather heavily," Flossie said as we stepped outside. "But if we run, it shouldn't be too bad."

She smiled and dashed off across the courtyard between the buildings. There was a lightness to her step that I found quite charming, and she kept looking back at me to laugh. Spending so much time with my grandfather (and any number of dead bodies) had the effect of making me feel rather old sometimes, but dashing through the snow was the perfect respite from more serious matters. We picked our way around the fountain, which had frozen entirely, of course, and followed the line we'd taken from the door to reach the large glasshouse.

It had occurred to me at the time that Flossie might have been lying when she'd said that she required a few minutes to lock the orangery before going off to find the body. I had questioned the need to secure an outbuilding on a private estate in a blizzard, but I now understood why she had done so.

"Parrots!" I said as I peered through the glass door in amazement. "They're real, actual, flying parrots!" I'd never been very good at telling one bird from another, but I knew this much.

"Well, they're a collection of parakeets, budgerigars and macaws, but we call them our parrots for short. My great-aunt bought the first flock, and I took over their care when she died."

She checked that I was ready to dash inside and then quickly pushed the door open and did just that.

"We mustn't let them out," she yelled as we darted through the doorway without any escaping. "We lost a Major Mitchell's cockatoo and didn't find him for a week. He turned up at the church in the middle of a service and made some particularly rude sounds that Father Goodman did not appreciate."

"They're incredible!" I had to marvel at the sight of all those exotic birds in the middle of a snowy landscape. "They help remind me that it's Christmastime."

I thought she might question this silly statement, but she smiled and agreed. "I know just what you mean. They're like flying baubles. They'd look lovely nestling on the branches of a pine tree."

I cast my eyes around in wonder at any number of the birds that flew about us. Some peered down from perches or the whitewashed beams of the building. There were bare trees in pots with ten or more brightly coloured creatures on each, and I even noticed a few hanging upside down from a net on the ceiling. It was quite the most unexpected sight I'd come across in my already quite unexpected existence.

There was a white metal bench in the corner between two palms, and Flossie pointed over to it. The orangery must have been heated by some sort of furnace somewhere, as it was much balmier than the main house, which was presumably necessary to keep the tropical birds alive.

"I didn't realise they could survive in Britain in the winter," I told her. "I've seen the odd one in circuses and at London Zoo, but never so many together."

As if to prove my earlier festive reflections, a small green bird landed on the arm of the bench by Flossie and a matching red one landed beside me.

"They're eclectuses," she explained. "The males are green, and the females are red. They must know what time of year it is."

The little girl parrot nuzzled my arm, and I was frankly amazed. "I didn't know they were so friendly." Admittedly, I proceeded to act like a brainless moonling. "Hello, madam. Would you like me to stroke you?" I believe I put on a babyish voice as I reached out to touch the beautiful beast's head, and she opened her beak to nip me. "Ouch!"

"How odd," Flossie responded. "They're normally quite sociable. I've never seen them do that before." She put her hand out to the small green gentleman, and he climbed on most calmly. "Try this one."

She swapped them over, and I had another go. "Ouch!" It didn't turn out too well, as there is presumably something very biteable about me.

With his nip issued, Mr Eclectus walked up my arm and sat on my shoulder to have a nibble on my ear. It didn't hurt too much, and I soon got used to it.

"They're gorgeous, Flossie, nonetheless." We sat enjoying the view for a moment until I remembered the dead man in the back salon and the threat to Lord Rivers. "I hope you don't mind my saying, but you seemed quite upset when you discovered your cousin's body." This was another point of interest as, despite her tears, she hadn't found anything nice to say about him over lunch. "Were the pair of you close?"

"No, not in the slightest," was her swift reply. "But it would take a heart of stone not to feel sorrow when encountering such a poor soul murdered in his own home, don't you agree?"

I had to lie then as I'd discovered any number of corpses and, unless my memory was playing tricks on me, I was yet to shed a tear. "Oh, quite! It would take an absolute monster not to show dismay when finding a dead body, but you seemed terribly distressed, even then."

She stroked the breast feathers of her little red bird as more parrots landed around us looking for attention. She was like a goddess of nature in her very own kingdom and was certainly striking enough for such a role. She had long brown hair that curled at the tips, much like the corners of her mouth, and her cheeks were pleasantly round except for a small, cheerful dimple on either one. However, I'd come to realise through the time I'd spent with my grandfather that murder investigations are not the place to meet prospective sweethearts – and besides, I was already half in love with Holly. There are only so many beautiful women with whom a young man can become besotted in a single Christmas holiday.

"I suppose it's because of everything that's happened," she eventually looked away from the bird to reply. "Uncle Perry likes us to come back here for special occasions, and I visit every week to see to the birds." (I had to hope someone was feeding them in the meantime, but I didn't like to interrupt her.) "We cousins have always mixed rather uncomfortably with one another, but over the last year or two, as the old man's health has steadily deteriorated, a new level of animosity has arisen that we'd never known before."

There was so much in this statement that could be important, and I wondered which thread I should pull first. "Is Lord Rivers quite ill then?"

"I'm afraid so." She had a truly soulful manner, and I didn't believe that she was putting on an act this time. "Until a few years ago he was spritely and active, but he had a fall and then another and, before we knew it, it was as if his whole being had been set to a lower gear. He wouldn't admit it, but it wasn't so long ago that he strode about his estate with the vigour of a much younger man. I think that even he must realise that he won't live forever."

"The possibility of his death must have made things more difficult between you all." I was still scrutinising every word she said. "I hope you don't mind my mentioning it, but we heard that you are in danger of losing your home. I can only imagine how that would weigh on your brother's mind."

Her tone became a little sharper for the first time. "I wouldn't say that. Luke isn't the type to think of wealth or status. He only wishes to do what's best for the family."

The response set me on edge. It sounded more like the vague, diplomatic statement a politician might issue when confronted with a scandal than a natural response. It made me wonder who the woman in front of me really was. We'd heard nothing negative about Flossie from the other suspects, but perhaps she was manipulating me just as

Nathan and Philip Acland had.

It suddenly came back to me when I had first heard her name. It wasn't that morning, but back on the train from Oxford. When discussing who could be to blame for the attempts on her grandfather's life, Holly had pointed to Silas – now dead – and Nathan – the obvious dark sheep of the family... or do I mean black horse? Whatever the expression, the third name she had mentioned was Flossie's.

When I replied, I chose my words more carefully to see what impact they would have. "I'm sure that your brother is a good man, but don't you think there's a chance that he took his sense of responsibility too far? Isn't it possible that he would have killed his older cousin in order to inherit St Audries? Surely the money that comes with this estate would be enough to restore your house at Grenham Manor."

It wasn't just her tone that had hardened. Her muscles pulled tight, and she shot to her feet as she considered how to respond to this aspersion. "No, I very much do not think it possible that my dear brother would indulge in a spot of murder."

The birds around us didn't seem to like her reaction, and a large grey one flew off to a tree in the opposite corner with a loud, meaningful squawk.

"I didn't mean to offend you, Flossie. My grandfather and I only wish to uncover whatever happened here today. I'm really not blaming you or your—"

"You can't possibly know how complicated life here is unless you're one of the family. And it is a far bigger family than you know." She wouldn't look at me now but delivered each word as if it was likely to upset.

"What does that mean? Are there not just five cousins? Is there someone we've overlooked?" I imagined a fugitive dressed in black, running about the house to murder his relatives.

"We're not all first cousins, you know?" she replied, without answering my question. "Peregrine is Holly's grandfather and our great-uncle. She's only my second cousin. And as for the family itself, almost everyone in the local area can trace their roots back to the Rivers clan. Our great-great-grandfather was an absolute bounder and fathered half the babies in the village. That was one of the reasons why Uncle Perry moved the locals off the estate."

I tried to think back a few hours, though it felt as though I'd been at St Audries Park for days already. "Your brother mentioned that. He said that Lord Rivers was paranoid and got rid of the last villagers. Do you think one of them was his lovechild, and he was worried that someone would make a claim on the estate?"

She took a few steps across the room and turned to look at me as though I were witless, which was fair. "No, of course not. We have enough potential claimants around without inventing secret offspring. And besides, if Perry had fathered any extra children, he would have been sure to tell us about it – especially if it was a boy. He would be only too happy to boost the notion of his overpowering virility. Why would you even imagine such a thing?"

I was surprised she thought it so unlikely. "Because that's just the kind of scandal my grandfather always exposes on our cases. Secret affairs, incognito lords, people who say they are one person when they're really someone else. It's all in a day's work for a detective."

She shook her head, clearly unimpressed with this notion. "What a strange existence you must lead. Let me put your mind at ease that there can be no clandestine assassin hiding in the coal cellar or holed up outside in an igloo of his own making. Whoever killed Silas was sitting at the dining table at lunch today."

"But you said that you're related to half the people in the area. Couldn't one of the servants be to blame?"

She at least considered this possibility. "Well, Daphne the maid and Ripon the butler are from some long-impoverished wing of the family."

If it turned out that Granny was correct in her theory that the maid was responsible for the murder, we would never live it down. "And what about Mary the cook?"

"No, she's just a cook, but I very much doubt any of them are guilty. They are only distant relatives and would have to murder a huge number of people in order to inherit this place. Even the local police couldn't fail to identify the killer if the butler suddenly became the master of St Audries Park with seventeen dead people before him."

I stood up to look at a beautiful blue-and-yellow macaw who was sitting on the top of a stone statue. I'd once seen a very similar parrot called Nora in London Zoo who could hum "The Keel Row" whilst performing a funny dance. I very much doubted that this would help us solve a murder, and so I returned to my previous chain of thought.

"It's hard to imagine how people believe they can get away with murder for personal gain. If you wish to inherit an estate, you should first conceive of a clever method to distance yourself from the crime. I wonder if that means you were wrong in your hypothesis and the killer wasn't really at lunch just now."

"Or it could be that…" She started this sentence with great confidence, but it soon ebbed away.

I looked across the tiled floor that was scattered with bright feathers. "You can trust me, Flossie. I'm not here to twist anyone's words."

"It could be that the killer isn't motivated by money after all. Perhaps there's another reason to want Silas and Uncle Perry dead. I know it may seem like the obvious motive, but if I wanted to kill my way to a fortune, I'd start from the bottom, not the top."

There wasn't a hint of viciousness in her words, but I couldn't help wondering whether she'd thought a lot about this topic. It had never crossed my mind to work out who I would have to kill to inherit my grandfather's estate, and yet this was a common pastime in the Rivers family.

"Starting at the bottom would at least confuse things," she continued. "So what if the killer attacked my great-uncle for another reason and Silas got in the way somehow?"

I'd assumed that she'd taken me there not just to show off her pets but to reveal something important. And yet all she'd offered were hazy thoughts and half-finished sentences.

"This is all too vague, Flossie. Why don't you just tell me who you think killed Silas?"

Her eyes became wider as she realised that the moment had come to stop prevaricating. "I don't know anything for certain, I honestly don't, but you must have realised that Victoria – that is, Mrs Stevans – well, she's not happy here. I've known for years, but she won't talk to us about it. She only ever spoke to Silas."

"Fine, but why would she have killed him?"

"I can't tell you that. All I know is that, of all the people in this house, when I learnt that someone was trying to kill Uncle Perry, hers was the first name that came to mind."

CHAPTER FOURTEEN

A great number of the birds suddenly took to the air to fly in a circle before landing back more or less where they started. I'd never seen such a display and, for a moment, there was a tornado of colour above us. Rising to my feet, I wondered how all those different species could get on so well whereas we humans fought and bickered over the slightest thing.

"I'm sorry," I tried one last time when I failed to understand what Flossie was trying to tell me and she seemed unwilling to clarify. "You must know something more than that. Victoria Stevans isn't happy at St Audries, and you think that means she was involved in Silas's death, even though she and Silas were confidantes."

"That's right."

I hoped that my brief summary would give her a clue as to the conundrum I faced, but apparently that wasn't the case. "Could you explain how any of that makes sense?"

"It's not my place to say anything." Her voice almost broke then, and she moved to leave the orangery. "I have to go. It's Christmas Eve and, even if there are dead bodies in place of Christmas trees, we still have tasks to complete."

I stood aside as she passed, but she stopped and placed one hand on my cheek unexpectedly. "You're a very nice boy, Christopher Prentiss. Thank you for being here to help us. I can't imagine what this holiday would have been like if you and your grandfather…" She paused to recall who else had landed on her doorstep. "…and mother, father, and grandmother hadn't come."

Turning to leave, she sniffed as though she'd been crying, but her eyes remained dry. I stood and watched her go as the flock took flight once more. For a moment, they seemed to stand in for the thoughts that were circling my brain. I had the definite feeling that various members of the household were trying to manipulate me, but that didn't mean I knew who was lying or even what they hoped to achieve.

Flossie wasn't the first person to point to Mrs Stevans as a potential killer, and that would be just the thing to do if she wished to distract me from the truth, but why would she? The only real anger she'd betrayed was when I'd mentioned her brother's potential guilt. She had shown more affection to her exquisite parrots than she had to her cousins.

I waited in that bubble of heat for a few minutes longer before braving the cold of that singularly pure landscape which stretched off from the house all the way to the coast. Of course, I couldn't make out the line between the snowy terrain and the sky. There was no hope of spotting the sea with those giant but gentle flakes still falling, but I could hear the wind howling as it reached the house and feel it lashing my cheeks and hands. Even the minute-long trek to the main house was an ordeal. Oh, and don't worry, I remembered to lock the door to the parrotry. We wouldn't want the multi-coloured flock to end up all white now, would we?

There was a fog in my head that would not clear even as I stepped into the warmth of the manor. I could have gone to discuss the strange affair with yet another suspect who would point me in the wrong direction and confuse me further, but there was one man who I rather hoped might shed some light on the situation. I eventually found my grandfather in the sitting room with his dog at his feet. He was playing cards with my father and grandmother, and Mother made a fourth.

"Don't you think we should be investigating Silas's murder?" I foolishly suggested as I sat down on the sofa to get warm near the fire which Ripon was stoking.

"I am investigating," Grandfather insisted, before yelling, "Snap!" and bringing his hand down on the small baize table in front of him.

"This is dreadful," my father bemoaned, rather ignoring the events of that day. "I've barely won a card since we started playing."

"Concentrate, darling," my mother told him.

"Yes, Walter. Concentrate!" his mother echoed. "You've never been a contemplative child, but it's not too late to change."

I allowed them another brief hand, which my mother won, before complaining once more. "You're not investigating. You're playing Snap. If you were at least engaged in a more intellectual pursuit, I might accept that you were exercising your brain muscles, but Snap? I haven't played such a juvenile game since I was a child."

Grandfather was about to lay a card down but held his hand in the air. "Would you like us to start afresh so that you can play, my boy?"

Oh, that sneak! He knew that, despite my claim to the contrary, I couldn't resist such a jolly pastime. He'd well and truly foxed me, so I sighed and pretended to see little joy in the prospect. "If I'm going to have to sit here waiting for you, I might at least pass the time in a more spirited manner."

"Wonderful. Another person to beat me," Father continued to moan. "How lucky I am."

"So, Christopher," Grandfather began as he shuffled the cards and dealt them out to each player. "Tell us what you have learnt whilst I have been here *investigating*."

I took a chair from the desk in the corner to claim a place at the table. "I spoke to Flossie in the parrotry."

"What's a *parrotry*?" Granny asked in her typically acerbic manner. Much like my grandfather, she could not stand neologisms and, as I'd only invented this word a few minutes earlier, I knew she would not approve of it.

"It's an orangery with parrots in it. But that's beside the point. I was talking to Flossie – she's Luke's sister and Holly's second cousin, in case anyone was wondering."

"Who's Luke?" my father was staring at the cards, and I very much doubted he could play the game and make sense of an already complicated case.

"He's Flossie's brother, of course," my grandmother snapped. "Do keep up, Walter."

I could tell that my father wished he'd left his mother at home.

"I was talking to her in the parrotry, and it just confused me more."

Grandfather managed to ruffle one eyebrow in sympathy, even while claiming a stack of cards with a resolute, "Snap!" He gathered up his winnings before speaking again. "Christopher, please tell us what it is that has so upset you."

I needed a moment to put it into words. "I can no longer decide who should be trusted and who shouldn't. I know you always say that I assume every person with a kindly attitude must be as innocent as they appear, but how am I supposed to tell who is good and who's not?"

The four adults looked at one another to see who would answer this tricky question. It inevitably fell to my grandfather to reply. I believe that my mother was too much of an optimist to give a fair answer, my grandmother too much of a pessimist, and my father was busy wondering how he might finally win a round of Snap.

"Sadly, there is no one trick for solving such a conundrum. All I can say is that you must take each person as they come and judge them not just on how they act but the tiny elements of a personality which are harder to disguise. Take Florence Rivers, for example. She was very generous to show you around the orangery and seems an open-hearted sort of person from our interactions with her so far."

"However…"

"However, we must also question why she would show you such kindness in the first place. What does she stand to gain from your thinking well of her? And what lies behind her words?"

I bit my lip, thinking over his advice. "So what you're saying is that I shouldn't trust anyone."

"Precisely!" Granny replied for him. She had a wicked glint in her eye and evidently sensed an opportunity to convert me to her way of thinking. "Trust no one. That's my motto, and it has served me well."

"I'm sorry, but I do not agree," my mother intervened. "We must give all people the benefit of the doubt, even as we remember that they may not be as good as they first seem."

Grandfather was only half paying attention and laid another card down in the middle of the table with a triumphant, "Snap!"

"Oh, I give up!" Father said and threw his cards down, much as he'd often told my brother and me not to do. "Let's talk about the evil-minded killer who haunts this house rather than this silly game. Christopher, who do you think is the culprit?"

Granny had occasionally eyed the butler as he dealt with the fire and, now that he had gone, she could finally say what she'd been thinking. "That chap who was just in here must be the killer!"

"The butler, Granny?"

"That's right. Didn't you see the way he lingered? There's no question about it; he was eavesdropping to determine what the famous Lord Edgington had discovered."

My mother was a very patient woman, yet even she struggled to remain calm around her mother-in-law. "Really, Loelia. Must you think the worst of everyone?"

Granny smiled her witchy smile. "As we've already established, yes, I must."

Grandfather was on hand to keep the peace. "I very much doubt that Ripon the butler has any reason to murder Silas or his employer." I decided this wasn't the moment to mention that the serving staff were distantly related to the Rivers family. "He may have been eavesdropping, but all the best servants do. I've trained Todd to be quite the efficient spy."

There were so many things that were wrong with this statement that I didn't know where to begin. Instead, I ignored it entirely and returned to my own frustrations. "Assuming that the butler is not to blame, I can no longer make sense of who might be. The person I considered the obvious troublemaker was murdered almost as soon as we arrived, and his slippery brother is both the least and most likely suspect."

This time, they really didn't know how to respond. Even Granny's pessimism offered no solution to my blue devils.

"Which is why you must not view the world through such fundamentally rigid blinkers." Grandfather tapped the table a few times, as if waiting for his turn in the game we'd abandoned. "Even after all I've taught you, you think that Nathan and Silas were the probable culprits because they were rude and combative. You feel such dispiritude because you've been forced to consider the guilt of the young, attractive and seemingly kind people who remain."

"That's exactly it. A few of the potential killers may seem self-interested and perhaps even manipulative, but none of them come across as violent criminals."

"Follow me, boy." Grandfather stood up from the table, and I realised that I hadn't laid down a card in the time I was sitting there.

Mother touched my hand soothingly as her father led me to the front door to look at the world outside. He sensibly put the lock on the latch before closing it behind us.

"Christopher, what can you see out here?"

This was a silly question, and so I provided a matching answer. "Snow."

His answer truly surprised me. "You're one hundred per cent correct." He didn't even roll his eyes. "And what is snow?"

I'd never been too bright when it came to science and that sort of thing, but I replied with a nice simple, "Cold water?"

He sighed and tried again. "Also correct, but I was thinking more of what it represents. Is snow good or evil?"

I would have asked him to repeat himself, but I was sure I'd heard the first time. "I don't think I've ever considered that question before. It's certainly very beautiful." I mused on this for a moment before realising the ambiguity of the millions of white crystals before us. "And yet it can be dangerous – deadly even if you spend too long in it without provisions. I suppose it's possible that more people have died over the millennia from freezing to death than bombs or bullets."

He considered my words himself then. "Until this century, at least, you may be right. And so you see my point, don't you?"

The Christopher from a year or two before, who generally blurted the first thing that popped into his head, would have answered in the negative, but I did understand. I'd understood even before I'd entered the sitting room, because it was the same thing he'd been telling me since our first case together.

"You mean that something, or someone, can look innocent and still be a killer."

"That's exactly it."

He almost looked proud as we stared at the flakes that the wind buffeted in the air before they could finally touch the ground. Even then they weren't safe and, like sand in the desert, a brisk gust whipped them back off the surface and around the estate.

"Now, my boy, I have another important question for you. Should we stay out here and have a snowball fight, or is it time to continue the investigation?"

CHAPTER FIFTEEN

"You cheated."

"How can you say such a thing?" Grandfather liked to claim that he did everything exactly by the book, but that didn't make it true.

"You threw a snowball in my eye, and I couldn't see anything. As a result, I fell over and got snow in the other eye and was completely blind when you ambushed me. That does not count as a victory."

"Huh!" came his indignant response. "Where in the rules of warfare does it say that one cannot make the most of one's advantage?"

"I'm not sure that a snowball fight counts as warfare, *your lordship*," I made sure to pronounce these last two words with just the right degree of sarcasm.

"Either way, you should not be a sore loser, Christopher. It is Christmas Eve, and we must be thankful that we have time to enjoy such frivolous pastimes." He stood in the hallway appreciating this fact for a good three seconds before saying, "Good. Now let's get back to work. We must speak to Mrs Stevans, whose name has come up several times in our discussions with the other suspects, but no one seems allied with her directly. In fact, in my observations, I have found her rather disconnected from the house and everyone in it."

I told him the details of what Flossie had revealed in the parrot house, and it only piqued his interest more. "There we go. You're having a crisis of confidence over nothing. I'm sure that Mrs Stevans will have a perfectly terrible personality and she will shoot to the top of our list of suspects."

I must confess, this idea was a little heartening, but when we found the lady in question, I instantly realised it was wrong.

"I felt sure you would want to talk to me." She was already crying before we'd asked a single question. "I've been dreading it since you arrived."

Just to give you a picture of the scene, she was sitting in the nursery on the second floor, surrounded by scraps of fabric and a pile of bodies. Very well, the bodies weren't human. In fact, they weren't even made of flesh. She had sewn and stuffed around thirty soft toys of different descriptions.

"Madam, may I ask why you're producing so many tiny animals?" my grandfather put to her in some amazement as she seamlessly stitched the seams of the silky creatures without looking at what she was doing.

"For the orphans, my lord."

"Of course," I said, as my heart sank a little deeper. "What would the orphans do at Christmas without such generosity?"

"There's an orphanage in Taunton that asks for donations at this time of year. I normally go down there on Boxing Day to deliver them, but the road is closed. They're saying we could be stuck here until New Year's Day."

It hadn't dawned on me before that the snow might keep us there beyond Christmas itself. I just had to hope we would catch the killer before we shared the festive feast the following afternoon. My grandfather's average was around two days to trap a killer, but I'm sure he would make a special effort to be more efficient, considering the date.

Mrs Stevans had other things on her mind. "When I think of all the children's poor little faces when they don't get the presents they deserve, it breaks my heart. It really does!"

My grandfather always had a clean handkerchief on his person for just such a moment, and he now produced it with a flamboyant flick of the wrist. Much like the handiwork of a stage magician, it seemed to appear out of thin air.

"Thank you, my lord. I am truly grateful for your kindness and attention." She had an upper-class voice and, judging by her manners, was clearly well bred, and yet there was something rather showy about her that I found quite unusual.

"Madam, could you tell me why you have been so nervous about talking to us?"

I thought that she might refuse to answer, but she wiped her cheeks and looked pleadingly into my grandfather's soft grey eyes. "The disturbance this morning truly unsettled me."

"You mean the confrontation between Lord Rivers and Nathan?" Grandfather tried to elicit a little more precision. "I believe the young man threatened your employer. But fear not. I rarely base my judgements on the words my suspects utter so much as the deeds they do."

She looked as if she might thank him again for his understanding, but then her expression turned grave. "No, that wasn't what worried

116

me. I was upset by the stone that nearly fell upon Lord Rivers's head. He could have been squashed like a French crepe." You see! She was clearly from the upper crust of society. Any average person would have compared the viscount's potential fate to a good British pancake.

"Did you see it happen, then?" I asked far too directly, before padding the question with unnecessary words to appear less rude. "Or rather, did you happen to be present at the time in which the brick so frighteningly descended from the door?"

She nodded in a fast, nervous manner without looking at us. "I was right there in the room with him. He opened the door, and it came plunging down. The sound was just dreadful; I believe it must have broken a floorboard."

"We will have to examine the scene forthwith," Grandfather replied, and this seemed to soothe her somewhat. "I can see that such an experience would be upsetting. It really is no wonder that you would feel the way you do. However, I'm afraid I still have more questions for you."

"Yes, my lord. Of course."

It was at this moment I realised exactly what had caused the unusual contradiction in her. She was a well-bred woman, but she had the obsequious manner of a servant. I knew she had served as a companion, and women in such positions rarely had high prospects in life. She was like a lady in waiting, minus the possibility of a high marriage or future title.

"May I ask how you came to live here in the first place?" Grandfather asked, to echo my own thoughts.

"I was Lady Rivers's companion before she died."

"Yes, but how did you know the family?"

She picked up the small figure of a bear in a Robin Hood outfit and held it tightly. "I grew up not so far from here, but my family did not have the same good fortune as the Rivers did. We were forced to sell our estate when my parents died. Lady Rivers and I were friends, and she suggested I come here to keep her company. Perry... that is, Lord Rivers, was often away on hunting trips or up in town. That lifestyle didn't agree with Lady Rivers, and so I moved into a spare room. We had a lovely few years here before poor Polly died."

"I'm sorry," I had to interrupt. "Are you saying that Holly's grandmother was called Polly?"

"That's right," she replied in the same quiet tone, and it was clear that neither of them found this strange. "Polly and Perry were a lovely pair. He was heartbroken when she died, especially as they had already lost their beloved daughter Molly."

I kept my lips tightly sealed then, but I would have liked to shout, *Who chose those ridiculous names?*

"It must have been hard for you." I believe that Grandfather moved to offer her a sympathetic handkerchief at this moment before remembering that he'd already done so.

"Molly was a kind and loyal friend to me for many years. But I was amazed when Lord Rivers offered to let me stay on here. He even moved me to a larger bedroom…" Her voice dropped away for a moment, though she managed not to betray any other emotions as she finished the sentence. "…right next to his own."

This brought to mind an obvious question that would go unasked. I can only assume that my grandfather deemed it impolite or perhaps too upsetting to broach the matter of Mrs Stevans's living arrangements with the viscount.

He found a way to address the issue from another angle. "Do you know what you would have done if he hadn't offered you a place to live?"

Mrs Stevans became more nervous again. "Oh, my lord, I don't like to think about it. I really don't. I had no money of my own. Not enough to buy a house, at least. I should likely have sought another position somewhere, but it's not nearly as easy as one might think. I might well have relied on the charity of my friends."

Grandfather had a… well, a rather grandfatherly smile when he needed to calm a witness, and he deployed it now to great effect. "How fortunate it is that such measures were not necessary. You have evidently built a life for yourself here. I believe that Flossie, in particular, spoke warmly of you to my grandson."

She looked at me as if she were grateful that someone had said nice things about her in my presence. Of course, this wasn't even true. All Flossie has told me was that Mrs Stevans was unhappy about something, but Grandfather was good at bending the truth to fit his needs.

"I am fortunate to be able to see a lot of the younger generation.

I wasn't lucky enough to have children of my own, and I feel that the people here at St Audries are, in some ways, like my very own brood."

"Indeed." The wily sleuth was clearly building up to something, and I was fairly sure what it was. "In fact, we heard tell that you were particularly close to Silas before he was killed. May I ask if that was another reason why you have been on edge today?"

As if she was a machine that my grandfather had rewired for a different purpose, her manner suddenly lost all its tenderness. "No. Not in the slightest. That boy was a disgrace. You know, people liked to say that the war changed him, but he was just as perverse before. As a child, he used to pick on his playmates and cut the heads off dead animals. The only reason I had anything to do with him was to make sure that he didn't end up murdering the lot of us."

I wanted to ask her why she took this responsibility on herself, but before I could, Grandfather spoke again.

"And do you believe that's what he had in mind? Do you think that this apparent reprobate wished to murder Lord Rivers?"

She hesitated, and I noticed that her fingers tightened a little around the teddy bear's tiny body. "I wouldn't have put it past him. He hated Perry; there's no doubt about it. He used to tell me his fantasy of becoming lord of the manor and what he'd do on the day that Lord Rivers died. But if he was to blame, he didn't share his plans with me."

"Is there anything you can remember that might prove he was responsible for the traps that were set during the summer and again this morning?"

She had a good think and touched the small bun of hair that was perched on top of her head. "I wish I could. But there's certainly nothing to say he's innocent, either."

"What of his brother?" I asked at last. "He was the one who threatened Lord Rivers today. Isn't it possible that he'd already tried to murder him?"

"Nathan?" she laughed in an oddly cynical manner. "I doubt he'd find the time to plan a murder. He's probably too busy looking in the mirror and dedicating poetry to his own reflection."

We had gone there to interview her as I'd considered the possibility that she was somehow in league with the two brothers, and yet she didn't have a good word to say about either of them.

"I do not believe that vanity, in itself, rules out the possibility of a man being a killer," my grandfather replied in a didactic tone.

"It definitely *wasn't* Nathan," she exclaimed even more confidently than before.

"But, Madam, how can you be so sure? I am not saying that he will turn out to be the culprit, but Nathan comes across as an angry and duplicitous fellow who puts himself before others. Can you really say that he's innocent of his brother's death?"

"Yes, I can." Her tone softened a fraction, and the fury drained out of her. "I know he didn't do it because, for one thing, he's my nephew and, for another, he was up here with me when Silas was killed."

CHAPTER SIXTEEN

"Your plan didn't quite go to plan, Lord Clever." I walked towards the stairs that led down to the room where poor violent Silas lay in three small pools of his own blood. "You promised that we'd identify some monstrous suspects. Now it turns out that Mrs Stevans sews teddies for unloved Christmas orphans, and slimy Nathan couldn't be the killer."

He ignored my sullen tone to ask, "What's a Christmas orphan? It sounds rather jolly."

He lingered outside the room we'd just vacated, and so I turned back to him. "Grandfather, what hope is there now? I just know that one of those nice, cheery characters like Luke or Flossie will turn out to be the killer and my faith in society, humanity and, dare I say it, Christmas will be forever dimmed."

"Oh, undoubtedly."

His perfectly empty response triggered a thought. "Of course, the fact that Mrs Stevans is Silas and Nathan's aunt could turn out to be important. For a moment, I wondered whether she had tried to kill Lord Rivers on her nephew's behalf. The problem is that she doesn't actually seem to like either of them, which means we're right back where we started.

He continued ignoring me but wore a perplexed expression. "Perhaps a Christmas orphan is a poor child who comes to spend Yuletide with a rich family, before being packed off back to the orphanage."

"Grandfather!" My voice rose. "Are you listening to me?"

"No, boy. I am not. I'm waiting for you to stop fretting so that we can explore Lord Rivers's bedroom." He pointed to a half-open door a little way along the corridor.

"Oh... I see."

"After you, Mr Prentiss."

I would have liked to continue grumbling, but there wasn't much point, and so I stomped off to look inside Lord Rivers's suite of rooms. Considering that he was the king of the castle, so to speak, I was left unimpressed by the simple apartment. It was not particularly luxurious or even tastefully decorated. The only treasures it contained were displayed on a shelf beside the door. There was a set of wooden soldiers, a tin of what looked like ancient conkers, and a small pile of ha'pennies. For some reason, it did not strike me as odd that the funny little man should have kept his childhood belongings there. For a viscount, there was something decidedly childlike about him.

"Christopher, look!"

Lord Edgington, of course, was a master of observation. He could have spotted an Easter egg in a room full of Christmas baubles in the time it takes to say, *What's that doing there?* The discovery he made in that room, however, was less out of place.

"My goodness," I whispered back to him, going over to look at the bulge in the bed. "He's still having his nap. You'd think my shouting and stomping would have woken him. What a sound sleeper he must be."

It was perhaps odd for two grown men to stand watching the old gent sleep, and Grandfather soon pulled me away to inspect the water closet in the corner. Just as Victoria Stevans had attested, there was a rather large crack in the bare floorboards and the immense lump of stone, which looked as if it had been stolen from a church, was still where it had fallen.

"That's disappointing," Grandfather said with a barely audible huff.

"What is?" I really couldn't guess.

"You know how you often complain that I don't let you in on my grand ideas until I can prove them."

"Yes?"

"Well, we can now rule one of them out."

I can only imagine that he was hoping I would show my excitement, as I would have a year or so before. Instead, I stood there and waited for him to explain.

"I'd been working on the principle that Lord Rivers himself had faked his brushes with death."

I had to think for a moment to understand why he would now dismiss the idea. "You mean that Lord Rivers wouldn't have had the strength to carry such a large chunk of rock up here, let alone set it to fall from such a height."

"That is precisely what I mean, along with the testimony from Mrs Stevans, of course." He knelt down to examine the block and poked it with a pen from his pocket on the off-chance it was much lighter than it looked.

"But why would he have gone to such lengths? What would he have gained from people thinking his life was at risk?"

He sighed, then tutted, then sighed again as he apparently hadn't communicated his frustration clearly enough. "I do not know, Christopher. I really don't."

I was frankly alarmed that he didn't have ten possible explanations ready to list off at will. "My goodness. I'm not sure you've ever admitted such a thing before."

"Oh.... Well, I clearly ate too much goose liver at lunch," he attempted to explain. "Indigestion sometimes leads to mental congestion." I very much doubted this was a scientifically proven fact.

"Yes, of course, Grandfather. And, you know, Lord Rivers might have set the traps in order to gain sympathy. Although his relatives regularly come here to win his favour, we have yet to find anyone who particularly likes him. Perhaps he just wanted a little of their affection."

"What a perfectly warm-hearted interpretation, Christopher."

I reflected on the idea. "Yes, but it wouldn't explain why Silas was killed."

He looked at the would-be murder weapon for a few seconds longer and then got back to his feet. "No, you're right, and that is why we must abandon the theory. Do you have another I might borrow?"

"Oh…" I had to scratch my head then, but sadly no flakes of an idea rubbed off. "I'm afraid nothing comes to mind unless… Well, I've been afraid for some time that Luke could be the killer."

He shrugged and was surprisingly open to the idea. "Very well. Luke is the killer. Now tell me his motive and the evidence against him."

"Yes, of course." This was easier said than done, and I racked the brains in my recently scratched head for an answer. "We gave Nathan a hard time because he seems like a bad apple, whereas I have been too easy on Luke because he comes across as a thoroughly good egg."

He'd been pushing me towards the corridor but paused to speak. "Christopher. I am not going to disagree with you." This in itself was a novelty. "However, you'll need more substantial evidence to convict a man of murder."

"In which case, I'll do all I can to get close to him and find some answers. We'll solve this murder in no time."

We both knew this was just bravado on my part, so we enjoyed a laugh or two at my expense.

"Ah, my dear grandson. You do know how to cheer me up."

I humbly bowed my head. "I try my best."

Slightly less cheery was the sight of Silas's body still laid out in the salon where we'd last seen him. It was horrible to leave him there for so long, but it wasn't as though a coroner was going to call by the house anytime. Had we possessed a sleigh of some variety, we could have pulled the corpse to the nearest village, but I very much doubted they had a mortuary there and so, for the moment, he would stay where he was.

To my surprise, the doorbell at the front of the house sounded, and the place rang with footsteps as half the inhabitants of St Audries Park rushed to see who had reached us in such treacherous weather.

"I'm P.C. Acland," the caller revealed and, though he didn't look much more than fifteen, he was apparently a police officer.

"Are you any relation of—" my grandfather began, but before he could finish the question, Philip Acland appeared from his office.

"Hello there, Ted," the clerk said over our shoulders, before explaining, "This is my little brother." Everyone in the area really was related to everyone else.

The constable stood smiling contentedly. His neat blue uniform, which looked three sizes too big for him, had a small pile of snow on either shoulder (and a larger one on the top of his flat blue hat). Granny was watching him from the door to the sitting room, but before she could declare that our new arrival was to blame for the killing, he spoke again.

"No one else wanted to come. I've always liked the snow, though, so I volunteered. I hear there's been some sort of murder?"

He was a very sunny person. I'd never heard anyone talk of such a crime in a cheery tone before. Well, except for my grandfather, who now ushered the boy inside to have a look at the body.

"Yes, indeed." Lord Edgington was ever so enthusiastic. "You know, it's becoming something of a tradition in my family. This is the third year in a row we've investigated a Christmas murder."

"Perhaps you should be my first suspect," P.C. Ted quipped, and the two men's sides were about to split when the victim's brother descended the grand staircase, and all joviality was smothered by his taciturn presence.

Delilah was at my side and reprimanded her master with a low bark, or perhaps she was upset that no one had given her much attention for some time.

"Nathan, dear boy," Luke called along the hall to his cousin. "You must do something to take your mind off what happened." The handsome fellow swept his hand through his hair as he considered what they could do as a distraction.

"Well, it is Christmas," I hazarded. "Perhaps we could make the place look a little more festive?"

"A tree!" Luke replied. "That's just it. We must go on a quest to find the perfect Christmas tree."

Flossie seemed most excited by this. "What a wonderful idea. You will join us, won't you, Nathan?"

The eldest remaining cousin looked supremely indifferent to the prospect. "I suppose I might as well."

Even poor tragic Holly became slightly less frownsome – if that is a word. It was the first time since we'd arrived that I'd seen her without a task to complete, though she evidently still had work ahead of her.

"I promised cook that I would help make the paradise pudding for supper."

"There's no need for that," I tried to convince her. "Your cook will have all the help she needs from the Cranley Hall staff. My grandfather refuses to travel without his favourite employees, and they will do a wonderful job in your absence."

She vacillated in her usual uncertain manner, but Flossie put one arm around her, and she soon yielded.

"Well, hurrah!" Luke said when Holly gave a hesitant nod. "Now all we need are warm clothes and some supplies."

With no one new around to suspect of murder, Granny had got bored and retreated to her spot by the fire, but Mother stuck her head out of the sitting room. It was our tradition when I was a child for the two of us to pick a tree together every December. We'd buy it from the farm along the lane from our house at Kilston Down, and then drag it home, singing Christmas carols all the way. We would decorate it as a family, and even my father and mopey brother normally enjoyed the ritual. It came as no surprise that Mother wished to be included now and joined the march upstairs.

We ran to our rooms to don extra layers of clothing in order to delve headfirst (hopefully not literally) into the snow. Todd had unpacked my bag in the adjoining room to my grandfather's, and I was happy to find several jumpers – all of which I put on, one over the other – along with my thickest winter coat. Admittedly, I was no longer able to lower my arms due to all the layers I was wearing – and I almost expired from the heat before I made it back to the front door, but it was worth it when I got outside and barely felt the chill wind.

Everyone assembled on the front doorstep, and Delilah looked particularly happy as she bounded about in the snow. There wasn't nearly so much cascading from the sky at that moment, and I felt quite positive about our excursion.

"Are you ready?" Luke asked the group, and when no one replied, he took this as a positive sign. "Then off we go into the unknown."

CHAPTER SEVENTEEN

"Christopher," Holly asked with concern in her voice, "are you supposed to look like a star that has fallen to earth?"

"That wasn't my intention. Perhaps I should have worn a jumper or two less. I don't exactly love the cold, you see. And this way I can help choose a tree without my body turning to ice. I don't have a great deal of flexibility in my arms, but I'm sure that won't be a problem." I tried to lower them again, but they popped straight back up to shoulder height.

Her magnificent blue eyes sparkled, and she gave a faint laugh that was as gentle as the tinkling bell on the bracelet that was restored to its rightful place on her wrist. "You know, you are funny."

"Holly, dear," Flossie called over to her and the enchanting young lady was stolen away once more.

My mother threaded her arm not exactly through but at least around mine as we circled the snowbound house. The wind was a little lighter on the eastern side of the property, where the buildings sheltered us from the sea. For a moment, I had a fantasy of frolicking across the nearby beach in the summer with Holly at my side, but even as the image formed in my mind, something told me that it would never come to pass.

Luke fell into step alongside us to offer a dose of positivity.

"Despite the biting wind and the frost forming on my toes at this very moment, this is beyond doubt my favourite time of year." In his navy blue, ankle-length coat with a rabbit fur collar, not to mention his impressively bushy black moustache, he looked rather like a Russian statesman.

"I bet it is!" I snapped, despite agreeing with everything he'd just said. What I was thinking in my head was, *There's no hope of my impartially considering you as a suspect if you're as much a lover of Christmas as I am.* Only I couldn't say that out loud, and so I had to think quickly. "I mean… I bet it is. Mine too!"

He looked nonplussed for a moment, then smiled his winning smile. "Oh, yes, I love everything about it. The sights and the smells… and the presents, of course."

"Ah, ha!" I once more uttered something that was supposed to stay between me and my brain. I was thinking, *At last! Whose favourite part of Christmas is the presents? He's clearly driven by material wealth and killed Silas to get one step closer to inheriting a fortune.* But before I could consider the point further, he spoke again.

"Or rather, I love giving presents. I'm not too concerned about receiving them. It's always such a joy to see the beaming faces of my loved ones. Don't tell Uncle Perry, but I've made him a hand-carved shield of the Rivers coat of arms for him to hang on his bedroom wall. That room is so bare, I decided that he needed something to display."

"What a thoughtful gift," my dear, trusting mother exclaimed.

If he was the killer, he was incredibly good at hiding his true personality, but I was determined to dig deeper. "You know what would be a rather special gift for you, Luke? If Lord Rivers finally named you as his heir."

He looked at me without turning his head. "I suppose it would, but I don't like to think about such things. I have never relied on my family's wealth or expected to receive anything from Perry. That's why I trained to become a solicitor. Some around here might deem it beneath the blessed Rivers Family to go in for a profession, but I believe in hard work. If I'm to secure the survival of my family home at Grenham Manor, I will do it myself."

He looked straight ahead as he said this, as though his goal was just in front of him, and he was determined to reach it. I rather hoped that he would turn out to be the killer if only so that I could say I had met such an accomplished liar.

"That's very impressive, Luke," Mother told him. "I think more people should have such an attitude."

"Yes, it's most admirable," Nathan said. He was a few steps behind us and still wore the velvet suit he'd had on all day. He'd added nothing more than a wide woollen scarf to fend off the cold. "You really are a thoroughly nice man, aren't you, Luke?" His voice was light and cheerful, but I had to assume there was a sceptical undertone to the question. "However, there is one thing you have overlooked."

"Oh, yes?" his cousin murmured, and I doubt that Nathan heard him over the wind.

"There aren't any pine trees on this estate. We've come out here on a doomed mission to freeze off our extremities. At least Scott of the

Antarctic made it to the South Pole before he and his men all died. All we have are oaks and yews."

Luke would not be discouraged. "Then we'll make do with oaks and yews."

It was true that we'd walked around three sides of the manor without coming across any conifers. But our fearless leader led us on towards a small, wooded area on the other side of a vast expanse of snow. It was odd visiting a grand estate in such conditions. There could have been sand dunes or marshes beneath our feet, and I would have been none the wiser.

"Here we are." Luke clapped his mittened hands together when we got to the cover of the trees. Even though they were largely leafless, they were so dense that little snow broke through. I must say that it was rather eery under there. The light was already dying and there was something fantastical about finding a piece of land that was not covered with that thick blanket. It was almost as if we had passed travelled to a realm in which the colour white had been replaced with a spectrum of browns.

"I thought we were looking for a Christmas tree, not fetching kindling," negative Nathan complained. "They tend to be green."

Before he could question whether anyone had even thought to bring the necessary tools, Luke pulled out an axe and saw from the knapsack he'd been carrying (that I'd forgotten to mention until now).

Mother pulled me to one side as we awaited our instructions. "Is everything all right? I thought your grandfather had made you feel slightly less gloomy about life."

My feelings were a strange thing to worry about when there was a killer to apprehend, but I appreciated her concern. "I'm still worrying that I'm too easily fooled by our suspects. For about three minutes, I had an inkling that Luke must be to blame for his cousin's murder. But after speaking to him for a short time, I'm back to believing he's the nicest chap I've ever met."

She laughed at me then. I appreciated it less than her previous concern. "You do worry about silly things. Despite what your grandmother might believe, pessimism is not the solution to all of life's problems. It's good that you can see the best in people."

The deep sigh I produced made my lips wobble. "I think there must be something wrong with me, Mother. Christmas is coming, but I don't feel the way I'm supposed to feel."

"There is a dead man in the back salon, Chrissy." She clapped her arms around her to keep warm. "It wouldn't be right to laugh your head off and play games all the time. I really don't think the Rivers family would be too happy if you did."

"That's not it. What I mean is…" I didn't know how to finish this sentence, but watched Delilah as she wagged her tail excitedly. Flossie had picked up a dead branch, and the expectant dog must have assumed that someone would throw it to her.

"Listen to me, my darling." Mother moved in front of me so that I had to look at her. "There is nothing wrong with the way you view the world. In many respects, you're just like me. I always look for the best in any situation. When I was young and I went to work with my father in Scotland Yard, he told me that I would need a hard heart if I was to be a great detective. Well, for one thing, I had no intention of becoming a detective of any stripe, but I managed to help him with his cases without giving up my humanity. As it happens, he told me I was rather good at what I did."

I'd heard stories of her youthful adventures with my grandfather before, but I was always eager to know more.

She put one hand on mine as she spoke. "My point is that it's not your job to think that the suspects are ultimately good or bad. You have to search out the discrepancies that will tell you who they really are." She looked at Holly, Flossie and Luke, who were surely three of the nicest people there. "You've already shown how capable you are at assisting Father. You've got nothing more to prove and, if anything, your positivity is an advantage."

The woman was a magician.

"You're right, mother. There are those who carry Christmas with them throughout the year and those who don't, and I know which I'd rather be."

She wrapped me up in a hug, and I felt three times warmer than before, which, let's be honest, is a bit too warm when wearing so many jumpers.

"Come along, you two," Luke called to us. "We need your help to choose the prettiest branches."

130

We returned to the group with all the enthusiasm of the golden retriever who followed us. Even Nathan seemed invigorated by the happy scene and, once we'd selected the barest, most wintery-looking offshoot, he climbed onto Luke's shoulders to chop it down. Flossie collected a bundle of smaller sticks. Holly said she knew of a holly bush and ran off to take cuttings, and we paraded back to the house.

We made such a joyful noise as we returned that everyone from Philip Acland to our footman Halfpenny stopped what they were doing to watch.

"A Happy Christmas, one and all!" Luke beamed and, having taken him for a Russian revolutionary, now he'd removed his coat, I thought him a good British gentleman who would have fitted perfectly in the cheery closing chapter of a Dickens novel.

Mother had found some mistletoe and kissed my father despite their son's presence. Todd appeared with a tray of mulled wine – because he has a sixth sense for these things – and I struggled to get out of my jumpers before I expired.

"Help," I weakly murmured when I got my head stuck halfway through shedding the first layer. "Please help!"

"Look everyone," Flossie said with glee. "It's time to unwrap our first gift!"

I could see through the tiny holes in my knitted prison that they all gathered around to pull, and Holly delivered the only joke she would make that day.

"It's a Chrissy present." Her smile was so sweet, as it curved her previously blank face, that I almost had to look away.

This inspired a good amount of mirth from the others. Even my grandmother enjoyed a titter, and she had once told me that laughter is as unwelcome a reaction as belching.

By the time I was down to a single jumper, Luke and Nathan had gone to fetch some decorations while the girls and I attempted to arrange the branches we had collected so that they resembled some sort of tree. A base was found, and Flossie tied everything together with the pretty red ribbon from her hair. Two large boxes arrived, full to the brim with shiny trinkets, and we took it in turns to deck out our makeshift Christmas tree, which we placed in the corner of the sitting room, not so far from that brightly blazing fire.

By the time it was finished, it didn't look like any tree I'd had in my house over the years, but it was all the better for being a product of our hard work. We stood back to admire a job well done, and there was a smile on every face.

CHAPTER EIGHTEEN

As heartwarming as this sight was, it didn't compare to the transformation of Nathan Rivers. His sullenness had been erased, and he was no longer set on charming everyone with empty words – which was far more charming, in my opinion.

The cousins enjoyed their task so much that they soon talked about decorating other rooms in the house. My grandfather appeared for a glass of hot, sweet, spicy wine, and having moved Silas's body to cold storage in the icehouse, P.C. Ted was convinced to have a snifter before he returned home to the tiny village nearby.

Lord Rivers had presumably finished his nap as he came downstairs with Mrs Stevans to inspect our handiwork. He wore a terribly serious expression as he regarded the now sparkling branches that were strewn with bells, beads and baubles.

"I suppose I am remiss in buying a tree in the first place." He turned to his group of young relatives. "You have my apologies, children. It is a worthy addition to the house, and we shall open our presents here tomorrow as a family." He turned to my grandfather. "And the party from Cranley Hall will be here with us. This may not be the Christmas any of us imagined, but we will put the sadness of today behind us and make the most of the season."

If Lord Edgington was a benevolent Father Christmas figure, then the lord of St Audries Park was more like a tiny elf. And yet, there was something quite noble about him at that moment, and I sensed that he was doing what he could to unite the fractured group.

"I think that's just wonderful." Nathan's transformation hadn't lasted long, and he was using that same excessively slick voice as when I'd first arrived. "Thank you, Uncle Perry, for your hospitality and sense of occasion."

Lord Rivers nodded, his face no longer quite so jolly.

Nathan spoke with sudden haste. "In fact, I was hoping I might speak to you in private. There are a few matters I would like to resolve before we begin the celebrations in earnest."

"Not right now, boy. I must talk to Lord Edgington before dinner is served."

Nathan was unrelenting, and it was surely apparent to all present that he was playing the inheritance game once more. "Of course, of course. I totally understand, but if you could just step into the library with me for a few minutes, I really won't take up—"

His great-uncle really lost his temper then. "Did you not hear me?" Despite his frail body and diminished stature, his glare was still powerful and sliced right through the man. "I don't wish to talk to you this evening. I've said all I have to say, and I'm not interested in going over the same ground once more."

Whatever goodness had emerged from Nathan in the woods, it was now buried. His lip curled, and he looked as though he wanted to snarl and rip the man to pieces. Instead of insulting his prospective benefactor or landing a cuff on him, Nathan muttered bitterly and retreated from the room.

"I'm very sorry about that, Lord Edgington," Rivers said, before turning to the others. "And to you, ladies and gentlemen. That is not what I wanted to happen this evening. None of this is as I imagined, and I wish…" His words trailed off and, of all the people in the room to show some sympathy, my cantankerous grandmother came forward to distract him with some light-hearted conversation.

"You mustn't worry, Lord Rivers. The scene we've just witnessed is nothing compared to one Christmas Eve when my father came home from the navy. I was only very young, and no one had thought to mention that he would be returning from Japan without his legs. They'd been blown to smithereens in the bombardment of HMS Euryalus in the Anglo-Satsuma War, and he was not happy about it – I can tell you that. On arriving at the house, he accused Uncle Maurice of attempting to steal my mother from him, and the two brothers fought a duel that, somewhat surprisingly, my father won. No one was killed, but it was all very exciting. Many in my family considered it the best Christmas we'd ever had, so I wouldn't worry about a little thing like a murder spoiling the celebrations."

She went to sit down in the corner and continued to hold court, with Mrs Stevans and the viscount offering her due reverence for some time. The rest of us drank our wine, and I had to wonder what P.C. Ted thought of all this. I'm sorry, I know his name was Acland, but he just looked so young that P.C. Ted was the only way I could think of him.

Whatever he thought, he soon finished his drink and hurried off the estate, back to civilisation.

Eventually, my grandfather could wait no longer and decided to risk interrupting my garrulous granny.

"…by which time the men were all covered in pig fat, the maids were standing on chairs waving fans, and my parents were on the point of disowning me."

It occurred to me then that I should have paid more attention to the rest of her story.

"My apologies, Loelia," Grandfather began. "I've no wish to interrupt such a charming anecdote, but I believe that Lord Rivers wished to speak to me."

The viscount looked a little disturbed by whatever he had just heard. It was hard to know whether he was relieved to be pulled away from the conversation, or worried about the troubled mind who had chosen to share this apparently alarming tale in polite society.

"Yes… Yes, we must talk forthwith. I suggest we go to my salon."

He led us from the room in that slow shifting manner of his that made it look as though either leg might give way at any moment. Had I been so cruel as to knock his elegant cane from his hand, he would have gone falling to the carpet.

It turned out that his salon was some distance to walk. Halfway there, I considered suggesting to my grandfather that we each take one of Lord Rivers's arms to carry him to our destination. Surely there was a library, lounge, or drawing room that wasn't an hour's walk away.

During this lengthy expedition, I was at least afforded the opportunity to take in the manor's opulent decoration, which was at odds with Lord Rivers's bedroom. The soft, woven wallpapers looked as though they had been imported from India or the distant east and had interesting patterns showing villages, lakes and passing birds in black on a rich red background. There were similarly ornate and exotic vases placed on either side of the many doors we walked past, and so it was probably a good thing that our very waggy dog had stayed behind.

"Here we are," our host said as he showed us into the largest salon we had yet seen. One wall was covered with shelves from floor to ceiling and the international theme continued. There were figurines from China, Japanese masks, Mongolian headdresses and a French beret for some reason. But the most striking thing of all was an exquisite stuffed peacock who sat looking at us from its perch, right in the centre of the wall.

It's interesting to note the different reactions two people may have to the same thing. I was quite entranced by the beauty of the objects on display, whereas Lord Rivers had probably been born with them already in the house and barely saw them anymore.

He sat down in an extremely soft chair that seemed to want to swallow him, and my grandfather and I took our places on the sofa opposite.

"I'm sorry to take you away from the festivities," he said when he had called for tea and Ripon the butler had left. "I wanted to ask you about your investigation without being overheard."

His eyes were hidden by drooping skin, and like brambles in the summer, his eyebrows were overgrown. In fact, it was a wonder he could see at all.

"It is no inconvenience," my grandfather assured him. "What would you like to know?"

Rivers was calmer and more considered than he had been that morning. I had to wonder to what extent the events that had occurred prior to our arrival had distressed him.

"I'd like to know whether you've identified the killer and we'll have to call P.C. Ted back to arrest him."

"Gosh," I replied, unable to believe the coincidence. "Do you call him P.C. Ted, too?"

"That's right. He's far too young to think of as P.C. Acland. I've known him since he was a toddler and, to be quite frank, he hasn't grown a great deal in that time."

It was rather nice to hear someone agree with my way of thinking, but Grandfather was there to return us to the matter at hand. "I am confident that we are on the right course, but I cannot guarantee that the culprit will be apprehended before tomorrow."

Rivers looked perturbed for a moment. "I suppose that can't be helped. I still appreciate your effort."

If this was all he had called us there to discuss, I really felt we could have avoided the hassle of the journey.

"I have a question for you, Lord Rivers." Grandfather tapped his finger on the armchair a few times in a syncopated rhythm before revealing what this would be. "I believe you must have chosen your heir by now. Are you ready to reveal who it is?"

Peregrine Rivers smiled. It was an uncommon sight, and there was something not quite right about it – as if his mouth no longer matched his other features. "I can tell you who it *would be*." He stressed these last two words, but I couldn't say why. "It *would be* that dear boy Luke. There is no question that he is the most deserving of my relatives, even if I cast the net wider to include more distant cousins and what have you around the area. He has worked hard in his studies, takes nothing and no one for granted and, unlike Nathan, he hasn't spent the last decade or longer trying to win my favour."

Grandfather caught his meaning before I could. "And yet you haven't chosen him. Can you tell me why that is?"

"I haven't chosen Luke because I can't."

"How can that be true?" I asked, as his attitude towards the future owner of the estate had baffled me from the beginning. Not only would he not leave it to his own granddaughter, just because she was a woman, he apparently wouldn't pass it on to the man he deemed the obvious choice.

"He means," Grandfather interpreted for me, "that he is forbidden from leaving it to the man he would most like to make his heir."

Rivers closed and opened his eyes in place of a nod. "That's correct."

"I assume the estate is entailed then?" Grandfather knew more about these things – and most things – than me. He was also a kind man and explained what "entailed" meant. "Legally, St Audries Park must be left to Lord Rivers's oldest male relative within the usual chain of succession. He has no direct descendants except Holly and, from what I understand, his brothers are dead. This would mean that, until today, Silas was set to inherit the estate."

"I don't understand." This was a lie; I understood every word my grandfather had just said. What I couldn't grasp was how Lord Rivers could be so cruel as to make his relatives believe that they had a chance of inheriting his fortune when it was always going to go to the first-born boy. "Why would you lie to them?"

Little Lord Dishonest showed no shame. "I had my reasons."

"Please share them." I was glad that my grandfather said this. I might not have been so demanding of a man I hardly knew.

Rivers looked from one to the other of us before turning to stare at the unlit hearth. Perhaps the reason he needed a salon of his own was because he preferred the cold. Our host was clearly a frosty type, and this was the first room I'd visited that wasn't heated.

"You learn a lot about a person when they think they can sponge money from you. It brings out the worst and, less commonly, the best in people. I wanted to know the true character of those who will be looking after the place when I'm gone, so I let them think what they wanted to think."

"That's a pity." Grandfather sounded disappointed. "I'd considered a more charitable explanation; I assumed you enjoyed your young relatives' company and didn't want them to forget about you. If you'd told them that Silas was set to inherit the house and the lion's share of the wealth, they might never have visited."

Lord Rivers didn't respond. Had he done so, he would have had to admit that he was a lonely old man in need of attention, and that the cousins' affection for him only extended to the bequests he would leave them.

"This rather changes things," I realised out loud. "If Silas was the presumptive heir, it explains why the killer decided he had to die before Luke or Nathan, who had seemed the likely favourites to inherit. Perhaps he is willing to wait for you to pass away, Lord Rivers. I assume you have already made a will."

"Of course I have!" He'd become tetchy as the story we'd pieced together tarnished his image. "I'm not a fool. If I died intestate and left this place to the courts to distribute, it might well have taken a decade and ended up in the wrong hands. My only interest was to ensure that St Audries Park would be well looked after."

"You could have bequeathed it to your closest relative – your very own granddaughter." I stressed this point, as I believed it got to the heart of his selfishness.

"Don't worry about her," Rivers responded, whereas my grandfather had a more pertinent point to make.

"He couldn't leave her the estate itself, Christopher. One of his ancestors made sure that, in order to continue the Rivers name, only men could inherit. However, there's nothing to stop him dividing the estate from his fortune."

"And let the old place wither and die without the funds to care for it?" He raised the less unhealthy of his two legs and brought it down noisily on the floor with a wince. "I wouldn't do that. I may not like the fact that Silas and now Nathan will inherit, but I respect what my forebears did to protect their legacy. Many good British families like ours have lost their ancestral homes because they couldn't afford the upkeep. I will not let that happen."

It was at this point that my grandfather's temper began to show. "You can phrase it however you like, Rivers, but the fact is that you played with your younger relatives' expectations because it gave you a sense of excitement. You told us that your uncle did the very same thing to you and your brothers when he was alive. You were the oldest and so you inherited everything. Has it not occurred to you to remove the entailment by legal means?"

"I didn't let you into my house to hear your moralising," Rivers snapped. "Ask the questions you need in order to catch the killer and nothing more."

"Very well. Who knew about the will?" he asked, perhaps realising that criticising the man would not help us find the killer.

Lord Rivers's mouth gave an involuntary twitch. "No one but me and my solicitor. All my most important papers are kept in a safe in the office downstairs. No one in the family has access to them."

"And what about your health? At lunch you said that you have plenty of living still in you, but if the killer knew otherwise, it might have changed things."

He didn't look at us directly but fiddled with one golden cufflink. "Ah, you have lived up to your name and discovered my secret. The doctor says I'm dying. I haven't got long to go, but I don't see that it changes anything."

I thought it changed a lot, though I didn't need a doctor to tell me that the old fellow was on his last legs; his legs told me everything I needed to know.

Grandfather crossed off the questions on the list in his head one by one. "And the process you went through to choose the theoretical heir. We hear that, at one point, Nathan was the likely winner. What went wrong?"

"He's stubborn and pig-headed," the viscount replied, and I didn't have to think long to imagine from where such qualities had come. "We argued and he wouldn't accept that I was right."

"What was the cause of your disagreement?"

Lord Rivers literally had to grit his teeth to answer the question. "He thought he was smart enough to choose a wife for himself, and I disagreed. After that, he turned into the charmless charmer that you've seen today. He knows he can't make up for what happened, and so he lays it on too thick. It's desperate if you ask me." He spoke with such disdain that it was hard to imagine he had ever liked the man.

"Are you saying that he found the woman he wanted to marry, and you counselled him against it?"

"I'm saying that he wanted to bring the ragamuffin here to the house, and I said no."

Grandfather could well have criticised the man's arrogance, but he restrained himself once more. Instead, he leaned forward as though he had reached the key point he wanted to address.

"When the first attempts on your life occurred, did you do anything to protect yourself?"

Rivers took a deep breath before answering. "Someone tried to squash me, poison me and send me over a cliff. There wasn't a great deal I could do if the swine wanted me dead. I took certain precautions. For a while I had my butler sleep in a bed in my room. That sort of thing."

"And there were no more accidents or attacks between then and now?" I asked to make sure.

"I haven't had so much as a grazed knee since the summer."

Lord Edgington's voice would sometimes drop when he got to the most significant questions, as if he wanted to make sure that our witness was paying attention. "Bearing in mind how likely it seemed that one of your young relatives had tried to kill you, why did you invite them all back for Christmas?"

"I thought I might tell them how sick I've become in the hope that the killer would leave me alone. I thought we could spend one last Christmas together. I was going to do it at lunch, but Silas was killed before I could."

"And when did the various members of the family arrive?" With each question he asked, Grandfather spoke a little more urgently.

"Silas never left. Holly got here at the beginning of the week." We

140

knew this much already. "Nathan comes and goes to London whenever it pleases him, but he arrived on Wednesday if my memory serves me correctly, and Luke and his sister came last night."

"Thank you, Lord Rivers." The old sleuth looked rather pleased with himself. "I believe this information may yet prove extremely useful."

CHAPTER NINETEEN

"What did you realise?" I asked my grandfather as we followed the labyrinthine path we'd taken through the house. "You only grin like that when you've experienced some sort of minor revelation."

"I'm not grinning, Christopher," he said whilst grinning. "I'm merely content that things are progressing as they should be."

"Would you like to give me a hint?"

His grin became a... what's bigger than a grin? "Very well. I thought it was fascinating that despite all his raging and talk of the Rivers family name, our host has a surprisingly tender side to him."

"That's what you took from our interview? That he's secretly soft hearted?"

"Yes, I did. Whatever else he might have done, he truly believed in Nathan at one time, and he feels the same about Luke now. Add that to the fact that he put his life in danger in order to enjoy one last family Christmas, and I would say he has the soul of a true sentimentalist."

"That is one way of looking at it, I suppose. And what about the entailment? You said that there were legal remedies to remove it. If he's such a good sort, why hasn't he done something to that end?"

He stopped for a moment to consider the question. "It is a notoriously difficult process, but it can be done. To be perfectly honest, I imagine that he thinks it his duty to respect his ancestors' wishes. He is a traditional beast, even if he isn't quite as fierce as he'd like everyone to believe."

I couldn't see the logic in this, as Rivers's ancestors were the ones who caused all the problems in the first place. Instead of puzzling over such conundrums, I cut to the heart of the matter. "Do you know now who killed Silas?"

"No, I do not. But as I told Lord Rivers, I believe that the information we have garnered may prove to be essential."

I pressed him for more as we cut through the long corridor that led towards the front of the house. "Are you referring to his explanation of when everyone arrived here? I've been thinking about that and while, on the surface, it could suggest that whoever plotted against Lord Rivers only just got here, any smart killer would wait until there were plenty of suspects around."

"That's a very strong point, Christopher." He sounded gratified but gave away nothing more.

"I was also wondering whether the crimes have to be connected." He didn't ask me what I meant, but I explained anyway. "I mean, is there anything to say that whoever wanted to kill Lord Rivers is to blame for Silas's bloody demise?"

He frowned as he considered my point. "Just as I was coming to believe that I could see a connection, you suggest that there may not be one." He showed no sign of dismay at the idea. "It is always a good idea to keep an open mind."

Our voyage was almost over, and we could hear voices. We reached the entrance to the Great Hall, where Luke and Flossie were still busy decorating. They'd even roped in Philip Acland to help them.

"Mr Acland, don't you have a family of your own to see for Christmas?" Grandfather asked. "Your people are from around here, are they not?"

"Yes, Lord Edgington, but…" He had a long string of shiny metal paper between his teeth, and he was balancing on a stool as Luke tried to pin the other end of the decoration onto the wall in the opposite corner of the room. This made it rather difficult to reply, but he managed it, nonetheless. "Well, except for my brother, who will be with his wife's lot tomorrow, my family are a few miles from here. I won't make it with so much snow on the ground. And our parents died some time ago, so it's only a lot of old aunts, uncles and cousins I'd be visiting. I can't say I'm sorry to miss out on yet another argument about whether the General Strike was caused by a bunch of greedy shirkers who were too lazy to work, or it represented the working classes' fight for a decent existence."

"I see." Grandfather looked uncomfortable even imagining such a scenario. "If that's the case, I quite understand why you haven't donned a fur coat and beaten a path to Bicknoller."

Acland had secured the spangled silver tinsel and jumped down from the chair. I must say, he looked a little sickly all of a sudden. "How did you know that my people are from Bicknoller?"

Lord Edgington was the picture of innocence. "Are they? I just picked a name that we'd driven past. I had no idea that was where your family live. What a strange coincidence."

I could tell that he was lying, but for some reason, he appeared to want Acland to know this, too.

"Oh my goodness. Look at that." Grandfather pointed across the hall to where Flossie was standing beneath a sprig of mistletoe that she'd just fixed to one of the arches.

"Come along, Phil," Flossie shouted over. "If you've got time to talk, you've surely got time to kiss a pretty girl at Christmas."

"Not that you sound the slightest bit vain, my dear sister," Luke teased her.

"Yes, come along, Mr Acland." Grandfather took him by the arm. "It is a tradition, after all."

Philip Acland had turned a deeper shade of yellow, but he made his way across to Flossie, who closed her eyes rather sweetly. He approached the matter as if it was pure torture, and I was about to offer to take his place when he gave her a quick peck on the cheek.

"Ahh, how festive." I couldn't say for certain why my favourite old stirrer had engineered this strange encounter. Was it to see how Acland felt about the Rivers family? If the clerk had killed Silas as part of a vendetta against them, the experience of kissing Flossie might well have been an ordeal. Had Grandfather just driven the killer out into the open?

Entertained by the awkward scene, cheery Luke smoothed his moustache and told us of the plan for the evening.

"It's time to get ready for dinner. We'll be eating in here, and then everyone will head to the midnight service at St Etheldreda's. It starts at eleven."

"Midnight mass starts at eleven?" I had to check.

"That's right. It finishes at midnight around here. Perhaps the priest doesn't enjoy late nights. Old Father Goodman has rung the bell there for forty-nine Christmas Eves and this is his fiftieth. Obviously, if the blizzard is blowing strong, then we'll stay here, but I think it's eased off for the moment."

"Thank you, Luke." Grandfather bowed his head appreciatively. "I look forward to it."

Acland still seemed out of sorts as we left the room. I knew there was no sense asking the ever-furtive detective why he'd done what he'd done. I'm sure he would have told me that he was merely trying to raise some Christmas spirit, but the truth would come out before long.

As the sitting room was now empty of everyone but our sleepy dog, we went upstairs to change for dinner. Or at least, that's what I thought we were doing as we climbed the stairs of the tower. When we got to the second floor, however, instead of continuing to our suite of rooms, Grandfather turned to walk deeper into the house.

"There's something important we must investigate while everyone is busy," he told me before I could ask.

I could hear the low strains of a mournful piano playing somewhere, but I didn't think anything of it at the time. Grandfather was busy inspecting each open room we came to in search of... whatever it was he required.

"This must be it!" he exclaimed as we reached a door in a nondescript corridor in the gloomiest part of the house. "Yes, this is just where I would have imagined him living."

Inside the room was the hideout of some nefarious criminal. Well, it was dingy, smelt of gunpowder, and there were weapons and ammunition scattered around it. The first thing I noticed, on a worktable in the corner of the room, was a huge Vickers machine gun that must have been used in the war. It was standing in position, pointed directly at whoever entered. There was a belt of bullets already threaded through it, and it was quite frightening to look down its barrel.

"Is this Silas's room?" I asked, still standing in the doorway.

Grandfather nodded, and I decided that it was unlike any bedroom I'd previously seen. It didn't have a bed, for one thing. There was just a narrow mattress on the floor in the far corner. Aside from guns in every shape and size that had been secured to the wall, the only decoration was a medal which hung below a small, square mirror. It was all rather squalid, and not somewhere I'd want to spend the night.

"This isn't a place to live so much as a shrine to death." Grandfather eyed the medal of King George with its maroon and white ribbon. "It's terribly sad. Silas was obviously a capable soldier, but it seems that all he had in his life was war."

"His aunt, Mrs Stevans, told us that he'd been just as odd before he went off to fight – though his brother and great-uncle claimed the opposite."

I wasn't desperate to incriminate myself in a future murder investigation, so with my eyes alone, I inspected a few items on the desk. I noticed knuckle-dusters, bayonets and hunting knives, mixed in with a variety of other nasty devices. "I've been wondering again whether her relation to the boys will turn out to be significant."

"Oh, yes?"

"Yes, we know she isn't happy living here, but it seems to me that she has no other choice. Perhaps she hates Lord Rivers and decided to kill the old miser knowing that one of her nephews would inherit the estate and let her live her for free. If that was the case, it would no longer be relevant whether she liked them or not."

"That, Christopher," Grandfather began before pausing for a few seconds to terrify me, "is a perfectly reasonable hypothesis."

"Oh… thank you."

He came to stand next to me and scanned the mess of objects in front of us. "You're most welcome."

"Would you happen to have any opinion on whether it is the right one?"

He froze again for a moment. "It is a well-balanced suggestion." This told me nothing.

"Yes, but is it the right one?"

Before he could answer, something caught his attention, and he inhaled sharply. I followed his line of sight to a revolver that was set apart on the tabletop. Sadly, I knew nothing about weapons, even after all the killings we've investigated. Off the top of my head, I'd come across five men who'd been shot to death, but I knew no more about pistols and rifles than I did when I was an innocent schoolboy. What I had learnt in the meantime, however, was how to read my grandfather's wide range of facial expressions, and I could tell from his critical gaze that there was something not quite normal about the black gun with its trigger, handle and long poky bit.

"Do you know what we have in front of us, Christopher?"

I really didn't want to give him an obvious answer and get told off for not using my brain, but I was looking at a gun and so I said, "Is it a gun?"

"Yes, boy, of course it is. But don't you notice anything strange about it?"

I knew there was only one right answer to this question and that I did not know it. With this in mind, I thought I might as well say something ridiculous, as he was bound to complain no matter what I said.

"Is it a special gun that can do things that no other gun can?"

"In a way, yes." He was surely about to admit that he was pulling my leg, but oddly, that didn't happen. "It has an attachment which screws onto the barrel and dampens the sound of the bullet being fired."

I'd read about such things in sensational stories from America, of course. Gangsters were forever running about the place, stealthily murdering their enemies in near silence. If the truth be told, I'd assumed it was just a fantasy.

"British soldiers wouldn't have had such weapons, would they?"

Grandfather's eyes roamed on around the table. "I very much doubt it, but then we know from his brother that Silas fought at the Battle of Belleau Wood." He spoke as if this was hugely significant but, when I didn't respond, he explained. "It was one of the key battles in the Spring Offensive of 1918 in which American troops took part. The U.S. Marines burnished their reputations there immensely."

"So you're saying that Silas could have received this device from them?"

"Silencers, such as this one, wouldn't have been standard issue in the army. In fact, they are much rarer than sensational cinema films would have us believe – even in America. It's possible, of course, that enthusiasts in the Marine Corps could have brought their own equipment with them, though. A lot of what we see before us must have been obtained during the war."

"It explains why we didn't hear the shot in the rest of the house." A sad thought came over me then, and I wondered whether the gun we were discussing had belonged to a soldier who had died there. There was another silencer lying loose on the desk, and I had to conclude that the oldest Rivers boy had picked up souvenirs from his fallen comrades.

"That's right. And it shows that whoever set out to kill Silas came here first, knowing that he possessed a device that could be used even when there were people nearby."

This raised the question of who would have known what Silas had in his room, and one name in particular came to mind.

"But it wouldn't suppress the sound entirely, didn't you say?" I looked at the spare metal tube and considered for a moment how it might work. "Flossie still heard it from outside, for one thing. So it was quite a risk to take."

"That's right. And much like the cushion that the killer wrapped around the gun, it would have been more useful in disguising the sound than eliminating it. We all know what a gunshot sounds like, and this would have changed that just enough so as not to be noticeable."

A rather neat thought came to my mind then. "Lord Rivers was asleep upstairs, too. We know he's a deep sleeper, but he would presumably have woken up at the sound of gunfire." Grandfather looked really very pleased with me, and so I decided to keep thinking out loud. "It occurred to me that Silas might have spotted the killer on his way to murder Lord Rivers and tried to stop him. Let's say Silas recognised his own gun and intervened. The killer stabbed him through the chest, and when that didn't finish him off, he completed the job with a bullet to the head."

"Another excellent theory, my boy. You're full of ideas today."

"Jolly good. Now all we need to know is who actually killed him, and we can pop open the champagne and play some party games."

In a moment, he was at the door. "There is only one way to find out!"

Animated by his positivity, I went after him. "Oh yes, and what's that?"

He looked a little flummoxed. "Through painstaking and thorough investigation, obviously. How else would you hope to find a killer?"

CHAPTER TWENTY

This time, when we walked through the house, the piano we could hear was a little louder. Grandfather appeared unconcerned about the short time we had to prepare for dinner and took another long corridor to seek out the musician. As we reached a room not far from Lord Rivers's own, someone started singing in a low, mournful voice.

> **"I heard the bells on Christmas Day**
> **Their old, familiar carols play,**
> **And wild and sweet**
> **The words repeat**
> **Of peace on earth, good-will to men!"**

I'd never heard such a mournful interpretation of that hymn, and when we looked into the music room to see the pianist, it did not surprise me to find that Nathan was the performer. He cut a miserable figure but, to give him credit, he had a pleasant voice and knew his way around the keyboard.

He came to a sudden stop when he saw us, and Grandfather was the first to speak. "That was beautiful. Did you know that the poem was written in response to the horrors of the American Civil War?"

He turned back to the piano with glum resignation. "Yes, I did."

"Oh." Grandfather wasn't used to people knowing as much as him on any given topic, which was inevitable considering how much time he spent with me.

Nathan continued playing sad notes on the piano. What is it about certain sounds that instantly make you feel such despair?

"I am sorry for what happened to Silas," I decided to tell him, as my companion had fallen quiet. "Obviously we'd only just met him, but I know how sad I'd be if anything happened to my brother... even if he is terribly irritating a lot of the time."

Nathan laughed, but even this involuntary gesture was filled with sorrow. "Thank you, Chrissy. I appreciate your sympathy, and I do miss my brother, despite his faults. But there is far more in my life to concern me than poor Silas's violent death."

I looked at my grandfather, who had taken a seat on a chair in the corner of the pale blue room. I had hoped he might know what to say, but he evidently wished me to conduct the discussion alone.

"It's hard being in any kind of family," I tried. "Especially one ruled by a despot like Peregrine Rivers."

This provoked another laugh. "Yes, he is rather a tyrant, isn't he?" His brief smile was extinguished, and he even stopped playing. "You know, I honestly believe that old Perry means well. I just don't happen to agree with how he goes about things. He treats some of us like devils and the rest like saints. He spoils his favourites – or rather, Luke and Holly – then treats Flossie, Silas and me as though we're baseborn traitors. I can't take it anymore. My nerves have suffered for years, and I think it's time I gave up on my place here for good."

Grandfather looked as though he wished to speak, but he changed his mind, and it made me wonder whether I should reveal who the heir to St Audries now was.

"I have more burdens than any of the others," Nathan moaned when we didn't say anything. "I have a house in London with…" He was more hesitant than normal and had trouble finishing his thoughts. "I've never been a confident person, despite the way I present myself. And when I'm here, it's even worse; I spend the whole time doubting myself. I lie and making up stories just to have something to say." His hands dropped to his lap, and I really did feel sorry for him.

"That must be difficult for you." I searched my mind for some piece of wisdom that could make things better. "But I think it's always a good idea to be true to yourself. I'm never the most confident person, either, but there's no sense in pretending to be someone that I'm not. Lies and exaggerations don't help because I always know the truth, even if others don't."

He finally swivelled around on his piano stool and looked straight at me. "Perhaps if I'd had someone like you for a brother, Chrissy, I wouldn't be in the mess that I am now."

"Everyone is getting changed for dinner in the Great Hall," my grandfather said, and the vulnerability Nathan had shown instantly disguised itself.

"Oh, of course, it's Christmas Eve. It's the one night of the year when we all act a little nicer, we smile a little easier, we cheer a little more… except, of course, it's all fake." That same swagger and swank was back in his voice. He was every bit the peacocking gammoner once more.

"You don't like Christmas?" I asked him in as soft a voice as I could manage.

"Don't you start! You say you hate Saint Valentine's or May Day, and nobody cares, but you say you hate Christmas, and people treat you like you're a leper."

"But your family—"

"They're not my family." He stood up and walked about the room to take in the various instruments resting on stands. "The only connection between us is that we've all stuck around in the hope of inheriting the old man's money. I did everything I could to get what I deserved. I even pretended to like him for a while, and it was all for nothing. You see, the one thing I couldn't do… The one thing I wouldn't do—" He broke off again and, to distract from the sentence he couldn't finish, he picked up a guitar.

"You wouldn't marry the woman he chose for you," Grandfather said out of the blue.

"Oh, so you know, do you?" He made a dismissive snort as he looked at the instrument in his hands.

I thought for a moment that he was going to produce the most beautiful melody, but when he thrashed the strings, a terrible racket filled the room. It was as though he wished to murder the guitar rather than play it.

He asked another question even as he strangled the cat. "And did he tell you that I'd already found someone on my own? Did he tell you that he didn't trust me to choose the woman I loved for myself?"

Grandfather sat up a little straighter. "He did not reveal any of the details, but he was evidently disappointed by what has passed between you." He took his time, and the room would most likely have fallen silent if Nathan hadn't been attacking that guitar. "I came to think that he was most disappointed in you, my boy."

"There's no need to remind me. All I ever hear is how I've wasted my potential."

"That's not what I mean. I believe that Lord Rivers once considered you the right person to take over this estate. When the pair of you fell out, he was hurt."

"The poor old creature. I must make it up to him." His voice was soaked with sarcasm, and there was a hint of fury in his eyes. "Well, have a lovely evening. I'll be in my room drinking my sorrows away. There's no time like Christmas for a bout of self-indulgent wallowing."

"You won't join us for dinner?" I asked. It was one thing for me to put myself in the shoes of a cruel and heartless killer, but I struggled to understand a man who had no love for my favourite time of year. I wonder if there is often a correlation between the two things.

"I will not." He put the guitar down with a resonant clang and wandered listlessly to the door. "In fact, I wish you goodnight, gentlemen. If I sleep through Christmas, feel free to wake me on Boxing Day. But please bring plenty of coffee."

CHAPTER TWENTY-ONE

I left that room with an unsettled feeling. I was no longer so concerned about my own role in our investigation, or whether I had the sense that my family promised I possessed. After this encounter, I had the definite feeling that the killer would strike again. Assuming that Nathan hadn't killed his brother, and it wasn't some form of personal vendetta against Silas, it would make no sense to leave the body count at one.

"Grandfather, I think you should ask Todd to keep an eye on Nathan tonight. I feel he may be in danger."

He looked troubled, and I was uncertain how he would view my proposal, but he finally agreed. "I was considering the very same thing. He and Lord Rivers are the next likely targets. I just wish he would tell us all he knows."

"I doubt he's the first person today who has held back secrets from us. All the witnesses have been very forthcoming when it comes to providing information on other members of the household, but they become noticeably reticent whenever we wish to know more about them."

"Yes. From the very beginning, I feel that they've been trying to shape our understanding of the case."

"You'll simply have to take a firmer line with them," a voice said, and we turned to see Lord Rivers approaching (ever so slowly) from the corridor that led to his bedroom. "Many of my relatives lost their parents at a young age. My brothers both bought it in the Transvaal Rebellion and their sons died during the war. I've done what I can to be strict with their offspring, but as soon as they went away to boarding schools or moved to the city, they lost their path."

"Thank you for your advice, Lord Rivers," I spoke in the same quiet, respectful voice that I'd previously reserved for my teachers at school. "We'll certainly try that."

"All in good time, boy. All in good time, but first you must dress for dinner." He had almost caught up with us by now. "And by the time you're ready, I should have just about made it down to the Great Hall."

He let out a wonderfully hearty laugh, and it was nice to see a jolly side to him. He was clearly in the mood for the celebration, even if his great-nephew wasn't.

We did as he suggested and returned to our rooms to dress. Grandfather's outfit for the evening was almost identical to the one he'd been wearing, except for a change of colour from grey to black. He wore an old-fashioned, knee-length jacket, as if he were off to a garden party at Buckingham Palace or planning to travel back to the 1850s. I had a rather more modern outfit to wear and opted for my favourite suit in a shade that was as black as badger's stripe. I'd brought my opera cloak with me, as well, but I felt that would have been overly flamboyant. In fact, I'd felt that every day since my grandfather had bought it for me. When does one get the chance to wear an opera cloak these days if one never goes to the opera?

However, when we arrived downstairs, I was far from the smartest there. I'd rarely seen such a sharply decked-out cove as Luke Rivers. His collars and cuffs looked as though they had been mathematically engineered to have the most perfect lines possible. His black suit had a certain gloss to it, too, and seemed to shimmer in the light of the fifty or so candles that the staff had lit around the room.

His sister was just as elegantly attired, and her long, curly hair had been unleashed about her shoulders. With her beige lace and black silk dress finishing – and I'm not exaggerating when I say this –two whole inches above her ankles, she was quite mesmerising.

"Look at you both." Grandfather held his arms out as we walked through the archway into the hall. "It's not often one sees such a sight. That is a charming dress, Miss Rivers."

Before she could answer, the two of them were blown out of the water like a rowing boat coming up before an oil-powered battlecruiser. They were eclipsed like a new moon before the sun. What I'm trying to say is that, just then, Holly appeared on the minstrel's gallery.

She wore a deep green dress that was once more similar to the coat she had worn in Oxford Station. Just like then, I was quite breathless when I looked at her. It wasn't merely the dress, of course. It was the way she peered down at us, her hands on the wooden balustrade, and her eyes the colour of fire. Well, the blue bit of fire, obviously. They burned from across the room, and my heart almost went on strike.

"Come along, child," her grandfather called up to her in the stern tone he used to address everyone in the family, with the exception of his dear Luke. "We're waiting."

I suddenly remembered Nathan referring to Holly as spoilt and one of Lord Rivers's favourites. If anyone was spoilt it was him, and I might have told him just that if I hadn't been so distracted by his inexplicable dislike for Christmas.

Holly smiled, and I wished that I could have flown to her so that I could be the first to tell her how beautiful she looked. Being hampered by gravity, I stood right where I was and waited for her to descend. She ran from the balcony, and it was nice to see a hint of the joyful person that I had no doubt she was inside.

In the meantime, my family appeared, and Todd went around the room offering glasses filled with a yellowy cocktail with a foamy layer on top that was the very colour of fresh snow.

"I'm confident that you'll like this one, Master Christopher," he assured me, but I did not believe him.

I sniffed it and there was a distinctive scent that I had not expected. Being far braver than I was, my family went a step further and actually tasted it.

"You've outdone yourself, Todd," Grandfather told him. "That's the very thing for this evening."

"It tastes like…" my mother attempted, before Father had a go at describing it.

"Yes, what is that flavour? It tastes rather like…"

"It tastes like Christmas," I told them. There was nutmeg, egg and sugar in whatever we were drinking, and I thought it was just wonderful. "I believe you've finally found my drink, Todd. Bravo!"

"Thank you, sir. It's a Champagne Flip."

"And it's superb." I shook my head in wonder as others around the room made noises of appreciation. "You can hardly taste the champagne."

"You'll have to come back every Christmas," Luke suggested, and it was unclear whether he was talking to my family or the talented cocktailian who was serving our drinks.

"I'll second that," Flossie added. "And I'll have a second drink, too, as soon as you have a moment."

"Yes, miss." Todd had a truly charming way about him, and I

believe that Flossie swooned just a fraction as she put her empty glass back on his tray.

I was busy wishing that I could have such an effect on women when Holly appeared, and I went back to feeling like I was floating in a bubble of some description; I was both as light as air and trapped by her beauty, which was most unnerving.

"You look sublime, Holly." Sadly, I was not the one to deliver this compliment. That dry fish Philip Acland had emerged from his office to steal my thunder. To give him his due, he did look suave. His hair was swept back off his face with brilliantine, and his cream suit had been exchanged for a more fetching dark one.

To my surprise, Holly was quite unmoved by his words and turned away to look at the food. "We've always had a buffet dinner on Christmas Eve – even back when my parents were alive. It's nice to give the staff some time off to enjoy the festivities."

She put her arm through mine, and we went to inspect the culinary offerings. It was easy to tell which of the two cooks in the house had made what. Our own dear Henrietta was responsible for anything that was architecturally impressive or entirely unrecognisable.

"It all looks… interesting," Luke exclaimed.

"Todd, old thing." My father squinted as though this would help make sense of the dishes before us. "Do you happen to know what any of it is?"

Our factotum needed a moment to examine the fare himself. "There are sausage rolls and mutton puddings. Three-cheese skewers and ramekins of minced fowl a la bechamel. Oyster patties, and I think that must be curried endives, but I can certainly find out for you, sir."

My grandfather answered before my father could. "That won't be necessary. Take some time to celebrate with the others below stairs. We can serve the drinks ourselves, though I'm afraid I may have a job for you when we go to church at eleven."

"Very good, M'Lord," he replied, then retired with a bow – just as soon as he'd provided us with another round of sweet and creamy cocktails.

Mrs Stevans was the only person yet to arrive. If you happen to have spent any time around murder investigations – and especially those that take place in snow-bound manor houses at Christmas –

you'll know that as soon as anyone is absent for any length of time, your mind is overrun with dark thoughts.

I doubt I was the only one who had noticed the lady's absence, as the room suddenly fell quiet, and a few of my companions glanced about. It wasn't so long ago that Victoria Stevans – Lord Rivers's rumoured mistress and the dead man's aunt – had burst into tears in an interview. She'd revealed any number of potentially significant details on the other suspects in her nephew's murder. And now she hadn't appeared for the evening meal and was surely—

Oh no, ignore me! She turned up a few moments later.

With our party complete, we enjoyed a fine informal meal, and the drinks were certainly appreciated, but there was a feeling of suspicion in the air. The joviality we had enjoyed now seemed inappropriate. I believe that we were all aware that the killer was amongst us – or upstairs in his bedroom, drinking the night away. Any polite conversation that my family introduced could not distract from our hosts' shifting glances and twitching muscles. We were alive to the fact that this was no normal Christmas Eve feast.

Holly had lost the joie de vivre she'd briefly shown and, perhaps to escape the awkward atmosphere in the hall, she took a plate of food up to her absent cousin. I was relieved when she returned a few minutes later and we discovered that, like Mrs Stevans, Nathan was still alive.

What with all the excitement of the decorations, drinks and dinner, I wondered whether Grandfather would give me a night off from the investigation, but he was definitely still working. The way he looked at our fellow diners told me that he was recording every unusual expression on their faces – every narrowed eye and curled lip. It did nothing to make the evening a more pleasant one.

"It must be time for church by now," Lord Rivers announced when it seemed that we'd been convened there for several days.

"It's still only half-past nine," Acland revealed in a sorry tone, and we all sighed in disappointment.

Mother opened her mouth to fill the silence, but nothing came out. I looked at my father in the hope he would think of some boring topic of conversation to make things less awkward, but he could only stare back, uncertain how to respond.

"Father," I tried, "weren't you telling me something interesting this week about your job in the city?"

"Me?" He pointed at himself to avoid any confusion. "Interesting? I very much doubt it."

"What about you, Granny?" I was becoming desperate. "You must have some story about Christmas when you were a child with which to entertain us all."

My grandmother's face turned sour... well, sourer. "Not at all. My parents did not approve of such hedonism. The word *Christmas* was rarely mentioned in our house."

"But you must have gone to church." I was becoming really desperate.

"That's right. We went to church, then went home to bed and, when we woke up the next morning, if we'd been well behaved all year, do you know what my brothers and sisters and I would find when we ran downstairs?"

"No?"

"Breakfast." She huffed out through her nostrils like a particularly unimpressed dragon. "And if our parents deemed us mischievous in any way, we'd go without our cold porridge and have to wait until lunch."

I was no longer so surprised that the best Christmas in her family was the one when her father came home from Japan with no legs and proceeded to fight a duel with her uncle.

"What a festive image that stirs in the mind." Grandfather's comment was so soft that I believe it was meant for me alone.

"My experience wasn't so different from yours, Loelia," Lord Rivers replied and, as they were both of a cantankerous nature, it did not surprise me that they were already on first-name terms. "People make such a fuss of giving presents and sending cards and all that diddle-daddle. As a child, I was grateful if I received an orange on Christmas Day."

So this made everyone a lot more miserable, and there was still an hour before we could even think about heading to church. But somehow – SOMEHOW! – after another twelve to forty-seven years, the time finally arrived to leave for the midnight service.

CHAPTER TWENTY-TWO

We wrapped up in our warmest clothes once more and the St Audries Park butler provided us with lanterns on long hooked sticks to light the way. Carrying one made me feel like a shepherd, so at least that was *in keeping* with the date. Ha! Innkeeping!

"Todd," Grandfather whispered to his right-hand man as we were preparing to leave, "you'll have to make certain that Nathan is safe in his room. If I were you, I'd take a book up there and sit outside his door. If he's in a sociable mood, he might even enjoy your company. But don't let him out of your sight… except if he needs to use the facilities, of course."

"Very good, M'Lord. I had much the same idea." Todd peered around to make sure that no one was paying attention before showing us a book and a pack of cards. "I believe it's one of your favourites, Master Christopher."

I looked at the name on the spine and it was almost enough to make me offer to stay home and guard Nathan myself. "'A Christmas Carol'! That's a fine choice indeed."

The two men nodded to one another in their usual confidential manner, and then it was time to go. Delilah was sitting beside the door and would not move when Ripon tried to close it.

"Of course you can't come with us," Grandfather told his faithful hound. "As a general rule, dogs aren't allowed in churches."

Delilah looked back pleadingly.

"I know you've been to one before, but that doesn't mean you can come now."

Delilah emitted a melancholy moan, but Grandfather remained unmoved.

"If you insist on being unreasonable, I've nothing more to say to you."

The poor creature looked so crestfallen that I went to give her a pat and whisper something in her ear.

My grandfather looked at me disapprovingly. "You spoil that dog, you really do. She used to be a far more disciplined creature. Presumably you just told her what you bought her for Christmas?"

His psychic abilities knew no bounds, but I tried to convince him otherwise. "A Christmas present for a dog? Who's ever heard of such a thing?"

"Well, last year when we got home to Cranley Hall, you gave her a marrow-filled bone. The year before that, I believe it was a pound of pork belly. And the year before that, you were not invited to my house at Christmas and my dog was not so spoilt." He smiled, as if thinking back on happy times.

"Gosh, I'm more generous than I realised," I replied with a smirk. "Perhaps I've been spoiling you, too; I've given you presents every year since I was six years old. I'll remember not to get you anything next Christmas."

He did not appear to approve of the idea but said nothing more.

Despite my feeling of ill ease, the walk to the charming church I'd previously spotted was a pleasant one. Luke took his great-uncle on the back of a horse from the stables, so at least it would not be a long journey. If we'd had to match the viscount's pace through the snow, we'd have arrived at the service just in time to go home again. As predicted, the wind had died down by then and, though a few pretty flakes fell around us, the weather had improved greatly since the afternoon.

It was really quite fun to walk through the high drifts of snow. The only way to make any progress was to take giant steps, and I did enjoy seeing my grandfather's ridiculous gait.

"Do not laugh at me, Christopher," he warned as I jumped behind him from footprint to footprint. "This is by far the easiest method to move through thick snow." He looked as though he was intentionally performing a very silly walk.

Philip Acland took Victoria Stevans's arm to help her to church, and the two of them fell back a little way. My father escorted Flossie, and it only seemed right that I should offer my arm to dear Holly. I was approximately a second too late, and she slipped in the snow as I arrived.

"Thank you, Chrissy. You saved me."

I held onto her coat to keep her steady, and she smiled up at me. I doubt that I would have needed the lantern with those bright blue eyes there to guide us.

"Really, it was nothing," I assured her, but she wouldn't accept such modesty.

"You're too kind. You genuinely are. I can never thank you for everything you've done – for driving all that way here in the first place and bringing your grandfather. I know we lost Silas this morning, but I'm sure it would have been a lot worse if you hadn't come."

"Really, it was nothing," I repeated, as I was holding her hand in mine now and it had put me in a state of shock. There were two pairs of gloves separating us, so it was hardly the most intimate gesture, but at least she hadn't let go.

She glanced behind us to see who was nearby. "You must find the killer, Chrissy. You really must. My family seem oddly indifferent to what happens, but I can think of nothing else. Do you have any idea who it might be?"

I hesitated. I didn't want to disappoint her but was uncertain how to answer the question. "Grandfather seems confident that we'll get to the bottom of the matter very soon. I know what the former bloodhound of Scotland Yard is like when he's on a scent. His tail starts wagging – metaphorically, of course – and it happened earlier when we were talking to Lord Rivers."

"That is such a relief." Her tone did not quite convey this meaning, and it was her turn to repeat herself. "I can think of nothing else."

"And so," I began cautiously, "is there anything that has occurred to you that could help us find the culprit? You said when we met on the train that any of your cousins could be behind the attacks on your grandfather, and yet I find Flossie and Luke to be thoroughly nice people."

"I suppose they might be," she said in a listless voice, before modifying her answer. "I mean to say, they've always treated me kindly, but I don't believe they're as innocent as they pretend. Flossie takes no interest in anything but her brother and those twittering birds in the orangery. She has never spoken of marriage or a profession. She treats her brother as though he is a saint who needs daily veneration. And as for Luke himself…" She didn't finish that sentence, but I thought I knew what she wished to imply.

"You're worried he's simply too good to be true?"

Her face fell a little more and her brow creased. "I must sound terribly unkind."

"Then what about the other members of the household? Mrs Stevans could be involved, or perhaps Philip Acland."

She moved from concerned to shocked. "But Philip has no reason to kill my grandfather. There's nothing he could gain from it. Unless you know something about him that I don't."

Her statements arrived in swift succession, and I struggled to reply. "Oh... no, I wouldn't say that. I just find him a little creepy, don't you agree?" I waited for a response and, when it didn't arrive, I explained myself. "He's always lingering in the background, and, when we arrived, he seemed intent on moulding our impressions of the other people in St Audries Park. He took particular interest in Mrs Stevans."

"Really? I don't see why." She squeezed my arm a little tighter as we navigated a tricky stretch of the path off the estate. The snow was up to our knees, but I thought nothing of it as I waited for her to continue. "Victoria has a kind heart. Admittedly, she doesn't seem to enjoy her life with my grandfather and, if the truth be told, she can't have much choice in any of it. But I very much doubt she would have killed her own nephew. Also, if she were to succeed in murdering the man who gives her a home and stipend, she would be in an even worse position than she is now."

"So there's all the more reason to think that Philip was distracting us from other possibilities."

She gave a violent shake of her head. "No, Chrissy. I refuse to believe he had anything to do with the terrible events that have taken place today. The killer must be one of my close cousins."

If true, this only left us with three suspects, and I couldn't choose between them. No doubt my grandfather had already solved the case – and perhaps one or two more that we hadn't started investigating yet – but I had reached another brick wall. Not that I told Holly that, of course. No, I pretended to be brave and confident for her sake.

"In which case, we'll find the guilty party before it's time to unwrap our presents tomorrow. You can always rely on my grandfather. I've yet to find a mystery that could boggle him for long."

The church came into view up ahead, and she patted my hand affectionately. "I'm sure you're an immense help. That's what all the newspapers say, isn't it?"

For fear of sounding vain, I did not answer. I'm sure that my cheeks were already scarlet from the cold, or I would have blushed uncontrollably.

The light spilling from the grand old church drew us forward. As we got closer, I saw families streaming towards us from the village that was visible a few hundred yards along the lane. I was glad we weren't going any further as I had no feeling left in my feet, and yet it was worth it just to see the excited looks on the children's faces. They were all aglow like the church.

Embellished with highlights of white, it was as pretty as a picture. In fact, it was as pretty as a picture book. St Etheldreda's was surrounded by snow-covered trees that covered the hill behind it. The stained-glass windows were all illuminated in the tower upon which a rather imperial spire scraped the heavens. It reminded me of a fairy-tale castle and was the very place to visit on that most magical of nights.

Grandfather waited at the front door for the rest of our party to arrive, and then we all sat down together on the left of the nave. It wasn't so grand a building as some I'd visited, but with the chatter and hum of expectant parishioners, it was as attractive as any famous cathedral.

I learnt that there has been a midnight celebration every Christmas Eve since the foundation of St Etheldreda's, and its steward, Father Goodman, turned out to be a merry chap. With his balding pate and bulging tummy, he rather reminded me of Friar Tuck. He delivered a jolly service with plenty of warm messages, good wishes for the season and one of my favourite hymns. It was 'Good King Wenceslas', and we all sang our hearts out.

It went... well, I'm sure everyone knows the words and I don't need to repeat them here.

My point is that everything at the church was perfect. I could feel the joy of the congregation almost as though it were a palpable force. I could not have asked for a more delightful midnight mass, and yet I felt a touch uneasy. As I listened to the priest's sermon and all that talk of faith, hope and charity, it jarred so strongly with the events of the day, and my encounters with some truly evil people over the last few years, that I struggled to resolve the discrepancy.

When the service ended and the bells rang out for midnight, the feeling had only grown. I couldn't be sure if it was the contrast between Silas's violent death and that cheerful scene in the church, but a knot had formed inside me, and I wanted to hurry back to St Audries and hide in my bedroom until it had passed. At the door to the church, the priest wished us all a Happy Christmas, and Mother clearly wanted to continue the conversation there with our new friends, but I set off through the snow.

"Christopher?" she called after me in alarm, but I ploughed on (if you'll excuse yet another pun).

It was even colder without Holly there to distract me, and the walk home felt twice as long. Luckily, Ripon was still awake to let me in when I arrived. My whole body felt as though it had been in the icehouse overnight, and I was more than relieved when he opened the door. The feeling didn't last long. I could already see on his face that something terrible had happened and, within a moment or two, I heard the screams.

The screams of Christmas Eve is not a phrase that trips off the tongue, but that is what I most remember from that night.

"We don't know what to do for him, sir." The butler was as pale as a ghost. "We just don't understand it."

I knew where to go without his saying anything, and it wasn't simply because the wails of agony coming from the first floor were so loud. Those hollow, clanging bells at the church had left me with the sense that, if anyone more were to die, it would happen soon. And there was only one obvious victim. I took the stairs three in one bound and followed the network of corridors to a room not far from Lord Rivers's suite.

Nathan's arm hung over the side of the bed like in the painting of 'The Death of Chatterton'. The sheets had become tangled around his legs to resemble the chains of a prisoner. His face was pale and sweating, his pupils were dilated and, for a moment, I thought he was already dead.

CHAPTER TWENTY-THREE

"Master Christopher!" As Todd stood over the suffering figure, he had never looked so distressed or dispirited. "I don't know what to do for him. The butler called the doctor in the village, but he didn't answer the phone until he was back from church. We don't know how long he'll take to get here, and I fear he may be too late."

I didn't know any better than my companion, and I must say that I was just as alarmed to see Todd so very scared as I was by the sight of the sick man.

"It will be all right," I said without evidence. "Grandfather won't be far behind me. I'm sure he'll know what to do if the doctor doesn't get here first."

This did little to calm my dear friend. He looked quite wild as he searched for a solution, or at least an explanation for what had happened. "He was fine just a short time ago. We were playing cards together, and he was in good spirits. I don't understand what happened to him."

If I had been discouraged on my way back to the manor, I now felt quite helpless. Nathan's infrequent movements were lethargic, then unnaturally fast as he fought with the covers and wiped away the cold drops on his forehead. All I could do was take his hand and whisper lies to him.

"There is a solution to whatever is wrong," I said. "You are suffering horribly, but help is on its way."

In response, he shrieked then mumbled, depending on which stage of pain he was enduring.

"Yellow," he said over and over when he found the strength to speak more clearly. "Yellow. Hazy yellow. And my heart." He clutched it then, perhaps to make sure I understood. "My heart is too fast."

My only comfort was that I'd been through this before. "I promise that, as soon as my grandfather arrives, he'll be able to help you. I saw this very thing six months ago." I had to pause then, as I couldn't recall whether my brother's wedding had been in June or July. "Or possibly it was five months—"

"I'm not sure that's the relevant detail, sir," Todd replied with a touch of anger in his voice.

I couldn't blame him in the slightest. "No, of course not. What I wanted to say is that my grandfather saved a man's life. He's still walking the earth as a result, and Lord Edgington will be here at any moment."

Even as I was speaking, I heard the front door slam shut and the sound of someone storming up the stairs. Nathan released an anguished scream to attract the help he needed and, in less than a minute, grandfather was there with us.

"Thank goodness you came, M'Lord," Todd reacted. "I assumed at first it was a heart attack, but I'm no longer sure."

Grandfather was at the stricken man's bedside in a moment. "Symptoms?" The situation was so grave that he didn't even take the time to form full sentences.

"He phases in and out of responsiveness and has spoken of his vision being blurred. He says his heart is beating too fast, and he's been terribly sick. I've tried to keep him comfortable, but this isn't my area of knowledge, sir. I'm so sorry I haven't done more."

Grandfather didn't respond at first. He was taking the man's pulse, and I could tell from his reaction that things weren't right with Nathan. Well, that's a silly thing to say; obviously things weren't right. He was in the middle of a full-body seizure and was shouting the house down. But my grandfather's expression told me that he was just as powerless as I was to halt the man's pain.

"The doctor has been called?"

"Yes, M'Lord. Do you think he'll have the right medicine?"

Grandfather froze then, and I was glad that Nathan had screwed his eyes closed as, in that moment, there was no doubt left. The patient before us would die that night. I didn't know how long it would take, but it was evident that no other outcome was possible.

"There are many things that doctors can try to correct the dysrhythmia of the heart," Grandfather explained. "Tell me what happened before he fell ill."

Todd's eyes scanned the elegant room once more and landed on a table on the far side of the bed with two chairs set beside it and two glasses on top. "We were playing cards together. He was actually very good company, and we enjoyed a drink together."

"You drank from the same bottle?" Grandfather couldn't hide his fear as he asked this.

"That's right, M'Lord, but I feel absolutely fine. I don't believe whatever did this to him was in there."

Grandfather retreated from the bed to examine the paraphernalia of the two men's evening. He inspected Nathan's dinner tray before asking another question. "Did you see him consume anything else while you were in here?"

Our factotum had to think for a moment, but then pointed to a small cabinet over a basin that was fixed to the wall in the corner of the room. "He took a bottle from there. He told me he struggles with his nerves and takes a tincture to help calm him."

Grandfather walked to inspect the medicine. He still wore gloves from our trip to the church but held the small bottle he found between the tips of his fingers.

"Lord Edgington, please tell me what I can do to help," Todd begged. "Cook has given Mr Rivers a herbal infusion and brought up warm water for his brow, but nothing seems to make any difference."

"For the moment, you must find the main store of medicine in the house and bring whatever analgesics they have there."

This sounded like a positive step to take, though I worried it would only control the man's pain and not cure him. Even as Todd left, Nathan screamed out again, clutching the sheets with his bent and twisted fingers as he did so.

"You'll catch him, won't you, my lord?" the dying man asked.

"There's no need to worry about that, Nathan. Just concentrate on preserving your energy."

His eyes now open, he looked oddly peaceful. "I'm not worried anymore. I see the angels coming for me. They've filled me with great peace." This was not the sort of Christmas visitation I would wish to experience, but anything that gave him courage was a good thing. "All I want to know is that justice will be done."

Grandfather stared at me across the bed. It was a night of reversals and, when he couldn't summon a response, the task fell to me.

"Of course we will, Nathan. We'll catch the man who killed your brother." I didn't feel this was enough and so I kept talking in the hope that my voice could soothe him a little before Todd returned. "I'm sorry for ever suspecting you. I'm sorry for not seeing that you were innocent, but the killer will get his just deserts. You have my word."

It seemed he had reached a spell of lucidity as he went from total distraction to clear focus. "You needn't feel any guilt. I am to blame for much else in life." His senses became muddied then, and he stamped his feet against the mattress as if fighting off the pain. "It's my family I pity. Tell them I'm sorry."

It didn't occur to me at this moment what a reversal this was of his previous position. I took water from a jug on his nightstand and poured a glass for him, but he didn't have the strength to hold it and, even when I pressed it to his lips, he struggled to drink.

His room was far tidier than his brother's and more comfortably appointed than his great-uncle's. It made me think that he'd been given it when he was younger and Lord Rivers still favoured him among the cousins. There were rich and elaborate tapestries hanging from the wall, and the bed in which the tragic creature was lying had a high wooden frame with damask drapes at each corner.

Grandfather eventually took my place at Nathan's side and found the words he should have summoned a few minutes earlier. "We'll find your killer," he murmured in a dejected voice. "Though I can promise nothing else, that is one thing I will achieve."

When Todd returned with a tray of pain relievers, Nathan gave out his last breath. There were no dramatic final words, no great agonising wails to cut the air. He was alive one moment and dead the next, and the stillness and silence that followed were the hardest thing I experienced that year. Nothing had prepared me for the sight of a young man dying right before me.

I did not stay there to watch his relatives pay their respects to the second dead brother of the weekend. One of them had killed him, and I couldn't bear to live through that scene knowing that the culprit was feigning his sorrow and sympathy. I should have stayed to examine their reactions, though I thought it unlikely that anyone willing to despatch two souls so violently would show much guilt.

I got changed into my pyjamas and lay in bed. My head had no room for thoughts of the coming day. For the first time in my life, I was disconsolate on my favourite night of the year.

So this is Christmas? I thought to myself and would have wallowed in pity for a little longer had my grandfather not knocked on my door.

"Was it digitalis?" I asked, having spent some time thinking about poisons instead of Christmas presents since I'd left the dead man's room.

"I believe so." He hung in the doorway as though uncertain what to do. "How did you realise?"

I let out a single, sad huff. "When you heard of the symptoms, your expression told me that there would be no cure."

"I still can't say for certain what was given to him, but it makes sense considering that he thought he saw angels. I put that down to the blurred vision associated with such toxication."

"He said it was all yellow."

"That fits too, and as you evidently remember, the killer already tried using foxglove seeds to poison Lord Rivers in the summer. He was more sophisticated this time. He appears to have dissolved the poison in the tincture that Nathan was taking for his nerves. Either that or the bottles were swapped."

"And what happens now? Are any of us safe here?"

He held his open hand to the side of his face and rubbed the white bristles. "I cannot say for certain, but I've made sure that the butler sleeps in the same room as Lord Rivers tonight, and Todd will bunk with Luke, just in case."

"What if we're wrong about everything? What if Silas and Nathan weren't murdered for the inheritance but some terrible grudge? It's surely possible that this was a personal grievance given that the two victims were brothers."

He came to sit down in an armchair beside my bed. "You're right, Christopher. It's too soon to tell, but if that is the case and the inheritance is not the killer's motivation, it is unlikely that the majority of people here are in any danger."

For some reason, I did not find this reassuring. Perhaps he realised this very thing as, instead of saying goodnight and going off to his room, he pretended that his eyelids were heavy, and his head started nodding. He was obviously faking, as I saw him peek out at me from time to time. I suppose he knew that I knew he was pretending, but this made the gesture all the nicer. I would not be sleeping alone that night and neither would he, which was reassuring on two counts. Delilah was curled up against the door, too, and my parents would be together in their room. As for Granny, I was fairly sure that, wherever she was, the killer was no match for her.

"Good night, Grandfather," I whispered when he really had fallen asleep, and his gently rhythmic breathing floated over to me. "Happy Christmas."

CHAPTER TWENTY-FOUR

He was still asleep when I woke up early the next morning. I didn't have the heart to wake him, and so I crept from my room as a strange mix of emotions passed through me. On the one hand, it reminded me of Christmas Day mornings with my brother when we were little. I would have invariably gone into his room at some point in the night because I was too excited about the coming celebrations and couldn't sleep on my own. When I woke up (approximately seventeen minutes later) I would have to wait several hours for Albert to join me in sleeplessness before we could tiptoe downstairs together.

Getting from upstairs to the rear salon where our Christmas tree and presents were always located was more difficult than one might think. My mother had the ears of an owl and would swoop from her room to tell us to be patient if we went too early. But if we timed it just right and trod as silently as church mice, we could reach our target without anyone hearing. And what a prize that was! Even if we didn't dare open one, or even peek beneath the ribbon-tied paper, the joy of sitting in front of those prettily packaged gifts was almost as good. Albert liked to speculate about what each one might contain – based on size, shape and, if he was daring, a brief survey of weight. I didn't need to anticipate what delights we would receive. I was simply over the moon that Christmas had come.

So, yes, I was reminded of that wondrous scene as I escaped from the tower at St Audries Park, but I was also thinking about the possibility that someone else had been murdered in the night. In place of a pyramid of sparkling gifts, I imagined a dead body waiting for me in the sitting room, and so I gingerly poked my head around the door. To my immense relief, the makeshift Christmas tree was just as handsome as it had been the previous night, and the room was corpse-free… for the time being.

I was about to begin the search for some breakfast, in case Grandfather sent me off on some impossible mission that almost miraculously avoided all food, when I heard a light step behind me. I turned to see an angel descending the grand staircase. Holly was not dressed in green for the first time since I'd met her. She had a heavy coat on in festive red with a soft white collar. I thought in that moment that she was glamorous enough to be one of the actresses I'd seen at the cinema. But she was far more beautiful than Alma Cavendish or Norma Shearer.

As she saw me, a smile came to her lips, but it didn't stay there long.

"Good morning, Christopher," she spoke in a cold, determined tone. "I'm going skating on the lake as I do every Christmas. The killer won't stop me today."

She marched over to a cupboard beneath the stairs to pull out a pair of ice skates, which she hung around her neck. With her prize secured, she walked past me and out of the door. I would have liked to join her, but there was one problem I couldn't resolve.

"Here you are, Master Christopher," that genie of a man, Todd, was standing just behind me holding a small cardboard box. Ignoring the fact he'd scared me half to death by popping up like that, I accepted the proffered package.

"They're skates," I replied rather dimly. "And in my size, by the looks of it. But how did you…?" My question faded out in a cloud of bemusement.

He pulled on his perfectly pressed waistcoat as though I'd said something to challenge him. "I'm sorry, sir, but I wouldn't be a very good servant if I didn't think to bring a pair of ice skates for my master's grandson when there were freezing temperatures predicted, would I?"

"No…" I began despite myself. "No, I suppose not, but the very idea you could be anything less than excellent has never entered my mind."

"You're very kind, sir." He gave one of his roguish smiles and I knew that, on some level, he must have been pulling my leg. I just couldn't work out in what way… or where he'd got the skates… or how he'd known to be standing there at that particular moment just when I needed them. "May I be the first to wish you a Merry Christmas?"

"Not until I do the same, Todd. A Very Merry Christmas, old friend! I hope my grandfather makes your time away from home a worthwhile endeavour."

"Lord Edgington is always generous, and, at Christmastime he positively spoils his employees. I'm only too happy to spend this time with you and your family."

"I'm glad to hear it." After a brief exchange of nods, I took the skates, and he returned to his work – or perhaps his imprisonment in

174

an Arabic oil lamp somewhere.

With the appropriate footwear in hand, I now had no excuse not to join Holly on the frozen lake. Well, that's not quite true. There was still one excuse. I hadn't a clue how to skate.

"Whoa… oooh! Ahhhh!" These were the first noises I made outside that morning.

"Chrissy, are you quite all right?" she asked as she glided across to check on me.

"Ummm… in a way." I was lying on the path that led to the lake. I think I'd made it seven steps from the house before I keeled over into the snow. "I didn't realise how difficult walking in these contraptions would be."

"Yes, that's surely the untold danger of skating. Perhaps you'll be more confident once you get on the ice."

"Oh, undoubtedly."

I considered crawling to her on all fours. My trousers were wet enough as it was, though, and so I got to my feet instead. With my arms extended at my sides, I just about managed to hobble across to her without falling over. This gave me all the confidence I needed to step on to the ice and fall over there instead.

Despite Holly's previously glum disposition, I'd managed to make her laugh. "I'm so sorry, Chrissy. Have you never skated before?"

"No, never," I lied, as this was at least the fifth time I'd made such a spectacle of myself.

She circled me in one impressive move and then came to help me to my feet. "Give me your hands and I'll show you how to remain steady."

I did just that and, to my amazement, I didn't pull her straight down on top of me or instantly break both ankles. She helped me to my feet, and I managed to stand still. I know this might not sound like a major achievement, but it felt like enormous progress to me.

"I'm going to go backwards, and you just have to hold on to me and follow."

I have no idea how she achieved it but, without moving a single muscle, she appeared to have the power of self-propulsion. Perhaps even more impressive, though, she effortlessly slid whilst attached to the big artless lump known as Christopher Prentiss.

"You're incredible," I told her as she increased her speed, and I felt the wind whipping my cheeks and the smooth surface supporting me.

"You're doing very well. Just keep your feet a little way apart and don't tip one way or the other. Try to balance your weight as much as possible on your knees and, when I let go of you, don't make any sudden movements."

"Yes, that sounds like a sensible— Let go of me? Why would you do that?"

Before I could complain further, she had released my hands, and I continued on the same path. I was tempted to close my eyes and prepare for impact with the ground, but to my unending amazement, I didn't fall over. After a few moments, she skated around me to thread her arm through mine.

"*How* did you do that?"

"I only corrected your stance a fraction. It's not difficult to learn if someone teaches you."

"Then you must be the best teacher on earth to achieve any such thing. I have the co-ordination of a pig on wheels."

"That can't be true." She sounded serious again, but then a smile broke out on her lips, and she looked shyly away towards the house. "You *had* the co-ordination of a pig on wheels, but not anymore."

"Now I have the co-ordination of a pig." I couldn't help mirroring her blithe expression, and I felt that unique tingling sensation when I remembered that her hand was on my arm. "Thank you," I muttered, as I couldn't think what else one might say in such a situation. "You're the first person who's managed to get me to stand up on something other than firm ground for more than thirty seconds."

"All you need to learn now is how to stop and you'll be a real skater."

Those perfectly blue eyes finally looked back at me, and I was anticipating a pleasant half hour gliding about arm in arm when she started to cry. She broke from my grip to skate into the centre of the lake, where she fell to her knees and sobs ripped through her.

I would have liked to check that she wasn't hurt but, along with stopping, I didn't know how to change direction. I tried leaning left a bit, but that almost sent me off balance, and so I straightened up just in time to realise that I was shooting towards a tree. It was lucky that the lake had flooded at some point, or I would have crashed into the bank. Instead, I breathed in deep, held my hands out to seize the trunk and merely swung around it. I was rather proud of the manoeuvre until I fell flat on my face.

"I'm sorry, Chrissy. You must think me such a fool."

This was an odd thing to say, considering that I had just slid over to her on my belly like a clumsy penguin. "Of course I don't. I think you're wonderful."

I've never known how to speak to beautiful women and, true to form, this made her sob even louder. "I'm truly sorry. Today is my birthday, and it always makes me think of my parents."

"It's your birthday?" I repeated like one of Flossie's parrots. I couldn't decide whether being born on Christmas Day was the worst or best thing imaginable.

She looked across the snowbound landscape towards the coast. "That's why they called me Holly. They had originally chosen Noël, but Grandfather told them it was too foreign for his liking, so they thought of something far more British."

"It's a shame you didn't have a sister," I joked. "You could have called her Ivy."

She laughed for a moment, which provoked another burst of tears. "I miss them so much at this time of year. I know I was only young when they died, but I've never forgotten them."

"Of course you haven't." As bad as I am at talking to women I admire, I'm even worse at commiserating with them over the death of their parents in a famous maritime disaster. At least I didn't try to stake some claim to her sorrow by mentioning my dead grandmother (or the pet rabbit I'd once owned).

In fact, I thought of something sympathetic to say. "You know, I never met my father's father. He died before I was born, but I still think of him sometimes. I don't even know what he was like, but I enjoy imagining him as a jolly, friendly sort of person who loved his wife and was the perfect balance to her bossiness."

"Then you'll understand how I'm feeling." She breathed in and out again, as though she was suddenly exhausted.

"Possibly, but I doubt it's just the memory of your parents that has made you so sad." A surge of courage pushed me to speak more candidly. "You've looked quite distraught ever since we got here, not to mention our nine minutes together on the train. I can see why you would be worried about your grandfather, but your cousins are in a similar position to you, and they don't seem nearly as concerned."

She dried her eyes with the soft white cuff of her coat, and I hoped I hadn't offended her.

"You're right of course, but then perhaps they don't feel as guilty as I do."

"Guilty?" The word shocked me, and I imagined that pretty face turning back to declare, *That's right, Christopher. I'm the killer. I murdered Silas and Nathan because… because…* Admittedly, I didn't know why she would have done such a thing, but it was still a mite scary.

"I told you when we first met that my grandfather can be a real devil. I feel guilty because, if he was killed, my life would be a lot easier."

I didn't reply as, compared to our first meeting, I now knew her family rather well. I'd seen the way her grandfather treated them all; he veered between monstrous and mild, cruel and kind. He'd evidently paid for her to attend university, but apparently wouldn't leave her any money in his will. He hungered for the attention of his young relatives, but then bullied and manipulated them.

When I said nothing, she continued. "I feel awful that my cousins are dead. I feel bad for suspecting them of trying to murder Grandfather and wish that I hadn't been so cold towards them for so long. What makes things worse is that I judged them so harshly when I'm the obvious culprit."

I tried to shuffle closer along the ice, but I only succeeded in slipping back onto my front like a now stuck penguin. It required some truly inelegant movements to swing my legs around and sit up on my knees.

"You're not the obvious culprit, Holly," I spoke with as much conviction as I could. "I promise that your name has hardly passed my grandfather's lips. Anyone who sees you here must realise how selfless you are. As your cousins argued or strutted about, you spent your time working to get everything ready for Christmas. You are a good, kind person, and I can't believe for one second that you could have hurt your grandfather or killed two men."

"You don't know everything about me, though. In fact, you don't know anything at all." Her cheeks were wet, and it was so cold out there, on that big block of ice, that her tears might well have frozen.

"I'm the likely culprit because Grandfather is standing in the way of what I want in life. He told me I had to marry Nathan, and I refused. He was so angry that I thought he might disown me entirely, but then Nathan himself went down in Grandfather's estimations, and he gave me another chance."

There was so much beneath the surface of that fractured family that it was hard to take in everything she was telling me. The least I could do was explain things from my own perspective.

"Grandfather knows that Lord Rivers wanted Nathan to marry someone of his choosing. We hadn't discovered that it was you he had in mind, but I don't see that it changes a great deal. You refused to marry Nathan, so you had no reason to murder him, and as for Silas, he barely comes into any of this."

"But that's not everything." Her fringe was sodden where it had stuck to her cheek, but she was too distracted to push it away. "After Nathan, he wanted me to marry Luke. I said no again, but he told me I didn't have a choice. He could still force me to do it. He could take away my studies, and any hope I have of fashioning a life of my own."

"That won't happen. It just can't."

"Either way, it makes me look guilty, and I can't stand it anymore." She looked up at the pure white sky then, and it wouldn't have surprised me if the snow had started falling once more. It wouldn't have surprised me if she'd told me that Hans Christian Andersen's 'The Snow Queen' was a true story and it was based on her... Now that I come to think of it, that would have surprised me, but it would still have been a fitting revelation for the unique woman in front of me.

"I know you're innocent, Holly," I whispered, as I didn't know how else to comfort her. "I haven't imagined for one moment that you could be a violent person. I promise that you're not in any trouble."

"Do you know something, Chrissy?" Her gaze wandered from the sky to the ground, before becoming fixed on the house in front of us. Her sorrow seemed to retreat then, and rather than continue what she was saying, she became uneasy. "Did you just see someone in the downstairs window beside the front door?"

It was hard to keep up with the shifts in her emotions, and I struggled to know how to reply, "Don't worry about that. Concentrate on what you wanted to say."

She was more than uneasy; she was anxious, and when she spoke again, a note of panic had invaded her voice. "I've taken up too much of your time, and I have to…" I don't know what she said then, as she was already on her feet and skating away.

I watched in confusion as she reached the path and picked her way through the thick snow.

"I'll be right here if you need me, Holly," I called before realising that, without someone to help me off the lake, I may have spoken literally.

CHAPTER TWENTY-FIVE

Luckily, Todd came out to clean the ice off the boots that had been left in the porch the night before. He must have caught sight of me as I attempted to get to my feet and fell straight back down again.

"Stay where you are, Master Christopher," he shouted from the house as he ran the length of the path to come to my aid. Delilah was there with him but wisely decided to remain on the bank.

"I don't think that skating is my forte," I admitted as he took small steps across the ice to retrieve his employer's idiot grandson.

"I don't think it's many people's forte," he told me, which made me feel a lot better.

"You know, Todd, it wouldn't be Christmas without you… and the odd murder to investigate."

"I feel just the same, sir. I don't have many relatives in St Mary-under-Twine, and I've come to think of you and your grandfather as my extended family. I really have."

I had my arm around him to stop from falling and offered a fraternal pat. "You're the best big brother I've ever had," I said before remembering I had a real big brother. "Joint first with Albert, of course. These days, I tend to forget that he's older than me."

Todd laughed in his usual easygoing manner, and I felt I could breathe more easily when we made it to the bank. I didn't let go of him, but I was relieved, nonetheless.

Delilah thought that whatever game we were playing was just marvellous. She jumped up on Todd before running around the porch with her tail spinning like the propeller of a boat. She was so excited I was surprised she didn't take off into the air. I doubt it was just the snowy scene that had lifted her spirits. For a dog, she was always very aware of the season and must have remembered the present I'd promised her the night before.

This happy greeting did nothing to banish the memory of the strange encounter I'd had with Holly on the lake, though. It was hard to know what to think anymore. I couldn't remember a case when we'd been handed so many pieces of the puzzle from so many interested parties. My thoughts were as tangled as a skein of thread after a kitten had spent the day playing with it.

"Pssst," a voice said and Granny once more stuck her head out of the sitting room to announce her suspicions. "I know who the killer is."

"Oh, yes?" I replied with less enthusiasm than I might have mustered if this had been the first such claim she'd made that weekend.

"That's right." She paused to allow Philip Acland to leave his office and head deeper into the house. "It's Lord Rivers. That's the only thing that makes sense."

I considered listing some of the problems with this assertion but didn't have the energy. "Thank you. I will certainly give the matter some thought."

She looked at me as though I had said something particularly stupid, even by my high standards. "Don't you want to hear how I know he's to blame?"

"Yes, fine. Why not?"

She smiled her crocodile smile and the skin on her particularly narrow face pulled tighter. "He's already murdered two of his relatives. If he keeps going, there'll be none left, and he can give everything to that fancy woman of his." A puzzled look passed over her face and she corrected herself. "Actually, that makes no sense whatsoever. She did it!"

"Who, Mrs Stevans?"

"Is that her name? Victoria something? Very well, Mrs Stevans did it. She might not seem like the obvious choice because she isn't related to anyone. But mark my words, she'll be the last one standing."

"Actually, the dead men were her nephews."

"There you go then!"

I didn't know how to respond to her dubious logic, so I repeated myself. "Thank you. I will certainly give the matter some thought."

Just at that moment, someone appeared at the top of the stairs, and Granny turned her attention there. "Ah, Mrs Stevans. How lovely to see you this morning. Terrible business with your nephew being murdered last night. Just terrible." My grandmother really wasn't the subtlest person I knew.

The pair of them discussed the most recent tragedy, and I went looking for breakfast. As much as I love that most timely of meals, I love it even more on Christmas Day. The duo of cooks did not let us down and, when I arrived in the eponymous room, there were all sorts of pastries, crumpets, muffins and buns just waiting to be devoured. As I picked from all those goodies, I would not have been distracted if Father Christmas himself had flown over the house. I was set on enjoying that singularly early repast and took a plate to fill with treats as our footman Halfpenny went to the kitchen to fetch me a hot dish or two.

I was so taken by the diverse exhibition of food before me that I barely noticed my grandfather and Luke talking in the far corner. Delilah was there too, her tail beating the ground to the rhythm of the conversation. I paid them little attention as I took a seat nearby and, when my plate was empty, I finally listened to what they were saying.

"I don't see why," Luke responded to whatever Lord Edgington had said. "The fact is that the only person it really benefits is me. It's quite possible that someone had a problem with the two brothers, but I can't imagine who that would be."

"So, did you do it?" my grandfather asked in a sudden turnabout, and I rather wished I'd heard the first part of the conversation.

Luke displayed his usual good humour. "No, of course I didn't. I just admitted that I will benefit most from the murders. If I was really to blame for them, would I come down on Christmas morning to tell you that?"

"No, I suppose you wouldn't." Grandfather cleared his throat weakly, as though he were embarrassed to have made such an obvious point. He was acting, of course, and wouldn't have believed Luke's argument for one second. "But the fact remains that someone in this house must have killed your cousins."

As I munched on a buttered muffin, Luke's face clouded with what I first thought was doubt but quickly identified as caution. "Isn't it possible…" He pouted for a moment as he considered his proposition. "Isn't it possible that my great-uncle's estate is not the motivating factor in any of this?" Whether or not Luke was the killer, he was terribly good at shifting our focus towards evidence that would not implicate him.

"It's more than possible," my grandfather replied. "Can you suggest another explanation?"

Again, Luke hesitated, but I was sure he knew the answer. "I can't say for certain, but I do know that Nathan wasn't what people here thought he was."

Grandfather was unimpressed. "What a perfectly vague response. Would you care to expand on the idea?"

Luke was either nervous to discuss the matter or just as good an actor as the old sleuth in front of him. "I haven't told anyone this before, but Nathan came to see me at Grenham Manor in the summer and revealed something quite out of the blue. He said that he had married without telling anyone here. He said that his wife was expecting a child."

"Did you believe him?" I asked, though I'm not sure why anyone would make up such a lie.

"He had a photograph of their wedding in London. And it wasn't just of him in a smart suit standing with a young lady in a white dress. There was a whole party of his friends there. He was evidently a popular chap."

"But how could that have led to his death?"

He looked from me back to the real detective. "I can't say for certain, but the only reason that Nathan told me was because he was desperately worried. He believed that he wouldn't inherit a penny from our great-uncle and that I would be the likely heir. I promised him that, if he was right, I would look after him and the other cousins when Lord Rivers dies."

"How very decent of you!" I couldn't help thinking that he was a truly nice person from head to toe.

Grandfather maintained a degree of scepticism. "Yes, and it underlines the fact that you would never have killed your cousins in order to assure your inheritance."

"Well, quite." Luke's mask slipped for a moment, and a smile bothered his lips. "Or rather, I would never have hurt them."

"Of course you wouldn't." Grandfather allowed this apparently sincere statement to die away before speaking again. "You're evidently not concerned about the fact that, if you don't come into money soon, your family home will be sold, and you and your sister will be thrown to the mercy of the miserly man who has been manipulating you both for years."

"I…" Luke suddenly didn't look so confident, and Grandfather went for the kill.

"It is also possible that, with your legal training, you were able to look into the details of the St Audries estate and realised that it was entailed to Silas, the primogenit in the family. You would have known that, no matter what Lord Rivers told you, no matter what games he played, it was not in his power to choose his heir, and the only way you would inherit was if Silas and his brother were dead."

"Lord Edgington…" Luke's voice rose in protest.

"Did you or didn't you know?"

He could see there was no sense in denying it. "Yes, I knew. I looked into the conditions of the estate in my first year of university, which is why I've never taken much interest in winning Uncle Perry's affection. I've been myself. If he liked me more than the others, it is a reflection of my good character and nothing else. He and Nathan were the most alike. They loved games. I prefer to build my life on hard work and honesty."

Luke held his interviewer's gaze and, when it was clear that his defence was complete, the imperious Lord Edgington said, "I can see that you will make an excellent solicitor."

CHAPTER TWENTY-SIX

The image of Nathan on his deathbed kept popping back into my mind like a bad dream that wouldn't leave me. Now that he was dead, I somehow liked him far more than I previously had. Perhaps it was the terrible violence of his demise. Crying, sweating and screaming as your heart beats a thousand times a second – and you're half out of your mind thinking that the people around you are angels – cannot be many people's chosen fate. However, I think it was the news that Luke subsequently revealed that most affected me. Nathan had seemed so smooth and slick, so driven by his desire for wealth, and yet he'd given up his chance to inherit the estate in order to marry the woman he loved.

His final words came back to me. He'd said, "It's my family I pity. Tell them I'm sorry." He wasn't talking about his cousins or great-uncle, but his wife and unborn child. And the worst part of it was that he'd only gone to his ancestral home in order to provide for them. As if I wasn't miserable enough already, this certainly left me feeling wretched.

"Buck up, butty," my grandfather said in a curious voice as we left Luke to his troubled mind and cold tea.

Before anyone worries about my appetite, I'd had enough time to devour some bacon and eggs in the breakfast room (and the blazer I was wearing had an inside pocket that was the perfect size for storing a crumpet or two). I wouldn't go hungry, no matter how much of the investigation remained.

"It's rather hard to be positive after everything that has happened," I lamented as we turned past the Great Hall.

"What if I were to tell you that I have another present for you?"

"I would say that you spoil me, just like I spoil your dog."

Delilah was walking between us and released a happy growl. She was evidently glad to be included in the discussion.

"The point is, Christopher, that the road ahead of us is a short one. We have already unearthed a great number of the Rivers clan's secrets. All that is left is to fit them together into some kind of narrative."

"That's the thing, though." I would not let him rob me of my negativity. "We're not storytellers. We can't just bend the facts to create an interesting plot. We have to stick to the truth."

"I'm well aware of that. Thank you, Christopher. It was a metaphor."

"Oh."

I hadn't considered where he was taking me until we ascended the main staircase and took the right-hand corridor in the direction of…

"Nathan's bedroom?" I was surprised to be back there, and reluctant to enter. "Why here?"

"We have some of those precious facts of yours to confirm."

As he swung the door open, I heard the sound of tears. They were rather a feature of our weekend.

"My apologies, Mrs Stevans," Grandfather said on seeing the woman on the ottoman at the foot of the bed. "I didn't mean to disturb you."

The place smelt of death, and her arms were extended as though reaching for her nephew's corpse.

"I'm sorry, my lord. I just wanted to say goodbye to him. He was not a bad young man. Not like his brother, at least. I believe that Nathan always meant well, and I can't say I was particularly kind to him. I don't like to imagine what his poor parents would have thought of all this."

Her tears soon returned as she looked at the body. Nathan had lost his colour and stared up at the heavens, or the canopy of his four-poster bed, at least.

"You must take all the time you need, madam." Grandfather bowed his head solemnly, and I'm sure he would have stood there for hours had the poor woman needed that long.

Luckily for everyone involved, she only required another minute or two. When she had finished, she put her hand on Nathan's bare foot, then pulled it away just as quickly as if the cold touch had burned her.

"Please find who did this to him," Mrs Stevans begged, and I remembered that she was not the first person to make such a request. She walked up to my grandfather and, standing closer than polite interaction normally allowed, she looked him dead in the eye. "I'll be forever grateful, Lord Edgington. Please find the man who killed my nephews."

Grandfather gazed down at her with great compassion. "I will do all that I can."

She mouthed her thanks and, much as she had touched the dead man's foot, reached out to squeeze the detective's hand. She drifted from the room, and I had to wonder again what part she had played in the mystery. Of everyone in that house, we had learnt the least about the woman who was both a relative and an employee, a friend to Lord Rivers's deceased wife and now his apparently reluctant companion.

"What an interesting woman." Grandfather stared after her as she descended the corridor. I couldn't say why he had formed this conclusion and wasn't sure I wished to know.

"Aren't we here to examine the facts of the case?" I reminded him, and he jolted back to life.

"Yes, very much so." He put on his white cotton gloves and gave a pair to me to do the same. Delilah knew not to go stamping all over the scene of a crime – or perhaps she just didn't like the smell – as she waited out in the hall.

"What exactly did we come here to find?" I asked after we'd been searching the room for a minute or two.

"Clues, obviously," he replied most helpfully.

There was a bookshelf on one wall and so I decided to look there. It was interesting, as it held volumes from various periods of Nathan's life. At the bottom were stories he would have read as a child. There were titles like 'Heidi', 'The Secret Garden', 'Little Lord Fauntleroy' and 'Robinson Crusoe'. Above those were adventurous titles about heroic young gentlemen faced with impossible odds, and the shelf at the top was mainly populated by crime novels and the classics. It wasn't so very different from my own history as a reader, and I was a little sad to discover this previously unexplored connection that Nathan and I had shared.

An idea occurred to me, and I pulled down 'The Lost Prince'. I could imagine Nathan relating to such a book. It must be hard to grow up aware that you might inherit a large estate while knowing nothing for certain. If anyone was to blame for Nathan's complicated personality, it was the man who had dangled a fortune in front of him for three decades. Somewhat ironically, it was Nathan's most noble act – marrying for love rather than money –that had angered his potential benefactor.

It was all such a sorry mess, but to my disappointment, there was nothing to discover in the pages of the novel, and I was about to move on when I noticed the book just next to it.

"Is this what you wanted?" I showed my grandfather the photograph I'd found.

"You clever boy. Where was that?" He came to examine the picture of Nathan with the pregnant woman it seemed safe to assume was his wife. She was dark skinned and exotic. I had met very few people from anywhere but England in my life up to this point, and so Scots and Welshmen already seemed intriguingly foreign to me. At a guess, I would say that the woman in the photograph was from some distant faraway land like India, Morocco or Belgium.

"It was in a copy of 'The Swiss Family Robinson'. I thought it fitted rather nicely."

Though he had been happy with me a moment before, his face now turned sour. "Excellent work, Christopher, but it scuppers my idea."

"My apologies for scuppering," I replied with a perceptible huff.

He crossed the room, gently hitting the photograph against the palm of his hand as he went. "It's not your fault." What a generous man he was. "But this would seem to confirm what Luke told us."

"And that's a bad thing?" I asked before realising what he was saying. "You mean that you suspected him of lying. You really thought that nice, moustachioed fellow was up to no good and had engineered a story to throw you off the scent. Well, I never!"

He looked at me with a calculating glare. "Whereas you appear to judge our suspects based largely on their facial hair! Nathan was evidently a rotter because of his devilish goatee, and now you're saying that a man with a moustache like Luke's couldn't be to blame. The concept is ridiculous."

"Oh, come along, Grandfather," I rebuked him. "By my standards, that is a fairly rational approach to solving a crime."

He ignored this and returned to my previous point. "And you needn't sound so smug, Christopher. We all make mistakes." (I would remind him of this the next time I did something utterly foolish.) "You must admit that what Luke told us at breakfast was a smart way of distancing himself from the murders. He essentially claimed that he couldn't be the killer, as he had already made a deal with Nathan that they would look after one another, come what may. Whatever else we might say about Luke, he apparently chose not to reveal the real details of Lord Rivers's will to his cousin."

I hadn't seen it in that exact light, but I accepted his point. "Does the photograph really change anything then?"

He stopped his pacing to consider, failed to come to a conclusion, and so paced some more. "Luke knew about the entailment. He knew that he wouldn't inherit and would be reliant on the kindness of Silas and Nathan in order to have the money he needed to preserve his own family's estate."

This struck a chord with me, and I was reminded of another question I'd had. "The same could be said of the brothers, too. I wondered for a long time whether Nathan had killed Silas for obvious reasons, but he told us that the two of them promised to share their good fortune, regardless of who inherited. Silas was the primogenit, whereas Nathan was previously the favoured heir. It would have made sense to come to an agreement."

"You're quite right. It's extremely unlikely they were aware of the entailment, and yet the killer must have been."

"Which means…" I was hoping he might finish my sentence for me. I wanted to believe that the name of the culprit was on the tip of his tongue, but he was staring at the body again and looked distracted.

"It may be important to discover exactly when the poison was left here. Assuming that Nathan took his medicine at least once daily, the killer must have come in here sometime yesterday."

"That hardly limits the possibilities. Anyone in the house could have done it. I could have done it!"

In one quick movement, he spun around to direct the full beam of his gaze upon me. "And did you, Christopher? Did you kill this poor man?"

"Grandfather, I—"

"After all, you were the one who made us drive across the country to save a young lady with whom you are clearly infatuated. Did you decide to kill her cousins in order to—" It was at this point he started laughing. "I'm sorry, I tried my best, but I couldn't keep it up. The very idea!"

"That's hilarious. But you didn't convince me for a second." This was a barefaced lie; I was still quaking from the experience.

I wasn't the only one with a downturned expression. My grandfather had presumably realised how insensitive it was to play a joke beside the corpse of a murdered man. "We're so close. I can feel that the right answer is under our noses, but I can't quite fathom how everything will come together."

I couldn't bear seeing my dear mentor looking so gloomy, and so I attempted to comfort him. "It's surely only a matter of time. Either the killer will give himself away, or the fuse has been lit and the revelation will spark in your immense brain at any moment."

I believe that even he thought this compliment beyond the mark, but he barely let it show. "Thank you, Christopher. I appreciate your vote of confidence." He clapped his hands together in frustration. "There's only one thing for it. I need a distraction. Sometimes, a murder investigation is like an optical illusion. If you stare at it too long, you can only see one version of the picture before you. We must take stock and look at the evidence from an entirely different angle."

I didn't totally understand how this connected to the murder that weekend, but if it made sense to him, that was all that mattered. "What do you plan to do? Go for a walk? Have a nap?"

"Far from it. I'm going to the sitting room to listen to your grandmother complain about the world for half an hour. By doing so, I hope the truth will slowly come to me."

Without another thought for his hardworking assistant, he strode from the room.

CHAPTER TWENTY-SEVEN

It was rare for my grandfather to give me a long lead on one of our investigations. He tended to treat me a little more strictly than Delilah, which was just one of the many similarities between me and his loyal hound. I considered padding along after him to see my family – it was Christmas after all. However, something he'd said stuck in my mind, and I decided to go in search of pen and paper.

There were whole wings of St Audries Park that I hadn't explored, and I soon found myself in a corridor on the ground floor that I had barely entered. On one side were a line of salons – because, in a manor house, one per person simply isn't enough – and, on the other, I found the library. I normally like to locate that most pleasant of rooms early on in an investigation. It showed how quickly everything had unfolded that I hadn't once questioned whether they had any first editions of Charles Dickens' novels, or perhaps a shelf devoted to Wilkie Collins.

To make up for this, the room itself was a thing of wonder. The whole place was of a colour scheme that matched the large walnut desk in its centre. The elaborate ceiling was covered with intarsia work, with relief carvings descending in a regular pattern all over the wooden surface. The bookshelves were of that same honey-coloured wood and, rather extraordinarily, the majority of the books were bound in light brown leather with gold writing about the spine. I can honestly attest that I have never, before or since, entered such a harmoniously decorated room.

There were two grand old armchairs positioned in the large bay window that looked onto the garden, and I would have liked nothing more than to sit there with a good book, only taking breaks to watch the increasingly heavy snow fall to earth. Entering that welcoming space was like slipping on a thick jumper or climbing into a bath that was just the right temperature and neither scalded nor froze me to the bone. It was something approaching paradise.

Sadly, there was no time for leisure that day, and having failed to find a recent copy of Burke's Peerage, and wishing I'd brought my grandfather's book in from the car, I searched the desk drawers for the necessary stationery. With pen and paper secured, I sat in a high-backed chair with the most intricate armrests that were covered in carved foliage and snarling animals. They were quite beautiful, completely impractical, and painful to lean on. Nevertheless, I set to work, talking to myself as I went.

"Lord Rivers had one daughter, who, in turn had one daughter. Holly is Peregrine Rivers's only living descendant." I drew this first line of the family in the middle of the page. I didn't know the name of Holly's father, though I remembered her mother was Molly and her grandmother was Polly. I doubted Mr Bridport would be important to the case so, to keep things simple, I put his name down as Wally. I was trying to get a sense of how everyone was related and work back from there. "It's only logical that Lord Rivers had a brother who had at least two sons. Nathan and Silas and Luke and Flossie were first cousins, and they all shared the Rivers surname. That means Peregrine Rivers is their paternal great-uncle."

As I proceeded with my domestic detective work, the tree in front of me was slowly taking shape. "Mrs Victoria Stevans is presumably Silas and Nathan's aunt on their mother's side, unless her name changed when she was married..." I thought about this for a moment before realising that, if this was the case, it would have made her Lord Rivers's relative. "No, no, no! It's bad enough that second cousins are being paired up for marriage."

"Happy Christmas, Chrissy." Flossie was passing the library and poked her head inside. "Who's being set up for marriage?"

"Oh..." I didn't know how to respond because I'd quite forgotten what was supposed to be a secret and what everyone knew. "Just my cousin and I..." I had to swallow at the very idea of marrying my cousin Eleanor. The best thing you could say about her was that she knew how to juggle. The worst was that she talked about horses a lot – to the extent that I sometimes wondered whether she knew the difference between animals and people.

Flossie looked puzzled. "Really? I assumed you were talking about Nathan and Holly."

"Oh, they were supposed to get married, were they?" I don't know why I even attempted such a ruse. I'm simply terrible at it.

"Either way, I agree with you. There are so many people in the world. Why would anyone marry within the same family?" She took a few steps into the room to look at the paper on the table in front of me. "Why are you doing that?"

"I'm trying to understand who's related to whom and how. I don't think it's any secret to say that the obvious motive behind the deaths is the killer's desire to inherit this estate."

"You misunderstood me." She showed her perfectly white teeth in a smile as she corrected my misapprehension. "I meant, why are you doing that when there's already a Rivers family tree just over there?" She pointed to the bay that protruded from the room and, sure enough, there was a frame on the wall between two tall windows. Admittedly, the printed paper inside was somewhat neater than the crumpled, ink-stained sheet that I had produced.

"That's wonderful," I cooed as she brought it to me.

She appeared to be one of those people who are only too happy to help others. "Apparently Uncle Perry has told us we must all meet in the sitting room before lunch. I expect to see you there." She gave a final amiable look and left me to my work.

One thing that my diagram had that the one on the wall was lacking – aside from the pretty wig-waggy tree I'd drawn around it – was a clear structure. It was essentially a list of names with some squiggles under them, which I eventually realised were the years that each person had lived. The numbers were almost indecipherable, but once I'd managed to read a few, I felt like I'd rediscovered the Rosetta Stone and could make sense of all that was before me.

Perhaps obviously, the names were organised by date, starting with the first Viscount Rivers, who was born in seventeen twenty… something. Running between the names were lines that sprouted off all over the place to connect parents to children and brothers to sisters, depending on whether the line was broken, wavy, thick or fine. It was quite the most complicated system imaginable, and I eventually gave up trying to decipher the whole document and instead looked for the names that I already knew. To be frank, I doubt that Holly's four-times great-grandfather had much to do with the crime anyway.

I quickly located the fifth Viscount Rivers. Peregrine was born in 1846 and had two brothers. Everyone in the family was listed, and I ticked them off one by one. The Bridport name had appeared a few times over the centuries, and so Holly's father clearly wasn't the first to marry into the family. As predicted, Mrs Stevans was Silas and Nathan's maternal aunt. Their father John Rivers had married Eileen Stevans in eighteen something-y something. It really was difficult to read.

I felt quite proud of myself for having worked out so much and wondered whether I should give up on becoming a detective and take up the presumably more relaxing life of an archivist or perhaps a librarian. I even managed to find the servants, Ripon and Daphne. My sense of accomplishment didn't last long though as, while it was true I had confirmed all my previous suppositions, I was no closer to identifying the killer.

The chain of inheritance was just as it had appeared. Silas would have had the estate if he hadn't been killed. Then came Nathan, then Luke. The only detail that might have been relevant was that, if I was reading the blasted thing correctly, the St Audries estate would then have passed to one Philip Saul Acland.

Oh my ears and whiskers!

CHAPTER TWENTY-EIGHT

As I ran about the house in search of the duplicitous clerk, a sense of what had really been happening that weekend came to me. My mind was going as fast as Grandfather's Bentley. You'll be pleased to know, however, that I kept my thoughts to myself this time.

If he's the next in line, then Luke… And if I failed to see that, then couldn't… But how can that be unless she… I really hope I'm wrong about all of this!

Philip Acland was not in his office, or the sitting room. I considered telling Grandfather what I'd discovered, but he was still busy listening to Granny. She had just finished explaining the problem with postmen and moved on to a funny situation that had occurred to the shopkeeper in her small town in Tatchester.

"Mrs Grout searched everywhere for her favourite wooden spoon and, when she eventually found it, it was the in the kitchen where it was supposed to be. You see, she…"

Grandfather looked bored out of his mind, but I left him there to have the revelation he required. If I'd worked out the solution, there was no way that he would be far behind, and I didn't think it was fair to give away the ending.

I went upstairs to look through the corridors where many of the bedrooms were clustered together. Of course, this didn't mean that Acland's room would be up there, even if he was a distant cousin or what have you. There was also nothing to say that he would be in his room and, as it turned out, he wasn't. I heard his voice before I caught sight of him. I'd never liked that slightly whiny tone. It was too desperate, too needy and, when I heard him pleading with Holly in the Great Hall, I hated just about everything about him.

On soft feet, I crept onto the minstrel's gallery to listen to their conversation from above.

"Please don't talk to me like that."

"You were foolish," Holly responded. "You were foolish last night and again this morning. You shouldn't even be talking to me now."

His voice fell to a whisper – a needy, whiny whisper. "I can't help it, Holly. I hate all this acting we have to do. I was only being myself. You know how difficult that is in this family. You should be congratulating me."

I crouched down behind the balustrade and could just make out their faces through a trefoil cutout in the middle of the wooden panel. I was fairly confident that they couldn't see me.

"Just stop, Philip." Her words were hard and controlled. It was perhaps the first thing she'd said that weekend that wasn't running with six different emotions at once. "We can discuss all this when the time comes. Not here. Not now. Not today."

Trust me to think, *Grandfather would not approve of her sentence structure,* at a moment like that.

Acland turned, and I didn't have to see the expression on his face to know how angry he was. The muscles in the back of his neck were tensed, and he balled his fists up as he strode away from her. For a moment, I didn't know what to do. I wanted to confront them both, but I was so confused, so turned around by what I'd discovered that I couldn't bring myself to move. Perhaps if I hadn't seen Holly there with him, I could have kept believing in her innocence, but there was no chance of that now.

When she decided not to leave but sat down in the window seat looking out on the gardens, I found my resolve and marched down to her. It was a relief not to bump into her accomplice on the way. If he'd been coming up the stairs towards me, I might well have knocked him back down again.

"Chrissy." Her face transformed as she saw me. She went from downcast to delirious in the space of a single second. "I was just coming to find you!" She hopped to her feet and hurried closer. Even if I hadn't caught sight of her previously dejected expression, this happy-hearted act would have been out of place. "Everyone is convening in the sitting room. It's time to exchange Christmas presents."

I'd never imagined responding to such a sentence with anything but whoops of jubilation. Instead, I stopped beneath the arches to shout at a woman I had held in such high esteem since the very moment I'd met her. "You did it, didn't you?"

"I don't know what you mean." She smiled more nervously but kept up the pretence. "Perhaps we should have a break from all the terrible things that have happened and enjoy some time with our families. I really think that—"

"Did you lead me here just to fool me?" I didn't need her to respond, as I already knew the answer. "My goodness, you did, didn't you?" Evidence came to the forefront of my brain as though it had been hiding there the whole time. "You left your bracelet on the train on purpose, knowing I would do whatever it took to get it back to you. You gave me just enough information to find this place, and I was so taken by the mystery that I failed to realise that it was actually a trap."

There was a look of fear on her face and, when she couldn't answer, I continued. "And the ticket I found! It was there on your seat, but you'd already given one to the inspector. You must have bought out the whole first-class compartment. You wanted to make sure that we would be alone together so that you could tell me your tragic story."

"Chrissy, I don't know what you think but—"

Another fact that had seemed so distant suddenly came into focus.

"You knew my name, too. How could I have been so blind? The first time we spoke in private after we arrived here, you called me Chrissy, not Christopher, because you knew exactly who I was." I wouldn't let her speak now and kept on without taking a breath. "You must have read about me in the paper and known what easy game I would be. Those articles make it clear that Christopher Prentiss is a brainless simpleton who's charmed by every pretty girl he meets."

"No, it wasn't like that. I just needed your help."

Until this moment, I had hoped she might still prove me wrong.

"You told me of your sorrows on the train, knowing that I would tell my grandfather and we would rush to your rescue. And when we got here, you put on a big scene to show how mistreated you are. You made it look as though Lord Rivers keeps you as a skivvy, but it's just not true. How could it be when he pays for you to go to university? Nathan told us you were spoilt, and I couldn't see it at first, but it's clear now. You made me think that you were a poor Cinderella who needed saving, and I believed you because I've always wanted to be a gallant prince."

Her lower lip trembled as she decided what she should and shouldn't admit. "I confess that I knew you would be on that train, Chrissy. I saw you with your friends one day in Oxford and found out through a mutual acquaintance when you'd be going home. And yes, I wanted you to come here, but I promise that I only had good intentions. You must understand—"

She walked forward as if to take my hand in hers, but I wouldn't let her touch me. I'd been duped by her for too long already, and I wouldn't let it happen again.

"I don't want to hear any more lies. You brought me here because you believed that I would never suspect you of murder – that my unswerving trust in you could even influence my grandfather. And all the time you were running around with your boyfriend, killing off the men who separate him from a fortune."

As she realised that I knew exactly what they'd done, the words caught in her throat, and she couldn't make a sound.

"You refused to marry Nathan or Luke as your grandfather wanted because you were in love with Philip Acland. I should have seen it last night when he tried to compliment you. I thought you turned away from him because you didn't want his attention, but that wasn't it. You didn't want anyone to know what he is to you. It was the same this morning on the lake. You saw him watching from his office and left me as soon as you could get away."

"No, Chrissy. No, you've got it all upside down. I didn't... I wouldn't..." Her tears broke once more, but as she'd been crying for most of the weekend, it was hard not to see them as another part of her act.

"You tried to kill Lord Rivers, and when that failed, you thought you'd start further down the list and go back when the time was right. Silas's room was full of weapons, so you borrowed a couple to kill him." I didn't need to pause to see how this theory fitted the scene of the crime we'd surveyed. "That must be why there were two wounds. One of you stabbed him and the other shot him through the head with his own gun."

My words seemed to weigh her down, and she dropped to her knees on the pine floor.

"Nathan was next, of course. You took him up a plate of food last night before we left for church." I think this was when I knew beyond any doubt that she had to be to blame. This was when I finally accepted that she was not the angel-eyed innocent that I'd wished her to be. She was a killer. "How simple it must have been for you to swap the tincture he took for his nerves with a bottle of concentrated digitalis – the very same substance with which you'd tried to kill your grandfather in the summer."

She couldn't look at me anymore. She sat with her knees bent beneath her as though she was about to pray, but even that wouldn't help her now. She was beyond redemption – beyond forgiveness – and she deserved whatever punishment was ahead.

"Is that it?" she said in a voice that was as quiet as whispering grass. "You've noticed a string of coincidences and now I'm a killer?"

"I know that Acland will inherit this place if Luke meets the same fate as Silas and Nathan. Your grandfather wouldn't let you marry your impoverished third cousin, so you took matters into your own hands." Silence filled the room for a moment, and even her cries fell quiet. "You had more reason than anyone to want the viscount dead. He could have explored the legal procedure to break the entailment on this estate, but he never even considered leaving it to you. He played with your cousins for his own enjoyment and overlooked his granddaughter completely. He wouldn't even let you marry the man you love, and so Peregrine Rivers had to die."

I hadn't noticed him until now, but Grandfather was standing under the arches listening to what I was saying. He must have made a faint sound as, just as I noticed him, Holly did too. It sparked something in her and she mounted a defence once more.

"I lied, my lord." I didn't say it was a good defence. "I manipulated your grandson to bring the pair of you here, but you must believe that I didn't kill my cousins, and I never tried to hurt my grandfather. It would have been insanity to involve Britain's most respected detective if I planned to commit a murder." Her voice was so soft and so appealing. She sounded just as she had on the train from Oxford.

"Don't believe her, Grandfather. She's just trying to influence you. She's already done the same to me."

"I'm not lying. Not anymore." She was more confident now and slowly pushed herself up to standing. "I tricked you both into coming here because I wanted to find out who was trying to kill my grandfather. I wanted to make him so happy with me for saving his life that he would allow me to marry the man I love." Her breath was loud and insistent. "Philip isn't the killer, and neither am I."

"I wish I could believe you, Holly." We were only a yard or two apart, but I don't think I'd ever felt such a gulf between myself and a person for whom I'd previously cared. "I wish you weren't to blame."

Those phenomenal blue eyes strayed across to look at my grandfather, and we waited to hear his verdict.

"I came to tell you that we are ready to open the presents in the sitting room. But I also have to say how sorry I am." At first, it wasn't clear what he meant or who he was addressing. He left a long pause between each sentence to make my heart beat faster. "I feel sorry for you, Miss Bridport, and the fact you had to go to such lengths to achieve your goal. And you, Chrissy, because Holly isn't the killer. It's just as she said, she lied to get you here, but that doesn't mean she's to blame. As you know, it's a common mistake to equate dishonesty with criminality. A mistake of which we have both been guilty."

"But how is that possible?" I peered up at the bare beams above us as I tried to understand how I could have been so mistaken. "It all fits together perfectly."

"Yes, but that doesn't mean a lot if you've overlooked certain evidence." He took a long, slow breath before explaining. "Although a killer willingly inviting a detective to her home might be one way of implying she was innocent, Holly never admitted until now that she led us here. The possible advantages of such a strategy would not have compensated for the presence of a former police officer in the house."

He walked over and put an arm around each of us. "I'm truly sorry. This isn't a pleasant outcome, but we can still find a solution." A loud, dry click came from his throat then, and I could tell how affected he was by the scene I'd caused. "Come along, both of you. Christmas is the time to be with the people you love."

I couldn't look at him anymore. I felt so low and stupid, not just for failing to solve the case after all the training my grandfather had given me, but for accusing an innocent woman of such terrible things. I was a bad detective, an even worse person, and I certainly didn't deserve any Christmas presents.

CHAPTER TWENTY-NINE

I brought my sullenness into the sitting room with me, and even Delilah putting her chin on my lap couldn't make things better. She looked up without blinking, and I stroked her head as I sat in an armchair beside the truly roaring fire. I had no doubt that Grandfather had given up his prime spot for me, as he stayed on his feet in a shady corner to observe the largely gleeful congregation.

Everyone was there, and it really was a testament to my mother's ability to set others at ease that my family's presence did not seem like an inconvenience. Lord Rivers sat in front of the cobbled together Christmas tree with his young relatives on either side of him, and they appeared to have put the murders behind them.

A few members of the party remained a touch more reticent. Philip Acland was standing beside the door and looked just as angry as when I'd last seen him. Victoria Stevans was not merely leaden-hearted; her silence suggested she was reluctant to be there at all. Oh, and Granny shot suspicious looks around the room, as she was apparently still trying to identify whoever had carried out the crimes.

To be fair to our host, he did everything he could to maintain a merry atmosphere. He put his cane to one side and handed out parcels to everyone in turn. He had even found gifts for us interlopers. Grandfather was presented with an original notebook containing the prosecutor Sir Richard Muir's thoughts on the Crippen trial. Mother and Father got a beautiful Royal Doulton dinner set, and I was given a pair of leather slippers. It must be very difficult to choose presents for me, as people are forever giving me slippers.

"You really shouldn't have, Lord Rivers," Granny told him as she unwrapped a tasselled Manila shawl from Spain. It was made of black silk with intricately embroidered flowers along the hems. I could tell that this gesture instantly crossed him off her list of suspects. She looked positively undispleased for once, which was rare for my grandmother.

"I have a stock of presents in the house for such occasions," Rivers explained. "My wife would always collect knick-knacks when we travelled, and many of them are still in their original boxes. That was one of them."

"Grandma would have enjoyed seeing everyone here together," Holly said, but she didn't have the energy to deliver this nostalgic comment with any warmth.

"This one is for you Holly," her grandfather said, and he handed her a slim, black box with a leather finish.

She looked up at him, her eyes full of hurt and pain even as she opened her gift to reveal a sparkling diamond choker. It was richly inlaid by anyone's standards, and I realised that this was something else about which Holly had lied. Lord Rivers might have been a cantankerous sort, but he was no miser. In addition to supporting a young woman's university education – which was rare enough for a traditional man like him – this Christmas present was worth a small fortune. If she really wished to escape from her unhappy life, she need only pawn her jewellery and start afresh elsewhere.

"That's really very lovely," Flossie said without a hint of jealousy in her voice but plenty in her eyes.

"Yes, Grandfather. You're too kind." Holly's tone was just as hollow as I'd felt since I left the Great Hall, but some cheery conversation burst out around the room then, and the mood changed once more.

Mother complimented Lord Rivers on his choice of gifts. He admitted that Victoria had helped choose many of them and then, with his usual rambunctious energy, good old Luke suggested that, if the presents had all been exchanged, we might continue with a game of some variety. He'd begun to explain the phenomenally complex rules of something called The Mousetrap when Grandfather interrupted him.

"I have a present for you all." There was no sunshine in his voice. No light or softness, and it jarred with the message of his words.

"Oh, yes?" Luke replied with a touch of hesitation that wasn't typical of him. "And what's that?"

"The truth."

Flossie took a sudden sharp breath. "You know?"

"You know who the killer is?" Holly echoed.

"That's correct." Grandfather left his gloomy corner and took the last remaining seat between his daughter and me. It was a good spot from which to address the assembled party, but he took his time before saying anything more.

Granny wasn't the only one surveying the faces of those around us. Glances pinged about the room like… well, ping-pong balls, as everyone placed their bets on who the culprit would finally be.

When this dramatic pause had almost lost its drama, Grandfather began. "It is not an easy task to come into a family and assess its component parts. Since our arrival here yesterday, my grandson has been trying to puzzle out the chances that every good person is as honest as they seem and every rotter a born criminal. This was a perfect case to explore such possibilities as the differences between many of you are so marked. Luke and Flossie appear to be kind-hearted, hardworking and genuine. Nathan was the perfect charlatan, his brother a violent recluse and Holly…" He paused to look at her. "…Holly is a different proposition altogether."You all told me that Silas was a troubled individual and, had he been the killer, no one would have been surprised." He turned to Victoria Stevans then, just as Delilah got tired of comforting me and went to chew on the dried beef lung I'd bought her as a Christmas present. "Even Silas's aunt told us of her negative perception of her nephew. His room here is not so much a museum of military history as a torture chamber filled with every sort of weapon. Many of the artefacts there were presumably stolen from the battlefield. Unless he had a hidden talent for making friends, I can only assume he took trophies from the bodies of his fallen allies and compatriots."

He had already led us down a twisting path, and yet he'd barely begun his tale. "I say all this not to tar the man, but to remind you that I was required to investigate the death of a less-than-sympathetic character. Although it was claimed that no one in particular held a grudge against Silas, none of you had a good word to say about him. Nathan suggested that he loved his brother out of loyalty and obligation rather than tender feelings, but to give the first victim some credit, he did appear to be loyal. They came to an agreement that, should one of them inherit Lord Rivers's fortune, they would share it fairly. Unlike some people in this room, the brothers did not realise that the St Audries estate was entailed to the current viscount's next male relative. No matter what any of you did to convince Lord Rivers of your suitability to inherit, it was always supposed to go to Silas."

"You despicable snake," Flossie complained, as she apparently wasn't one of those in the know. "How could you have led us all on like that?"

Rivers raised his hands. "Now, now, Flossie. Don't say anything rash. I had a perfectly good reason for wanting to test your mettle."

Grandfather quickly explained his point. "That reason being that you are a vile meddler who takes pleasure in seeing your loved ones squirm and degrade themselves before you. You are a lonely old man who played your young relatives off against one another when you should have cherished and nurtured them if you wanted their affection. The Victorian era has many crimes for which to answer, and you are the perfect microcosm of its folly."

The old devil was speechless, and his eyes sank within their sockets as he tried to understand how anyone could speak so rudely to him, in his own house, on Christmas day!

My dear old gent maintained a stern expression as he continued. "Although Nathan had a silver tongue and a dubious relationship with the truth, I became confident fairly quickly that he had not killed his brother. For one thing, he didn't know about the entailment and had no reason to think that Silas was ahead of him in the order of succession. This really only left us with one obvious conclusion and, when Nathan himself was murdered, the link appeared to be confirmed."

He allowed a few brief moments for us to consider what this meant for the other suspects, and those judgmental glances ricocheted about again. "If the killer was murdering his relatives in order to inherit the family fortune, he wouldn't even have to kill the existing viscount. I must say, Lord Rivers, that the attempts on your life were half-baked. May I ask whether you told anyone of your poor health?"

Rivers had recovered somewhat from the previous slight and found his voice. "Yes... Luke knew about it. He has been a trusted confidante to me during a difficult period."

"I thought that might have been the case." Grandfather turned to the sweet-natured man with the truly impressive moustache. "So, Luke, you knew that Lord Rivers was dying."

He instantly became defensive. "I did. But I was sworn to secrecy."

"With Silas and Nathan both dead, and Lord Rivers's health deteriorating, you will soon inherit your family's estate. As a fledgling lawyer, you had the resources to learn about the entailment and, from what I can tell, you told no one else about it."

"That's right," he confirmed. "I realised what it would do to my cousins if they found out, and so I decided not to say anything. I knew how they would treat Uncle Perry."

Lord Edgington just nodded. "Very well. But it occurred to me, and no doubt everyone else in this room, that with your older cousins dead, you now have the money you require to preserve your own home at Grenham Manor." Though his stare was hard, he did not leave Luke to suffer for long. "However, several factors made it unlikely that you would have gone about things as the killer did. For a start, you would not have targeted your uncle, as you knew just how little time he has left."

With his eyebrows scrunched together, Luke looked truly baffled by all this and offered a weak, "Thank you?" as though uncertain whether it was the right response. Grandfather's language had been suitably vague, and I still couldn't say whether Luke's name had actually been cleared.

"The reality is that a motive does not make a killer." Lord Edgington paused to look at each suspect in turn. "A good detective must provide real evidence to link a suspect to the crime. I found no definitive proof that Luke had stabbed and shot Silas or poisoned Nathan. In fact, I am sure my grandson will be happy to hear that Luke is every bit the upstanding young man that he appears. I can't think of a better person to inherit this fine estate when Lord Rivers dies."

In a small, scratchy voice, the viscount gave the missing information. "The doctor says I may have six months if I'm lucky."

Flossie walked across the room to put a sympathetic hand on her great-uncle's shoulder. I was amazed by how quickly she had forgiven him.

"It was easy enough to assign motives to each of you," Grandfather continued. "Flossie clearly holds her brother in high esteem and may have wished to ensure that he would be the one to take on the viscount's mantle. Mrs Stevans…"

I believe that he held his tongue then for the sake of discretion. He might have mentioned the financial position that had forced the poor woman to share a bed with her employer, but instead he said, "Mrs Stevans had no great love for her nephew Silas and might have killed him to secure a better life for Nathan, though that wouldn't explain the second murder. As for Philip Acland, I was puzzled by just how strongly he wished me to believe that Mrs Stevans was the killer. He was one of the first people to speak to us after we arrived, and he presented his suspicions as though they were facts."

Acland had been rooted to the spot since my grandfather had started his explanation but, as those around us considered his potential guilt, he shuffled his weight from one side of his body to the other and back again.

It suddenly occurred to me that my suspicions might not have been as wide of the mark as I'd believed. What if Holly wasn't to blame for the killings, but her paramour was? Perhaps he'd convinced her to lead us to St Audries, believing that he could direct Grandfather's attention to Mrs Stevans before killing the remaining heirs and inheriting the estate. Was this the explanation? Was this the moment when we discovered the name of the killer?

No. No, it wasn't.

"Mr Acland may have been a distant enough relation for us not to realise that, should all the men in this room die, he would be the next owner of St Audries Park, but any such plan will always fail. Whoever remained would be the first person to arouse the suspicion of the police. Unless Holly was in league with him, she would have confirmed whatever plotting had taken place, and her sweetheart would have hanged. A clever person like Philip Acland would not have risked such an endeavour."

Delilah sat with her eyes half closed as she luxuriated in the waves of heat coming from the fire. You might think that she was the only creature there who didn't care who the killer was. However, until a scientist proves otherwise, I prefer to believe that dogs know exactly what is going on at all times. She had probably sniffed out a whiff of gunpowder on the killer and solved the case a whole day before her esteemed master.

"Holly herself, of course, was forbidden from marrying the man she loves and might well have murdered her grandfather to break free of his yoke, but she would have faced the same problem if she'd set out to murder half the family to benefit Philip Acland." With each minor revelation, one or two people gave a tiny gasp of realisation. To my surprise, it was my father who was most surprised to discover that Holly and Philip were in love. He'd sat there in silence, smoking his pipe throughout, but this really brought him to life.

Lord Rivers folded his arms across his chest. "So that was why you disobeyed me. It was Acland you loved, was it?" he asked in a resigned tone, and Holly could only nod.

"I found motives for all of you, but I could not say who was responsible for the murders until just half an hour ago." Something about the tensed muscles in my grandfather's hands told me that we had almost reached the end of his tale. "At the scene of the first killing, two things stood out to me. Christopher was confused as to why Silas had been both stabbed and shot, but I was more puzzled by the fact that both weapons had been removed. That a gun had been used in the first place suggested the killer had planned the attack and would have worn gloves to avoid leaving fingerprints. But if that was the case, why remove the knife from the body when he was surely more likely to drip blood on his clothes? The fact that there was no sign of the gun was also telling."

"Perhaps the killer wasn't wearing gloves," Luke proffered. "Perhaps he hadn't expected to find Silas in that room, and so he made the most of the opportunity." He still seemed a little nervous, and I had to hope that Grandfather had told the truth when he'd ruled out likeable Luke's involvement.

"It's possible, but I think a more likely explanation is that the weapons that killed Silas would have revealed a lot about what happened. The gun made very little sound and so only Flossie, who was on that side of the house, actually heard it."

"That is strange," Acland said, from his position by the door. I still hadn't given up on the idea that he was guilty and had positioned himself there for an easy getaway. "Where would someone get a gun like that?"

"In Silas's bedroom," I answered for my grandfather, as this was something we knew for certain. "We found a very similar one there yesterday."

Lord Edgington shook his head resolutely. "That's where you were wrong, Christopher. That's where we were both wrong. I now believe that the gun we saw was not merely similar to the weapon that killed Silas, it was the very same one."

"Then why did the killer hide it back where he'd found it?" Holly's tears had dried, and I got that same sense of her quick mind that I'd had when we'd first met. She was tying together the threads of the case, just as my grandfather had.

"Because the killer didn't take the gun from Silas's bedroom." In the glow of the fire, Grandfather was as rosy-cheeked and smiley as any Father Christmas just then. "Silas was carrying it when he was stabbed through the chest."

CHAPTER THIRTY

There was a burst of energy as the cogs in my head started whirring, and two clear doubts sprang forth. *What was Silas doing with the gun? And how was he stabbed if he was holding it?*

To my immense gratification, Grandfather immediately told us, "The two questions you should be asking yourselves are, what was Silas doing with the gun? And how was he stabbed if he was holding it?"

Holly was the quickest off the mark. "It must have been Silas who kept trying to kill grandfather. When the accidents he staged failed, he decided to shoot him!"

My own dear grandfather passed his cane from one hand to the other. "That is correct. As the oldest in your generation, he no doubt believed that he should be the one to inherit this estate, and so he hated Lord Rivers for the games he made you play."

The viscount himself sat looking disgruntled. I must say that he deserved it. His chickens had not just come home to roost, they'd built a great big smelly hen house on his front lawn to spoil the view!

"Silas set the stone to fall on his great-uncle and when that failed, and Nathan and Lord Rivers argued, Silas could wait no longer. Soon after we arrived, he fetched a gun from his room and would have murdered his enemy, not caring a fig for the consequences, but someone stopped him."

A crisp silence filled the spaces between us, and I tried to resolve this final mystery in my head. For a few moments, the only sound was the spitting of the fire and my granny's occasional tutting. She rarely went long without finding something that failed to meet her approval.

"You asked how Silas was killed when he was carrying a gun," Holly began, but then she came to an unexpected halt and could do nothing but look at the detective, the fear plain in her eyes.

Much like a fire catching, a sense of what had happened spread about the room before Grandfather could confirm our thinking. He rose from his seat and walked slowly towards Philip Acland.

"The killer had a knife, but Silas had a gun." He stopped just inches away, his hand still wrapped around the polished amethyst on top of his cane. "For the killer to get anywhere near, the victim would

211

have had to assume that the man in front of him offered no threat." In one swift movement, he mimed the stab that would have incapacitated Silas, and then knocked an imaginary gun from Acland's hand.

The poor clerk looked quite terrified, but Grandfather turned away to address the group once more. "Silas never imagined that the killer had a weapon because it was concealed in a walking cane, just like this one."

He held up the silver stick, but no one was watching anymore. We'd all turned to see the bitter old man in front of the Christmas tree. Flossie had removed her hand from Lord Rivers's shoulder and his other relatives looked at him with contempt.

"He was trying to kill me," Rivers shouted in the arrogant voice that had echoed around the halls of St Audries Park so often.

"I believe he was, and you had every right to defend yourself."

Luke darted from his seat on the opposite side of the room to inspect his great-uncle's silver cane, which had rolled a short distance away from its owner. He looked it up and down for a moment, then pulled on the rounded top to reveal a long, thin and ever-so-nasty blade that had been concealed within the main pole.

"But if you killed him to save yourself, why didn't you just tell us?" Luke had never looked so innocent. His eyes were enormous, and his jaw hung open as he studied the tricky old man before him.

Lord Rivers said nothing, and so Grandfather spoke on his behalf. "Because, with Silas dead, he saw an opportunity and seized it."

This was when it all made sense. Until this moment, I'd overlooked the second killing and thought that the viscount's only crime was failing to reveal what had happened to Silas. However, it was obvious, even to me, that you can't claim self-defence in cases of pre-meditated poisoning. I could just imagine Rivers before the judge saying, "I had to do it, your honour. If I hadn't swapped his medicine for the extracted poison from a foxglove – which I'd kept for several months and prepared on the off-chance I would need it – Nathan might have killed me after I came back from church that night with a large group of people, any of whom I could have told of the danger he presented."

My grandfather evidently agreed and continued to lay out the charges against him. "You couldn't forgive Nathan for falling in love with a woman you'd forbidden him from marrying, especially after he refused the hand of your granddaughter. You couldn't abide the idea of his inheriting this estate, but there was no way that your favoured choice, Luke, would get it unless Nathan died, too. You had the foxglove seeds from one of Silas's clumsy attempts on your life, and you decided to finish the job."

"This is nonsense, and you'll never prove it." The grumbling viscount wouldn't look at his accuser now, but peered into the fire as though contemplating the infernal destiny that awaited him.

Grandfather would not be intimidated. "You're just like your own old-fashioned ancestors. If you'd taken the necessary measures to change your will so that your own granddaughter could inherit, none of this would have happened. Of course, you would never conceive of such a thing. Your small-minded attitude would only allow one of the boys to inherit. And so now, instead of dying surrounded by your closest relatives, you will see out your days in prison."

"Evidence!" Rivers shrieked, his teeth grinding together, and his lips pulled back like a dog about to bite. "How are you going to prove any of it?"

"For one thing, you did nothing to protect yourself from further attack. Someone had already tried to murder you before we arrived yesterday and yet, when you went for your afternoon nap, you didn't even station a servant outside your open door. I thought it foolish at the time, but as soon as I realised that you had killed Silas and knew that the threat to your life had passed, I understood how you could afford your devil-may-care attitude."

Rivers was a rat trapped in a corner. He would never go quietly and continued with the same furious defence. "What fiddle-faddle. That isn't evidence; it's circumstantial at best."

"And yet you haven't denied any of it."

As this clash of grandpas continued, I plumped the cushions on my chair to enjoy it all the more.

"That's not my job. You're the one throwing around accusations. Now prove them!"

Grandfather raised one finger. I thought he had saved his best argument for last but, when he opened his mouth, not a sound emerged.

A sense of deflation was felt across the room. I looked at my ever-wise mother in the hope that she would be able to help her usually faultless father. Luke was a trained solicitor, and yet he couldn't produce the evidence to condemn the murderous tyrant before us. Holly was smart, Flossie enterprising, and Acland must have had his good points, so it came as an immense surprise to me when I was the one to land upon the proof we needed.

"You have a wound on your leg where Silas injured you."

"The boy's a jabbering idiot." Rivers stared at the fire again, and I realised that he'd done so each time he was facing defeat.

I got up from my comfy seat by the fire. "Luke, check his left leg. He was hobbling on his right when we arrived, but both seemed weak a short time after we found the body. I think Silas must have landed a blow after all."

Still unable to meet my gaze, Rivers tried to play on our sympathy. "Shame on you for using my infirmity against me. I'm an old man. My body isn't what it— Owwwww!"

He didn't get to finish his sentence as, just in the middle of it, Luke walked over to prod the spot where Silas had hurt him.

"Stop!" Lord Rivers moaned. "I did it. I killed them both. Just stop poking me." He was snarling again, but it would do him no good. "That swine Silas pulled the knife out of his chest to stab me in the leg. That's why I shot him, and you should have seen the look on his face as I did it."

A mournful cry fell from Holly's lips and, for perhaps the first time that day, I felt it was warranted. Discovering that your grandfather is a murderer would be bad enough at Christmas, but on your birthday too? That's beyond the pale.

"You're an arrogant man, Rivers," my far more loveable grandfather explained. I was glad he'd found his voice again, as I doubt that I would have done a good job. "Perhaps you invited me into your house before you knew that you would kill again, but you certainly thought you were clever enough to commit a second murder and not suffer the consequences."

Lord Rivers hadn't given up on defending himself just yet and turned to his granddaughter for one last attempt to convince her of his good intentions. "I did this for you, my darling. I've done everything for you. I wanted you to marry Nathan, as I knew that Silas would have shared the estate with him. When he let me down, Luke was my next choice. The two of you can still marry. He'll be the owner of St

Audries Park. You'd make a wonderful pair."

There was something wrong with his argument, but Holly put her finger on it before I could. "You're a liar, and you always have been. Everything you say is twisted and cruel. If you wished me to inherit, you could have found a way to change the will, just as Lord Edgington said. You didn't want me to marry Nathan or Luke for my sake. You wanted to see how far they would go to make you happy." There were tears in her precious eyes, but her voice remained strong and clear. "You decided that Nathan deserved to die just because he'd derailed your plan, whereas Luke lived up to his promise because he didn't say no to you."

Her elder cousin cleared his throat as though he wished to apologise for entertaining the old man's schemes. "I didn't say yes, either, Holly. And I wouldn't have. Uncle Perry told me that he was ill and how happy it would make him if we were to take over this place. I didn't want to hurt his feelings."

"I don't blame you, Luke. I don't…" The energy had drained from her, and it looked for a moment as though she would faint. Mrs Stevans stood up to give her the nearest chair, and Philip Acland knelt down before her to make sure that she was all right.

A certain hush had returned after all that shouting, and it was hard to know what to do next. I thought of calling the police, but it seemed a little cruel to make poor P.C. Ted come all the way out there on Christmas Day when there was a perfectly good coal cellar to contain Rivers until the snow melted.

Perhaps realising that the last word belonged to Holly and not us, Grandfather sat down again without further comment. As Flossie sobbed on her brother's shoulder and the others fussed over Holly, the future convict didn't know when he was beaten and issued one last angry remark. "I'll be dead before I see the inside of a court. I've had a good life, and I got what I wanted. Oh yes, I—"

The one thing he hadn't banked on was the channel of icy wrath that was now directed towards him. "Oh, do be quiet, you pitiful little man." My grandmother turned to me then and stated quite confidently, "I knew it was him all along."

CHAPTER THIRTY-ONE

Everyone felt a lot better once we'd rung for Todd to lock the still yelling and fighting Lord Rivers away somewhere uncomfortable. I don't think it was the coal cellar, but I doubt it was a great deal more luxurious. There would be a party below stairs that evening, not just to mark the day, but to celebrate the change of master.

We had something to celebrate too as, after we'd all dressed for dinner, a bell was rung to summon us to the banquet room, which I hadn't realised existed until I arrived there for the feast.

I don't know when the staff had found the time, but someone had decked that hall, not with boughs of holly, but with long golden garlands dotted all over with Christmassy shapes. I had a feeling that Todd had cut them out from pieces of foil and stuck them together to make the decorations. There were similar chains before us on the red tablecloth and, knowing how capable the man was, it would probably only have taken him a minute or two to make them.

What hadn't taken a minute or two was the Christmas dinner we would consume. I very much doubted that the staff in the kitchen had slept the night before, as the food we ate was so varied and elaborate that they had even drawn up a bill of fare which I will now reproduce for your (and my) pleasure. I took the liberty of adding certain annotations.

Menu – *Service a la Russe*

Ox-Tail Soup – Julienne Soup
(that second one is just carrot and celery by most people's standards)

Turbot and Lobster Sauce – Boiled Salmon
Stewed Eels (faugh!) – **Cod's Head and Shoulders with Oyster
Sauce** (the shoulders were particularly tasty)

Croquettes of Game aux Champignons – Canard (that's duck!) **à
la Rouennaise** (no idea!)
Perdrix aux Herbes (I imagine that means partridges with herbs)

217

Larded Sweetbreads
Roast Beef – Haunch of Mutton – Gammon Joint (Good, easy to understand British dishes)

Grouse – Pheasant – Larded Quails
Stewed Celery – Artichokes – Assorted Vegetables

Punch Jelly – Italian Cream – Neapolitan Struffoli
Bombe glacée – Christmas Pudding (hurray!) **– Croûtes Madrées aux Fruits**

I won't even hazard a guess at what that last dish was. I'd eaten so much by then that I may no longer have been conscious. Every last dish – except those disgustingly slippery eels – was just delicious, and I developed a particular taste for the Italian sweets that Henrietta had (surely) made. Perhaps it was our cook's subtle way of telling my grandfather to hurry up with the European tour he'd promised some months before.

But it wasn't just the food that was exquisite. The company and conversation were simply sublime, and, with the bad apples now removed, the Rivers family were a pleasant bunch. Once the formality of the current viscount's last few months of life had been dealt with, it was clear that Luke would be a much better replacement.

"The first thing I must address," he told us as I sat clutching my stomach after the meal, "is the breaking of the entailment on the estate."

"That is a good idea if you wish to avoid any more potential murders," Acland replied with a mischievous smile that he hadn't showed us before.

"That's not the reason," his second … or third … or maybe even fourth cousin answered in a solemn tone. "If I have a daughter, she deserves just the same rights as her brothers." Luke was a first-rate fellow, and I felt no small amount of relief that he was just as nice as he seemed – and his moustache implied.

"That is an admirable gesture." Grandfather raised his glass above the long table.

"Actually, no," Luke said, to correct his previous proposal. "The

218

first thing I will do is find Nathan's pregnant wife and make sure she has everything she needs for their baby. Nathan told me that his daughter Natalia was born this week, and despite my great-uncle's belief to the contrary, the estate is rich enough to support everyone." He was sitting at the head of the table and already appeared to be taking his new role seriously.

"I'm glad you see things differently from him," Holly told her (definitely) second cousin… or perhaps her first cousin once removed. I'm never sure how those things work. The point is Holly looked appreciatively down the table at Luke. "Perhaps grandfather had a better taste in heirs than I gave him credit."

This inspired a few shy smiles, but there was one person there who still looked shocked at the events of that day. Mrs Stevans could no longer meet our gaze, but if she was worried what might happen to her now that her employer was no longer in charge, I had a feeling that she would still have a place at St Audries Park.

"Lord Edgington, what I don't understand is how you knew that Peregrine's cane had a knife inside it," Flossie marvelled. "I thought that frightfully clever."

My grandfather finally had a chance to show off. "It was really very simple. He talked of the precautions he had taken after the attacks in the summer and, as it happens…" Before he could say anything more, he reached down to the floor and produced his own cane. "…I have a similar one myself."

I imagine I was more astonished than anyone else there. I'd seen the thing five hundred times and never noticed a small catch beneath the rounded amethyst. He pressed it and, just like on Lord Rivers's cane, the top pulled away to reveal a fine but frighteningly sharp blade that was normally concealed by the main silver shaft.

"Well, I never!" Flossie declared in joyous voice. "Perhaps every pensioner in the country is walking about with a deadly weapon on his person."

"I certainly hope not," I replied, as I could only imagine that this would lead to any number of new murder investigations.

"I think it would make things a lot more fun," Granny purred like the old tabby that she was. "I'll have to buy a pistol to conceal beneath my garter."

Everyone in my family clearly thought this was a terrible idea, but before Father could warn his mother off such a purchase, Luke had a new question for the master sleuth.

"And what about the gun? How did you realise that the one you'd seen in Silas's bedroom was the one Uncle Perry used?"

"That was thanks to my friend Loelia here." He nodded in my grandmother's direction and dear Granny returned the gesture with a not particularly humble hand to her chest. "She was telling a fascinating story of how Mrs Eileen Grout, the shopkeeper in her local town of Condicote, spent weeks searching for her favourite wooden spoon. When she finally found it, it was in amongst the other utensils right where it was supposed to be." The story was met with a range of blank looks, and so he explained what he had extracted from the anecdote. "Sometimes the normal place to find something seems too obvious, and so we discard the possibility out of hand. But where better to hide a gun than an armoury?"

I wasn't quite sure of his logic but offered an appreciative "Bravo!" nonetheless.

Halfpenny and his counterpart from the house had poured champagne in each of our glasses, and now Holly stood up to make a toast.

"I imagine that we have all lied or prevaricated in some form this weekend," she admitted, "and perhaps that's the Rivers family way."

Flossie wore a doubtful expression then, as if to imply, *I've been perfectly honest throughout,* and I must say that I believed her. In fact, as I looked down the table at that really very beautiful young lady, I rather wished I'd met her on a train instead of Holly. Just think of the fun our children could have had, misidentifying the parrots in her aviary.

Anyway, back to Holly's toast. "What I want to say is that this holiday has not turned out as any of us would have hoped. And although we will surely miss Silas and Nathan – no matter their faults – I can't help thinking that, when we come together next Christmas to celebrate, it will be the best we've ever had. And so I'd like to raise a toast to next Christmas. And if the Edgington family happen to be in the neighbourhood, you are all more than welcome to join us... though please ring ahead in advance."

"To next Christmas!" I said rather loudly. In my defence, Todd had been plying me with champagne flips and, for some reason, I was having trouble controlling the volume of my voice.

One by one around the table, we raised our glasses and a feeling of wonder, hope and – yes, I'm not afraid to say it – love for my fellow man flooded through me. As Holly had said, it was not the perfect way to celebrate Christmas, but the end result wasn't so different from my brother and me squabbling all morning over presents when we were little. Well, perhaps it was a touch different, as I don't remember our arguments ever resulting in a pile of dead bodies.

When the snow began to clear and it was time to leave St Audries (some six days after we'd arrived), the family came out to see us off. Father had spent most of the morning checking, cleaning, and then rechecking his car for the journey home. Mother bid a heartfelt farewell to every last person there – including the cook whom I'd only spotted once that week. Granny put her arm out of the window of Grandfather's most regal car to wave as she pulled away, and then it was my turn to say goodbye.

"I really do regret everything I said, Holly," I told her for possibly the seventeenth time that week.

"That's the one good thing about regret, Chrissy. It's never too late."

I smiled at the sweet sentiment and looked at Philip, who really was a much nicer person than I'd initially imagined. "I'm so happy for the pair of you, but I still feel that if—"

Grandfather interrupted me before I could say anything more. "How many times have I told you, Christopher? If ifs and ands were pots and pans, there'd be no work for tinkers' hands." He shook his head in despair, and I replied as politely as I could.

"Many times, Grandfather. But I must admit that I've never quite understood what it means."

This earned a laugh from Luke before Holly pulled me closer for a hug. "Thank you so much, Christopher Prentiss. Thank you for being every bit as good as I knew you would be. I don't know what I would have done without you."

I'm sure that I was blushing like a schoolboy and things would only get worse when Flossie repeated her cousin's friendly gesture. As Grandfather shook Mrs Stevans's hand, and Delilah jumped about in the driveway, I couldn't muster another word.

In fact, I didn't speak again until I was safely in the car, and we'd pulled off along the lane. I might have stayed quiet all the way to Cranley Hall if Grandfather hadn't spoken first.

"It's strange, isn't it? Each man's life touches so many other lives. Rivers made all his companions miserable in different ways. Silas was wrong to try to murder him, of course, and yet with the old rascal gone, the rest of the family are so much happier."

"And best of all, we can finally answer my question. The people who seemed like friendly sorts all turned out to be just that, and the rotters really were fairly awful… except for Nathan, perhaps… and I suppose we should have some sympathy for Silas. I doubt it was his fault that he turned out the way he did. Now that I come to think of it, Lord Rivers himself is surely just a product of his upbringing. Who are we to cast judgement on him?"

"Does that mean that, whichever case we next investigate, you will base your opinion of each suspect on the first impression they give?"

"Oh, no, not at all." I laughed at my own idiocy just then. "That would be a very silly thing to do."

"I'm glad to hear it." He smiled at me without taking his eyes off the road, and I felt perhaps that we were both learning in our own ways. Of course, I still had a lot further to go than my brilliant mentor.

"I have a question that I didn't feel I could ask in front of our hosts," I confessed. "I have no doubt that you considered Philip Acland's guilt in the murders. In our first interview with him, he directed our attention away from Holly and Flossie. I thought perhaps that was why you suggested that he kiss the latter of the two under the mistletoe. You could tell from his reaction that it was Holly that he was trying to protect."

He risked a glance at me as we were only going very slowly along the icy lane. "That's right. I thought he could be working with one of them and I was curious to know which. But that isn't a question."

"You are right, and you have my apologies. My question is how you knew he would inherit the estate if the other cousins were killed?"

He laughed silently. "Because you told me, Christopher."

"I did?"

He pointed down to the copy of Burke's Peerage that was by my feet below our very waggy dog. "On our way here. You read out his name. That was how I knew his family were from the town of Bicknoller."

"Remarkable!" I was so impressed by his memory, and the fact he'd been able to make sense of my reading as I fell asleep, that I began to reflect on my own failings. "Grandfather, does this case show that I'm back to where I started?"

"What on earth do you mean, boy?"

We were driving past the church, and I looked up to see old Father Goodman sweeping a flurry of snow from the front steps. "I mean that I made a real hash of things. I picked the wrong killer and only succeeded in upsetting a kind and innocent girl."

"A kind and innocent girl who repeatedly lied and manipulated you," he corrected. "And, no, Christopher, you do not lose all your knowledge and experience just because you struggled with one investigation. If that was the case, I'd never have improved as a detective. In my first few years as a police officer, I was more often wrong than right."

This certainly surprised me, not least because he rarely sounded quite so humble.

He spoke again before I could say anything. "And besides, without you, I'd never have wiped that disgusting look off Peregrine Rivers's face. You noticed a key piece of evidence that I'd overlooked and that doesn't happen too often… these days, at least."

"Thank you, Grandfather. I really mean it."

He smiled at me, and I suppose I must have still looked glum as he searched for something more cheerful to discuss. "I told you that I still have a present for you, Christopher. If you look on the shelf in front of you, you should find it."

I did just as he'd instructed and pulled out a small rectangular package wrapped in navy blue silk paper with a black ribbon around it. With one tug, it gave up its secrets and there before me was a map of Europe.

"It's about time we started planning our grand tour in earnest," he explained, and a thrill passed through me as I considered all the different countries I longed to visit.

"Do you really mean it, Grandfather?" I asked, as it had been at least six months since he'd raised the possibility of a trip abroad. "Are we really going soon?"

"Without a doubt." He hesitated then, and I knew he had a caveat to add. "We will leave for the continent just as soon as there's nothing to interest us over here."

He'd made me smile. "That sounds like a plan."

What I didn't tell him, as we pulled onto the main road and he accelerated away from St Audries Park, was that it was easily the best Christmas present I'd had in years.

It was even better than a pair of slippers.

The End (For Now...)

Wherever you're reading this, we hope you have a very Merry Christmas and an incredible New Year. With best wishes from Benedict, Marion, Amelie and (he wasn't born when this photo was taken) Osian Brown.

Get another

LORD EDGINGTON ADVENTURE

absolutely **free**…

Download your free novella at

www.benedictbrown.net

"LORD EDGINGTON INVESTIGATES..."

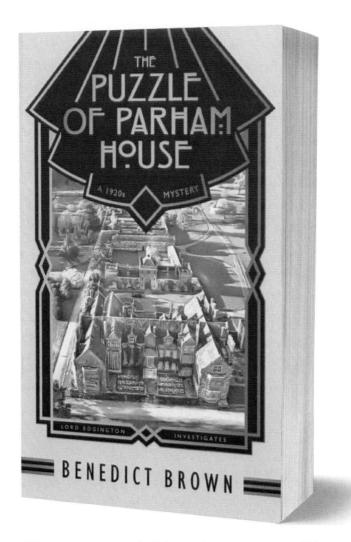

The thirteenth full-length mystery will be available in **Spring 2024** at amazon.

Sign up on my website to the readers' club to know when it goes on sale. The cover and title may change, as all this was a bit last minute. Whoops!

ABOUT THIS BOOK

It was the image of Chrissy heading home for Christmas on a steamy platform which sparked the rest of the plot and it's definitely one of my favourite openings so far. My father loved steam trains and we still have the Hornby train sets he had when he was young. My mother even has a cousin who previously lived in an abandoned train station where he kept a vast model railway, so my ever-growing Lego Winter Village has precedent in the family.

There are a lot of connections to my family in this book, not least the Christmas traditions that Chrissy discusses. It is my and my mother's tradition to go to the farms near our house on the outskirts of London and spend far too long choosing a Christmas tree each year. Chrissy's sheer horror at the absence of a tree at St Audreys Park is a joke for my family, as I reacted in much the same way on a number of occasions when I came back home from university to discover that my lazy brothers had done nothing to decorate our house. I would have to spend the days just before Christmas raiding the loft for decorations and stringing them up as swiftly as possible to create the cosy atmosphere that my ridiculous high standards demanded.

I really am over the top with Christmas decorations and try to recreate the special feeling I remember from childhood when the glow of the Christmas room was visible from the top of the first-floor landing. One year, I stayed up until two in the morning wrapping presents, made sure to leave the tree lights on, just as I like them, tidied the room so it would be perfect and went to bed full of expectation. When I sneaked from my room the next morning and crept downstairs, my dad had got up before me, opened the curtains, turned off the lights and was sitting watching telly. Dream ruined!

I'll be getting home to London with my wife and children a few days before Christmas this year, and I hereby warn my brothers, Dominic and Daniel, that if there isn't at least a prettily decorated Christmas tree standing in our lounge when I arrive, I will make Chrissy look like a very reasonable person indeed.

On a less angry note, one of my favourite traditions is still getting up early to sit with the presents and watch old cartoons, as Chrissy describes doing with his brother. My aforementioned siblings have long grown out of such practices, but I have kids now, so they're more than willing accomplices, especially if my daughter is allowed to raid her stocking for chocolate.

Since I grew up and met my brilliant wife, we found some new customs of our own. Marion was homeschooled so that she could train to be an ice skater from the age of three to eighteen. She competed in the national championships in France and every time I see her skating, I love her a little more. The scene on St Audrey Park lake was inspired by all the times she has held my hand and amazed me (with blades strapped to her feet on top of a slab of ice). When I see her pirouetting for minutes on end or zooming around at speed, I question how anyone so exquisitely sweet, talented and beautiful could put up with someone like me.

Even more personal, perhaps, is the search that Chrissy undergoes in order to find Holly. I wasn't conscious of it at the time, but I'm fairly confident this was suggested by one of my favourite anecdotes in our family, the story of how my Mum's twin sister met her husband. Auntie Valerie was hitchhiking to see a friend in Swansea in Wales when an incredibly dashing man with James Dean-esque looks stopped his flash car to give her a lift – which could be the beginning of a romance or a horror film. He told her his name was Aubrey just as they were driving past a pub called the Aubrey Arms, and Val didn't believe him.

Uncle Aubrey was so taken by the beautiful young lady, he later called her college, claiming that she had left her purse in his car and he wanted to give it back to her. This was back in the sixties, before data protection and GDPR, and so they gave him my grandparents' phone number. His request to contact their daughter caused a big argument as Nana wanted to put the two future lovebirds in touch and Grandpa thought it was a terrible idea and said that the strange young man must have "a wife in every port". My mum says this was the only time she can remember her parents seriously falling out, but Grandpa eventually gave in. It's a good thing he did, as otherwise I wouldn't be here. After Val and Aub got married and moved to London together, my uncle introduced Val's twin sister to a man called Kevin Brown, but

230

that's another story, and I'm pretty sure I've already written it in one of these chapters.

Oh, and there's one last little family story I slipped into the plot. There's a moment when Chrissy's seventy-seven-year-old grandfather rushes forward to stop Lord Rivers from toppling over. This is something my five-foot-nothing, eighty-seven-year-old grandmother did to stop an old man from falling. He toppled backwards; she zoomed over to catch him and, as she weighed about five stone and was no weightlifter, she was inevitably flattened. You'll be happy to know that both would-be rescuer and rescuee were absolutely fine. At the very least, she broke his fall!

I love hearing from my readers and will occasionally receive an e-mail that particularly moves me. One reader told me about a friend of hers called Sharon Stevans who is going through cancer treatment, and I also heard from a granddaughter and grandmother, both called Victoria, who read my books together. To say thank you to all of them, I lent Victoria Stevans their names. Three people celebrated in one character is pretty good going. I hope that Sharon is recovering from her surgery and the Victorias have enjoyed reading this book together.

And last but by no means least, what about St Audries Park itself? Well, it is a real place on the southwest coast of England, and I've tried to be geographically accurate with Grandfather and Grandson's mad dash across the country. Since the house was sold by the original owners in the thirties, it has been a school, a Buddhist centre and is now a wedding venue, which is how I came to find it. It is owned by the same group as Clearwell Castle, from the seventh book in this series, which is seventy-five miles north from St Audries. I have to say a big thanks again to the incredibly kind people at Country House Weddings for allowing me to use the image on the cover and the name in the story. I love making use of real places and the book would have been very different without their permission.

In fact, until a couple of days before I started writing, I'd been planning to use Parham House in Sussex, but because of a particular plot point, I decided to delay that until the next book. This left me scrambling to find a wintery-looking house to use on the cover, which is a lot more difficult than you might imagine. St Audries Park was the perfect option though, and as soon as I saw the snowy photo with the frozen lake, a plot began to take shape in my head.

I didn't find as much historical information about the house as many I've used, presumably because it is a little more isolated than Clearwell, for example. It's easy enough to learn that the estate historically belonged to the Acland family and the house itself was built between 1835 and 1870. However, I had to dig a bit deeper to find out about the abandoned village on the estate that is a plot point in my novel. Also unlike previous books, I decided not to use the real family in this one, but still included names that were appropriate for the area. If you look at the entry in a book like "Burke's Peerage", you'll see that there were connections between the Acland, Rivers and Bridport families, which is why I chose those names.

I love the way that a brief mention in a historical or architectural document can set my mind wandering and lead to new developments in my story. Sometimes my best ideas are there in my head when I wake up in the morning – the twist in the first Marius Quin novel, 'Murder at Everham Hall', being my favourite so far. I like to think that everything I read and research gets thrown into the cauldron of my subconscious and, when the time comes to whip up a plot, there's already something there stewing. Extended metaphor over.

If you loved the story and have the time, please write a review at Amazon. Most books get one review per thousand readers so I would be infinitely appreciative if you could help me out.

THE MOST INTERESTING THINGS I DISCOVERED WHEN RESEARCHING THIS BOOK...

I'm feeling peckish after that final menu, so let's start with food.

I had one major advantage this time that made my food writing a lot swifter than before; I invested in a copy of "Mrs Beeton's Book of Household Management" from 1861. Mrs Beeton was the superstar cookbook writer of her day and had an incredible impact on Victorian Britain, especially considering the fact that she died aged just 28 after she gave birth to her second son. Her first book sold sixty thousand copies in its first year and covers everything from how to manage one's servants, household poisons, slaughtering animals, first aid and, importantly for me, cooking.

One of the most incredible things in the eleven-hundred-page text is at the back of the book, where you can find menu suggestions for different party sizes. The bill of fare that Chrissy reproduces at the end is – would you believe it – a slimmed-down version of what might have been found at an elaborate winter gathering of the time. I cut down the meat, fish and game dishes by half, and it's amazing to me that anyone could have such an appetite.

One of the dishes I selected from her book was *eggs a la tripe*, which is fairly self-explanatory but sounds dreadful. I'm not much of a fish eater, so matelot of tench (a French fish stew made with wine) is not a great deal more appealing. Tench is also known as the doctor fish because, so legend has it, this slimy creature, which is as slippery as an eel, could cure other fish that rubbed against it. My favourite find, though, was vicarage pudding. I don't just love it for the very murder-mystery-appropriate name, it also sounds rather Christmassy. Raisins, currants, ginger and, of course, a quarter of a pound of beef fat. But what I really love about its inclusion here is that, when I tried to find out more information about it, I uncovered a crime!

I discovered absolutely nothing on the origin of the name of the dish, but I did find an article in an Australian paper from 1908 which claimed that a list of recipes included in the paper were "Specially Written for this Column. All Rights Reserved" before going on to print several of the recipes from Mrs Beeton's own book. Burrowa News from New South Wales, I'm onto you! Your perfidy may have taken one hundred and fifteen years to expose, but expose it, I did! Of course, as one of the biggest criticisms of Mrs Beeton was that she often plagiarised her recipes, it is hardly the crime of this (or, indeed, the last) century.

As for desserts, we have a couple of nice international dishes in Neapolitan Struffoli and bombe glacée. Struffoli are somewhat similar to French profiteroles and Spanish Buñuelos. They are deep-fried dough balls, sweetened with honey and decorated with colourful nonpareils (or hundreds and thousands/sprinkles, as I would call them). Funny story: When I was a child, we were having ice cream, and I told my mother that I wanted "Lots and lots". She didn't take kindly to this and told me not to be greedy. I replied, "But I want lots and lots!" I would not back down and got increasingly upset until my mother realised that what I really wanted were hundreds and thousands, which, though I might not have possessed the necessary vocabulary, is still pretty good paraphrasing for a four-year-old. Oh, and bombe glacée is an iced dessert which is frozen in a rounded mould and often covered with chocolate. Apparently, the legendary French chef Auguste Escoffier included over sixty recipes for bombes in his first cookbook.

The first thing I researched when writing this book were the train lines that ran across the country in 1927. There were four major rail operators through much of the 20th century and the Great Western Railway was in charge of most of the west of England and Wales. I'm not going to lie. I spent far too much time reading through timetables and consulting maps and the first two hours were enjoyable before I realised how long it was taking and accepting that what I'd discovered was accurate enough. Aside from station names, journey durations, types of train in use and potential routes to Somerset, the most interesting thing I learnt was that, at the time this book was set, the railways in Britain were at their peak with over 32,000 kilometres of track. This was over thirty years before the British government decided to close thousands of local stations and cut over a quarter of the existing track in the sixties alone. By 2019, the original number had halved. Sadly, trains in my country are now crazily expensive and, outside of major cities, not commonly the most efficient option for travelling (but I still love them).

This is probably the Lord Edgington book for which I had to do the most reading up on the First World War. The impact of the war has been clear in other stories – especially "The Tangled Treasure Trail" – but since I started writing a new series with a protagonist who served as a soldier, I've become increasingly fascinated by that terrible conflict that was supposed to be the war to end all wars.

The first thing I had to learn about was weapons from the time and I'll get the elephant in the room out of the way first. Silencers were not commonly found in the UK in the twenties, but they were fairly easy to get hold of in the States. The Maxim silencer was first sold in 1902 and patented in 1909. It was widely advertised and so it was presumably possible that an American marine could have taken a couple to war with him. British and American soldiers fought at The Battle of Belleau Wood together and so Silas could well have picked them up there. Done. Incidentally, the man who designed the first commercially available silencer was a fascinating chap.

Hiram Percy Maxim designed his own combustion engine, without knowing of the advances taking place in that field in Europe at the same time. He also used the technology he developed for his silencer to muffle car engines, set up the American Radio Relay League which still exists today, (and the Amateur Cinema League, which doesn't). He wrote two books: one about contemporary views on extra-terrestrial life and another about his family, and especially his father who had himself invented the first automatic machine gun, a popular amusement park ride called the Captive Flying Machine, a type of hair curling irons, the first fire sprinkler and, according to him, the lightbulb. What a family!

Sticking with weapons, I looked into marksmen and found out that, in the early part of the war, the scopes that German sharpshooters possessed gave them a massive advantage during battles. The allied forces couldn't understand how snipers were able to kill over such long distances until they happened to find the equipment and soon copied the technology involved. The word sharpshooter comes from the company that made rifles in the American civil war and had nothing to do with the shooters' sharp eyes. The Sharps rifle was the first ubiquitous breech-loading rifle and became an icon of the American west.

To counteract the threat of the German snipers, Britain set up "The First Army School of Sniping, Observation, and Scouting". It was run by Major Hesketh Hesketh-Prichard who was sent to observe the British troops in action and soon realised how poorly they dealt with long-range attacks. He started by ordering telescopic sights from the UK, which he paid for himself, and the training he offered was said to save thousands of lives over the course of the war.

This wasn't all he did, though, as Hesketh was another real legend. I particularly liked his Wikipedia summary which describes him as an "explorer, adventurer, writer, big-game hunter, marksman, and cricketer", but that doesn't do him justice and some of the things he achieved were to campaign for the end of seal clubbing in Britain. He wrote adventurous novels, which mirrored his own incredible life as he travelled to lands that no European had visited. He explored remote regions of Haiti (where someone tried to poison him) and gave an early western account of the unusual practices there, such as Voodoo. He was friends with the creators of Sherlock Holmes and Peter Pan and, in a series of ghost stories commissioned for a magazine, came up with the first psychic detective, Flaxman Low. Actually, that's not quite true, as he wrote those stories with his mother, Kate O'Brien Ryall Prichard, who was also his regular travelling companion. I rather imagine them as Chrissy and his mother might one day turn out to be. What a family!

Sticking with explorers, a far more famous but less successful figure was Captain Robert Falcon Scott, or Scott of the Antarctic as he's often known. Sadly for Scott, he is best remembered for his disastrous expedition to the South Pole, in which he and his four companions froze to death on their way back from reaching their target. This would have been little comfort, however, as the Norwegian explorer Roald Amundsen had beaten him by several weeks.

To this day, there is debate over whether Scott was a hero or a horrific leader. In his defence, a written note has recently come to light which had instructed dog teams to meet his men on their return leg. This never happened, and they were only twenty kilometres from the next supply point when they died. However, they were also hampered by temperatures forty degrees below zero and strong blizzards that left them unable to venture further. The whole thing is like a horror story with the bad weather as the unseen killer.

What is true, however, is that the Norwegian expedition was much better organised. They had prepared in advance with skis and dog sleds, whereas Scott relied on ponies that soon died and motor sledges that stopped working in the cold, which left him and his men to haul their equipment themselves. This was made all the more difficult by the fact they were a scientific expedition and had taken heavy rock samples – including fossils which proved that the Antarctic had once been forested – which slowed them down a great deal.

Scott's sole navigator wasn't entirely up to the challenge, and so the depots of supplies that they laid were not in the right places. They were twenty-five kilometres from the South Pole when they discovered that Amundsen was ahead of them. They arrived a month after the other party and found a tent with a letter inside it proclaiming Amundsen's success. The Norwegian expedition made it safely back to base camp two months before Scott died. He was the last of his men to go and had time to write several letters, including one to the public, declaring,

"We took risks, we knew we took them; things have come out against us, and therefore we have no cause for complaint, but bow to the will of Providence, determined still to do our best to the last… Had we lived, I should have had a tale to tell of the hardihood, endurance, and courage of my companions which would have stirred the heart of every Englishman."

He believed that the purpose of his expedition was not just to be the first to the pole but to indulge in a great adventure. For his part, Amundsen said, "Adventure is just bad planning." Perhaps it was this attitude that was the ultimate difference between them.

Sticking with disasters now, the sinking of the Lusitania was one of the great disasters of the first world war and helped convince America to mobilise in support of the allies. What was particularly tragic about it was the fact that the Germans chose to sink a civilian vessel, killing almost 1200 of the 1962 lives on board. 128 of those who died were American, and this caused an outcry in the States, though there had been warnings in newspapers that Trans-Atlantic voyages were no longer safe, as Germany had declared the seas around Great Britain a war zone. The ship sank in just eighteen minutes and, like many such tragedies, there were small margins between its sinking and survival. Due to rules over secrecy and plain poor judgement, certain messages concerning the sighting of the U-Boat that torpedoed the Lusitania were never communicated or came too late. As Chrissy says, the sinking was also one of the defining images of the war and was used as propaganda by both sides of the conflict.

Right, that was all very dark and depressing. What can I tell you about that's a bit cheerier…? Poison? No. A famous murderer? No, we'll come to him later. How about jewellery? That'll do. I had to check that charm bracelets were common in the twenties, and I shouldn't have worried. They had existed for some time but were boosted in their popularity by that old trendsetter, Queen Victoria. She was known for wearing such jewellery and often gave them as presents. She even started a fashion for mourning charms after her husband died. People would wear lockets of hair, black jet charms or small portraits to remember their loved ones by. It wasn't until 1889 that Tiffany and Co. released a bracelet with their famous heart-shaped charm, but the item is still available today. I wonder if the original decision to sell it was influenced by the English Queen.

Sticking with the Victorian era, through a chance e-mail I received from another writer, I discovered that Dickens was a creature of habit. He would sit at his desk from nine to two each day whether he wrote several thousand or just a few hundred words, and then he'd go for a three-hour-long walk to think about his books. He wrote fifteen (and a half) novels and five novellas in his lifetime, whereas I've managed twenty-three novels and seven novellas in the last four years. Oh, fine. His are a lot longer than mine and he also did a lot of journalism and toured performing his work, but my point is, I wish I had three hours a day free to go for a walk! I wish I had three hours a week free!

My own writing routine is to work from the time I wake up until I no longer have the energy to continue. This process is interrupted by occasional breaks for me to eat, play games with my daughter, and cuddle my baby son. But one thing I'm promising right now: I am not going to write eight books next year and if I change my mind and attempt to do anything so silly again, I hereby give my wife permission to slap some sense into me.

Sticking with Dickens, the book that Chrissie is reading "The Cricket on the Hearth" was one of his four Christmas novellas and, much like the first, was a publishing sensation when it launched in 1845. In that first year, seventeen stage versions of it opened in England, including an official one on the same day as the book came out. Dickens also performed the story in full and, for a long time, the stage version of it was more commonly performed than "A Christmas Carol". One person who did not like it, however, was Russian revolutionary Vladimir Lenin, who left halfway through a performance, as he found it sentimental and boring. There's no pleasing some people.

I've been pretty happy with my segueing between topics until now, but the rest of this chapter will be increasingly higgledy-piggledy.

The poet Alexander Pope was born with some major disadvantages in life. In addition to being trampled by a cow at twelve, and contracting tuberculosis of the spine, which meant he was only four foot six, he came from a humble background and was hampered by draconian laws. As Catholics, his family were not allowed to live within ten miles of London, and he was forbidden from attending public schools and universities. Despite all this, he was so bright that he taught himself multiple languages and was a devoted reader. He went on to be one of the great poets of his day, but was not one to avoid a fight, and became famous for his use of satire to cut down his enemies. In fact, he upset rival poets, critics and politicians so greatly that he carried pistols as a precaution when out and about. I suppose you could think of him as a very eloquent and well-read troll.

That's enough of that. I'm changing to bullet points!

- While digitalis, the chemical found in the plant of the same name (commonly known as foxgloves) is famously poisonous, it also has incredible therapeutic properties. It is one of the deadliest drugs that are still proscribed and even a small overdose can kill, but it is so useful that it is worth the risk. It is still used in cardiology and is effective in slowing heart rate and increasing blood pressure.

- When wife-killer Dr Crippen discovered that he would be up against the brilliant prosecutor Richard Muir, he said, "I wish it had been anybody else... I fear the worst." Muir's handling of the trial became a textbook case for prospective solicitors and barristers to study. Muir demanded such thoroughness that even his colleagues and seasoned police officers feared him.

- The snow in England in 1927 was intense. This may be the first book I've written where I had to play down rather than exaggerate the snowfall. A great blizzard raged from Christmas Day onwards and there were apparently twenty-foot-high drifts on Salisbury Plain.

- I found a brilliant book from 1896 called "Hood's Sarsaparilla – Book of Home Games". It was evidently produced as a promotional item to promote their multi-purpose remedy, as it intersperses testimonials with descriptions of games. Titles include "The Minister's Cat", "For Rheumatic Cramps," "Blow the Feather" and "Rash Disappeared!" I'm sure you can guess which is which.

- While we're on the topic, The Mousetrap game really does sound like the most complicated pastime you can imagine. I liked its connection to Agatha Christie, of course, and had thought to use it in the scene when the Cranley family are playing together on Lord Edgington's estate, but I couldn't begin to understand it. It involves a complicated sentence that keeps changing, two rows of chairs with men and women (or rats and cats) facing one another, and various gestures that everyone must learn.

- Chrissy mentions Nora the parrot from London Zoo, and she was a real parrot I read about in a newspaper article from the twenties. She could hum 'The Keel Row' whilst performing "an appropriate dance". And the reason I decided to create a parrotry (which is a word, Chrissy, but it actually means mindless repetition!) is because another nearby manor house in the Acland family had an orangery that at some point housed a collection of parrots. I also think that, as birds go, they're rather Christmassy! We went to Peruvian jungle on our honeymoon and got to see incredible flocks of thousands of parrots circling and then feeding on the clay cliffs there. It was one of the most incredible things I've ever witnessed.

- Badgers? Badgers?! We don't need no stinking badgers! Wait, yes we do! Badgers are incredibly cool animals and deserve out attention. Some of the amazing things that I learnt about them are that, when a badger dies in its sett, its companions will seal up the room it is in, much like a mausoleum. They are fastidiously clean animals and dig latrines, indulge in spring cleaning and regularly change their bedding, even going so far as to take it in and out of their setts to air out the grass, leaves and moss they use. They sometimes share their homes with rabbits or foxes, and can help rabbits stay safe from other predators. So it turns out that badgers aren't so stinky after all. And if you haven't seen the underappreciated "Weird Al" Yankovic film UHF or "The Treasure of the Sierra Madre" that it was spoofing, half of this paragraph won't make much sense to you.

Okay, enough titbits. Let's talk about colours. Arsenic green was a real shade that really was produced from real arsenic. It was used to colour clothes, fake flowers and wallpapers. The women who worked with it suffered terrible health problems – with some even dying – and their protection became a major cause for social organisations of the nineteenth century. The practice was eventually banned and, for some time after, it was considered improper to wear similar shades. Arsenic green may have claimed another victim as, when Napoleon I was held prisoner on the isle of St Helena, his rooms were painted in such a tone. He died of stomach cancer, which may have been caused by the arsenic on the walls coupled with damp. There were high levels of arsenic in his body after death, so he may have been inhaling the stuff all because his favourite colour was green.

A more positive association, of which Chrissy's mother (and the mother in Mary Poppins) would approve, is Suffragist white. The colour was chosen in order to show the world that these social rebels were pure of purpose. It was also to counteract the idea that the suffragettes were dowdy or masculine and, by 1908, the Women's Social and Political Union had adopted the colour as their official uniform. White was also the common colour of mourning dress for centuries in Europe and there is a painting of Mary Queen of Scots in white mourning attire in the sixteenth century. Black began to be worn by royals and the uber-wealthy, as it was more expensive. However, it was not until Queen Victoria lost her husband in 1851 that black was cemented as the colour of bereavement. She wore the colour for the next forty years of her life – even though three-years of wearing black was the standard rule for widows. I doubt that the men were held to such high standards.

The university which Holly attends, Somerville College, was one of the first women's colleges in Oxford, opening in 1879, ten years after the first in Cambridge. Despite this, it wasn't until 1957 that quotas to limit the number of female students were done away with. And it wasn't until 2015 that a woman became the Vice-Chancellor of the whole university, after eight hundred years of men in the position. Important alumni of Somerville College include the authors Iris Murdoch, Dorothy L. Sayers and A.S. Byatt. In a nice little coincidence, one of the members of the Acland family of Somerset helped in its founding.

Jumping back in time once more, I was curious to read about duelling. Though the practice was outlawed by the nineteenth century, it was rarely prosecuted, even in cases in which one of the combatants was killed. In fact, soldiers could be court martialled both if they refused a duel or failed to demand one when insulted. In 1840, the 7th Earl of Cardigan killed one of his own officers in a duel, but he was found innocent in court thanks to a loophole. There was something of an uproar and The Times newspaper claimed that "in England there is one law for the rich and another for the poor."

Sticking with outdated practices, entailment continued right into the twentieth century, though it was less common after the Law of Property Act 1925 – which I didn't know about until after I'd written this book, and which enabled those estates under entailments to be released. The original idea of an entail (or fee tail) was to ensure the continuation of a patriarchal line by pledging the estate to the first surviving male heir. This meant that both women and illegitimate offspring were circumvented. Some families were so set on the right son inheriting that they would give all their firstborns the same name, and there were at least eight Fulks in the FitzWarin family back before entails existed. It also forms a major plot point in stories from Pride and Prejudice through to Downton Abbey.

The major downside of entails was that they would often separate the land and title that the heir would inherit from the money the family owned, which tended to be split between offspring. This meant that the lord in question would not have the funds for the upkeep of the large estate he had inherited. By the nineteen twenties, many aristocratic families had fallen on hard times and entails played their part in the process.

Sticking with musty concepts, to my surprise, it wasn't until the seventeenth century that the idea of morganatic marriage – or marriage between royals and non royals – was considered in any way taboo in the English monarchy. Until then, it was common to marry a commoner, with four of Henry VIII's six wives of non-royal stock. However, there soon followed a period of 264 years during which kings only married princesses. George VI (our current king's grandfather) married the Queen Mother – who was a mere daughter of an earl. Of course, George VI was never meant to be king and only took on the crown when his brother Edward VIII abdicated to marry a divorcee. British royals can only marry with the permission of the monarch and, as that was Edward himself, he had to ask the government for permission to marry Wallis Simpson. I'm glad I only had to ask my father-in-law whether I could marry Marion. Thanks to the language barrier, he thought it was a rhetorical question and replied, "Well, you are very different". Thank you for your honesty, Gerard.

I'd never questioned before why Prince Albert became George VI, but there is such a thing as a regnal name. In Bertie's case, it was because Queen Victoria had placed a ban on future kings having the same name as her beloved husband, so her great-grandson took one of his middle names to honour his father and suggest continuity after the scandal his brother had brought about.

Sticking with names, Chrissy found some good ones on the map this time. All the silly place names I've used in my books have been real – the only exceptions being those in the fictional county of Tatchester from What the Vicar Saw. Perhaps the most famously odd place name in the UK – possibly behind Llanfairpwllgwyngyllgogerychwyrndrobwllllantysiliogogogoch – is Westward Ho! It was named after a popular novel from the 1850s and was chosen in order to attract tourists to a hotel that was built there. That's right, it was called "Westward Ho!-tel" a village built up around the hotel and took on its name. It is the only place in the UK with an exclamation mark, however Saint-Louis-du-Ha! Ha! in Canada holds the Guinness World Record for most exclamation marks in a place name with the grand total of two!

As for songs, I delivered a mere four this time. "God Rest Ye Merry Gentlemen" dates back to at least the 1650s and is referenced in both Dickens's "A Christmas Carol" and George Eliot's "Silas Marner" both of which left their mark on this novel. "Here We Come A-Wassailing" is a folk song from at least the nineteenth century that would have been sung by roving carollers and beggars at Christmas time, when the well-off were more likely to be generous. It essentially amounts to a request for coins, food or a sip of drink from the wassail bowl, which would have contained a hot, spiced drink made with mead, beer and apples. There is a similar song from my favourite place in Britain, the Gower in South Wales, which has various lines that the homeowners would sing back to the beggars. The tradition of wassailing is also connected to guising, in which people would go from house to house in fancy dress to bless the home in exchange for a treat. This tradition spread to America at the turn of the twentieth century and would come to be known as... Well, you've probably already worked that part out.

Sticking with America, I knew I would include "I Heard the Bells on Christmas Day" as soon as I picked the title for this book. I'm going to be honest, I settled on that name as I hope it will interest people who love Christmas but haven't read any of my books (of which there must be a good few million). I've tried to thread the motif of bells through the book, without ever really defining what a Christmas bell might be. The song that Nathan sings at the piano does this for me, though. It was written as a poem on Christmas Day, 1863 by Henry Wadsworth Longfellow in reaction to the American Civil War. His son had enlisted without his knowledge and was badly wounded eight months into his service. If you read the whole poem, it becomes increasingly dark as the ringing of the bells is drowned out by the thunder of war. In the final verse, the bells ring once more, and the poet rejoices in the belief that…

> **"God is not dead, nor doth He sleep;**
> **The Wrong shall fail,**
> **The Right prevail,**
> **With peace on earth, good-will to men."**

I knew nothing of its history or message before writing this book, but there's something in the imagery within the poem that reminds me of William Blake's "And did those feet in ancient time". It's a beautiful and powerful poem which was turned into a song by an English organist in 1872. That version remained the most popular until the 1950s, when Bing Crosby had a hit with a reworking. Both are good.

Right, that's it. As of writing this, I still have to decorate for Halloween so that we can leave up the decorations for far too long and then pull them down in time to put up the Christmas ones. Thank you for putting up with my waffling in all its forms.

ACKNOWLEDGEMENTS

I didn't have to consult too many experts on this one, which means I avoided bothering my friends and family, but I do have to say another thank you to the owners of St Audries Park. I love using real houses in my books as borrowing the décor and setting of such a unique property makes the books much richer. Have a look at *audries-park. co.uk* to see the more photos of the house as it is quite stunning.

Thanks also have to go to Ben Simmonds who took the brilliant picture on the front cover. Judging from *bensimmondsphotography.co.uk*, he is a seriously good wedding photographer and, if you happen to be getting married in the South West of England, he's the obvious choice!

Thank you, too, to my crack team of experts – the Hoggs, the Martins, (fiction), Paul Bickley (policing), Karen Baugh Menuhin (marketing) and Mar Pérez (forensic pathology) for knowing lots of stuff when I don't. And to my fellow writers who are always there for me, especially Catherine, Suzanne and Lucy.

Thank you, many times over, to all the readers in my ARC team who have combed the book for errors. I wouldn't be able to produce this series so quickly or successfully without you…

Rebecca Brooks, Ferne Miller, Melinda Kimlinger, Emma James, Mindy Denkin, Namoi Lamont, Katharine Reibig, Linsey Neale, Karen Davis, Terri Roller, Margaret Liddle, Esther Lamin, Lori Willis, Anja Peerdeman, Marion Davis, Sarah Turner, Sandra Hoff, Karen M, Mary Nickell, Vanessa Rivington, Helena George, Anne Kavcic, Nancy Roberts, Pat Hathaway, Peggy Craddock, Cathleen Brickhouse, Susan Reddington, Sonya Elizabeth Richards, John Presler, Mary Harmon, Beth Weldon, Karen Quinn, Karen Alexander, Mindy Wygonik, Jacquie Erwin, Janet Rutherford, Anny Pritchard, M.P. Smith, Molly Bailey, Nancy Vieth, Ila Patlogan, Lisa Bjornstad, Randy Hartselle, Misty Walker, Carol Vani, June Techtow and Keryn De Maria.

READ MORE LORD EDGINGTON MYSTERIES TODAY

- **Murder at the Spring Ball**
- **Death From High Places** (free e-novella available exclusively at benedictbrown.net. Paperback and audiobook are available at Amazon)
- **A Body at a Boarding School**
- **Death on a Summer's Day**
- **The Mystery of Mistletoe Hall**
- **The Tangled Treasure Trail**
- **The Curious Case of the Templeton-Swifts**
- **The Crimes of Clearwell Castle**
- **The Snows of Weston Moor**
- **What the Vicar Saw**
- **Blood on the Banister**
- **A Killer in the Wings**
- **The Christmas Bell Mystery**
- **The Puzzle of Parham House** (Spring 2024)

Check out the complete Lord Edgington Collection at Amazon

The first nine Lord Edgington audiobooks, narrated by the actor George Blagden, are available now on all major audiobook platforms. There will be more coming soon.

"THE CHRISTMAS BELL MYSTERY" COCKTAIL

This is the third Lord Edgington Christmas book, which means we've exhausted some of the obvious Christmas drinks. We've had eggnog, hot apple cocktails and Tom and Jerrys, so I had to go looking for something different. I found a really good cocktail book from 1924 which organises the drinks by season. There were so many drinks I could have chosen in there, but the champagne flip stood out to me. And it will henceforth be known as Chrissy's drink of choice.

It's suitably Christmassy thanks to the nutmeg, egg and sugar, not to mention the champagne itself. I also particularly liked the book 'Cocktails: How to Mix them' by *Robert,* the mononymous London barman of the twenties who worked at the Criterion and the Embassy Club. At the back of the book, he gives you some facts about the different ingredients and has this to say about the quintessentially luxurious French drink.

"Champagne is a stimulant to the body and mind. Physicians declare that good champagne possesses therapeutic properties. Nelson, Byron, Dickens and Napoleon I were extremely fond of it. It is of great value to those suffering from dyspepsia, neuralgia, influenza and gout. It had proved to be a stimulant when no other stimulant can be retained in illness."

So keep drinking champagne, everybody. It is a cure-all for countless diseases – just like Hood's Sarsaparilla!

A flip meanwhile is distinguished from eggnog as it doesn't feature cream or milk. And, according to Jerry Thomas, the trick to making one is beating the eggs well and pouring the mixture back and forth between containers to get the required smoothness. The drink dates back to the seventeenth century, though it has changed greatly over the centuries and was once served hot. Here's how you make the champagne version from the early twentieth century, according to Robert.

"The best way to make a Champagne Flip is by thoroughly shaking the yolk of a fresh egg with ice, then open the shaker and add the Champagne.

Strain into a wine-glass and grate nutmeg on top. Sugar or Sugar Syrup is only added when required sweet."

Which is a bit vague, so I looked around for another recipe which suggests using ¼ pint of champagne, one whisked egg and a teaspoonful of icing sugar. Modern recipes include brandy, cream and even orange liqueur, but this will do Chrissy just fine!

You can get our offical cocktail expert François Monti's brilliant book "101 Cocktails to Try Before you Die" at Amazon.

WORDS AND REFERENCES YOU MIGHT NOT KNOW

Ozymandias – a tyrant or megalomaniac.

Grumbletonian – a grumbler – this word was originally applied to a group within English politics and became an insult for those in opposition. It's probably fairly anachronistic for Chrissy to be using it two hundred years later, but it was too good a word not to revive.

Tunis cake – a sponge cake with a thick chocolate layer on top that is eaten at Christmas.

Reverend Crawley's Game - The Victorian equivalent of Twister, involving people all holding hands across the circle and then trying to untangle themselves.

Couilles De Mouton – Ummm… that would be sheep's testicles.

Cachinnation – laughter.

Dead Woman's Ditch – a real place located near St Audries in Somerset where, according to a council-erected sign there, a man murdered his wife before being hanged for the crime. However, it already had that name before he did so.

I'll be your *second* if you like – a second in a duel is the person who is responsible for choosing the weapons, setting the rules and overseeing the engagement.

Toplofty – haughty, self-important, snobbish.

Funking out – quitting before you do something.

Dangler – someone who chases after a woman.

Piccalilli – a horrible English sauce made with mustard, spices and vegetables.

On the cards – a couple of my American readers have tried to correct this, but, I promise, it's what we Brits say instead of "in the cards" which, I'm sorry, my dear transatlantic cousins, makes less sense than "on"!

Totem crackers – as mentioned in the notes to last year's Christmas book. They were a big sensation in 1927 and came with elaborate prizes connected to the hit musical, Rose Marie.

Moonling – a foolish person or simpleton.

My blue devils – your bad mood or misery.

Frownsome – No, Chrissy, this still isn't a word!

Paradise pudding – an apple, lemon, raisin, nutmeg and brandy pudding which, according to Mrs Beeton, is boiled in its mould.

Gammoner – a person who chatters away in order to charm people.

Cocktailian – a mixologist, which is also an old word but sounds so new I decided not to use it.

Brilliantine – a type of hair wax. Apparently, in Quebec, Canada, the film Grease is known as "Brilliantine". Brilliant!

Diddle-daddle – stuff and nonsense.

Butty – a slang word for a friend – unlikely to drop from Edgington's mouth, but I liked his playful mood here.

Beyond the mark – over the top / excessive.

Intarsia – a type of intricate woodwork, like marquetry, in which contrasting materials and tones are inlaid together in floors, ceilings and furniture.

Wig-waggy – not straight, winding.

Undispleased – I thought I was making this word up and was very happy to discover that I wasn't. I like the idea that Loelia can't be pleased, she can only be undispleased.

Beyond the pale – like beyond the mark / excessively cruel or unfair.

252

ABOUT ME

Writing has always been my passion. It was my favourite half-an-hour a week at primary school, and I started on my first, truly abysmal book as a teenager. So it wasn't a difficult decision to study literature at university which led to a master's in Creative Writing.

I'm a Welsh-Irish-Englishman originally from **South London** but now living with my French/Spanish wife and presumably quite confused infant daughter in **Burgos**, a beautiful mediaeval city in the north of Spain. I write overlooking the Castilian countryside, trying not to be distracted by the vultures, hawks and red kites that fly past my window each day.

When Covid-19 hit in 2020, the language school where I worked as an English teacher closed down and I became a full-time writer. I have two murder mystery series. There are already six books written in **"The Izzy Palmer Mysteries"** which is a more modern, zany take on the genre. I will continue to alternate releases between Izzy and Lord Edgington. I hope to release at least ten books in each series.

I previously spent years focussing on kids' books and wrote everything from fairy tales to environmental dystopian fantasies, right through to issue-based teen fiction. My book **"The Princess and The Peach"** was long-listed for the Chicken House prize in The Times and an American producer even talked about adapting it into a film. I'll be slowly publishing those books whenever we find the time.

"The Christmas Bell Mystery" is the twelfth novel in the "Lord Edgington Investigates…" series. The next book will be out in Spring 2024 and there's a novella available free if you sign up to my **readers' club.** Should you wish to tell me what you think about Chrissy and his grandfather, my writing or the world at large, I'd love to hear from you, so feel free to get in touch via…

www.benedictbrown.net

THE IZZY PALMER MYSTERIES

If you're looking for a modern murder mystery series with just as many off-the-wall characters, try **"The Izzy Palmer Mysteries"** for your next whodunit fix.

Check out the complete Izzy Palmer Collection in ebook, paperback and Kindle Unlimited at Amazon.

CHARACTER LIST

Suspects and Victims

Holly Bridport – a mysterious young lady whom Chrissy meets on a steam train home for the holiday.

Lord Peregrine Rivers (Viscount Rivers) – Her slightly tyrannical and miserly grandfather. Someone wants to kill him; you can be sure of that!

Silas Rivers – former soldier, Holly's second cousin and Lord Rivers's great nephew. He is the oldest male of the generation.

Nathan Rivers – a smooth, silver-tongued playboy. Silas's brother. Second oldest after Silas.

Luke Rivers – Nathan's cousin, and also Lord Rivers's great-nephew. A seemingly kind and jolly young man. He is studying to be a solicitor (lawyer).

Flossie Rivers – Luke's much younger sister. She adores her brother and her parrots.

Philip Acland – the clerk of the estate who lives in St Audries Park.

Victoria Stevans – Former lady's companion to Lord Rivers's wife, she stays on there as a general head of household.

P.C. Ted Acland – local policeman, Philip's brother.

Ripon – the St Audries Park butler / Daphne – the St Audries Park maid / Mary – the St Audries Park cook. I'm not sure any of them say anything, though.

Regular Characters

Lord Edgington – the man, the myth, the Marquess himself. He is a former Metropolitan police superintendent and the owner of a palatial estate in Surrey.

Christopher Prentiss – his well-meaning grandson and assistant in training, who is coming along rather nicely.

Violet Prentiss – Lord Edgington's daughter – Chrissy's mum. A good egg!

Walter Prentiss – Chrissy's father. He is rather set in his ways, but can you really blame him, considering…

Loelia Prentiss – Walter's mother, Chrissy's grandmother, and a real tough cookie.

Halfpenny – Cranley Hall's aged footman.

Henrietta ('Cook') – the Cranley Hall cook.

Todd – Lord Edgington's factotum and right-hand man. He acts as a chauffeur, barman, stand-in butler, and all-round great guy.

Made in United States
North Haven, CT
17 January 2024

47592579R00155